I0818043

INKED NOVELLAS

THE GALLOS

CHAPTER 1
MARIA

SITTING ON THE COUCH, I watched my husband, Salvatore, as he spoke to our eldest son, Anthony. The holidays always made me feel happy, but I longed for the days when the kids were young. The yelling, giggles, and kisses that came with youth had passed, leaving me with five grown children with no one to call their own.

As they grew, I wished they'd find that special someone and settle down, starting a family of their own and bringing a grandchild or two into our lives. But not my children—no, they lived as if they had all the time in the world, enjoying life on their terms and making no apologies.

Part of me envied them. They were young, unattached, and following their dreams. It's not that I was jealous of my children because I wasn't. There wasn't one moment in my life I would change, but I'd love to do it all again. Time passed so quickly that it was hard to savor the moments as they happened. I wanted to experience it again. Falling in love, having children, raising a family, and every moment in between happened in the blink of an eye. The years passed with greater speed each year, no matter how slow I tried to make it go.

As I looked down at the floor, Izzy was stretched out next to Anthony with her chin resting in her palms. She listened to Sal and Anth laughing and teasing each other, throwing in a crack or two herself. She was stunning with her long brown hair, big blue eyes, and high cheekbones. She was a knockout and single.

Izzy, my only daughter, was most like me. She was a free spirit who didn't take shit from anyone, most of all men. I raised her to be strong, independent, and fierce. I wasn't sure there was a man on the planet who could wrangle her and keep her attention. She was easily bored with the opposite sex or found them too demanding. Izzy did everything on her own terms. The quickest way to end a relationship with her was to lay down rules or have expectations.

Growing up with four older brothers made her rebel against any kind of restraints a man tried to place on her in adulthood. No one bossed her around, except for maybe Sal and me. She was a daddy's girl and never wanted to disappoint him. Even now at the age of twenty-two, she'd do everything in her power to make him happy. I loved her for everything she was, seeing so much of myself in her.

Today was New Year's Day, a day for new beginnings and fresh starts with new dreams for the upcoming year. If someone were to ask me what I wished for, I would answer for my children to find the one person who completes them, bringing them peace and love in the new year.

"Is it going to be the year the Cubs finally win the pennant, Pop?"

Anthony laughed as he spoke with Sal, seeming happier than he had in a while. By trade, he was a tattoo artist at Inked, a shop the kids owned together nearby. If you asked him, he'd say he was a musician. It was his true calling, his passion for as long as I could remember.

He hummed before he could talk, quickly learning to sing as soon as he was able to form words. I'd hear him in his crib, babbling to a beat until I'd grab him in the morning. He was content to lie there, signing to himself until I could drag myself from my bed. Music was his love, always had been. Preferring it to a real relationship, he told me that it was the one thing in life that never let him down. He had soured on women after high school, maintaining playboy behavior into his thirties.

Someone would capture his heart, but it would take that rare breed, a woman so spectacular that he'd fall in insta-love, and fall hard. I prayed she wouldn't break his heart, turning him off to any possibility of a lasting relationship. His focus now, besides tattooing and music, was the groupies. I wasn't a fool. I heard him talk with his brothers about the women who threw themselves at him. Manwhore is a term I've heard Izzy use, and Anthony seemed to fit the bill. My baby needed someone to knock him on his ass and steal his breath. He'd find her if he wasn't too busy with the trash with whom he spent his nights.

"I'm so hungover," Mike groaned, throwing his arm over his face as he stretched out on the love seat.

"You never knew how to pace yourself, man," Joe replied, leaning back, his foot resting on his knee as he kicked back on the couch.

"I watched how much I drank for the first few hours, but then it all turned into a blur. Fuck!" Mike spat, clutching his head.

"Want me to make you something to help with it?" Joe asked, grabbing Mike's foot.

"I don't pollute my body this way. I just need time to adjust, Joe."

Mike was my fighter—more prone to violence ever since the day Anthony punched him in the gut when he was three. From that day forward, Mike wanted to learn to protect himself and usually tested out the moves on his siblings. More shit had a red hue in our home, caused by the blood that was often lost during a fight. Having four boys hadn't allowed for peace and tranquility.

Mike had beefed up since high school. Working out during his free time, training for a championship bout, and piercing at Inked left him little time to fall in love and settle down.

He was a man driven with a purpose. He wanted a championship, proving that he was the biggest, baddest Gallo brother. He'd deny it, but I knew it was about him showing his superiority over the others. It was an internal drive, set at a young age, and combined with the unhealthy competition that developed between the siblings over the years.

Mike needed someone like his sister. One who could put him in his place and love him at the same time. It wasn't going to be easy, but a mother could dream.

Joe was in a league of his own. He was a no-nonsense guy, so much like his father in looks and attitude that he held a special place in my heart. I'd never admit to having a favorite child, but being so much like Sal, the love of my life, often got him brownie points. He was tough but kind. His heart was bigger than any of my other boys, but he didn't take bullshit from anyone. He was always quick to rescue someone in need, chip in when required, and loved his family with a protectiveness that made a mama proud.

The only thing about Joe I didn't like was his love of motorcycles. When he was a teenager, his friends started with dirt bikes, riding through the woods and doing things I never want to know. I probably would've had a heart attack if I had witnessed most of it, and I am thankful to this day that he survived in one piece.

He hung around with rowdy guys, preferring the company of the bikers at the Neon Cowboy above any other crowd. I worried that they'd lure him into the biker world, turning my son into a hellion and criminal. Joe assured me they were good guys and many of them repeat customers at Inked. Over the years, I learned to let go of my fear, seeing as my son stayed out of the world of the Hells Angels and other MCs in the area.

Although Mike was the fighter, Joe probably came home with torn clothes and bloodied fists more often than any of my sons. It was the protective nature engrained in him, unable to walk away when provoked or rescuing a damsel in distress. No matter how many times I told him violence wasn't the way, he'd assure me "it was my only option, Ma. I don't look for fights."

I was proud of the man he became—tough, independent, rugged, and caring. Even though he was a bruiser, he'd do anything to help a friend. If he loved you, he loved you intensely and with his entire being. Joe didn't give up on people, trying to bring out their good sides and rescue them, even if it meant saving them from themselves.

He was so much like Sal. I could see the passion he felt toward his family at an early age. He chased away every boy who tried to kiss his sister. Lord help anyone who wanted to date her.

Although the four of them were a handful when it came to Izzy, Joe was the most overprotective. I never had to worry about something bad happening to Izzy. Every male in the city knew she was a Gallo and that touching her meant risking your life. Even today, I smiled when I see Joe get in the face of her boyfriends. I had to remind him that she was grown and could make her own decisions.

"Thomas called me this morning, Ma," Izzy said, pulling my attention away from Mike and Joe.

I smiled, thinking about my other son. Thomas wasn't with us today and made my heart ache with the loss. "Me too, baby."

"He sounded good." She smiled, pushing herself into a sitting position and pulling her knees against her chest.

"He did. I don't like not hearing from him every day. I don't know how I'm going to get through the next couple of years."

Thomas was the one who wasn't content with the family business and declared he had other plans. He was always my little rebel, not going with the program, and declaring himself boss. Oftentimes it led to his getting a punch to the gut, but he never wavered from his self-imposed authority above the others.

A few months ago, he finished his training at the Drug Enforcement Agency, DEA, and was prepping to work undercover. Right before Christmas he was given his assignment, the details of which we weren't privy to, and he made it clear that contact would be minimal. He couldn't tell us for how long he'd be gone or where he'd be, just that he'd check in when he could.

I spoke with each of my children a couple times a week, stopping in to the shop sometimes just to see their beautiful faces. I wouldn't have that luxury with Thomas. Not knowing if he was okay would tear at my heart, slowing taking away a chunk until I'd be able to touch him again.

I always thought Thomas would be an actor. The classic looks of James Dean with blue eyes and a strong jawbone. He made the girls swoon at an early age, giving me hope that he'd settle down first and start a family.

Once again, I was wrong, although I'd never admit it. He'd kissed us goodbye, leaving home and dedicating his life to putting away the bad guys, making the world a better place. That was my son. He was always the enforcer, the one trying to keep everyone in line when even I had given up. To say I was proud of him for joining the DEA would be an understatement, but I was worried and mourned for my son who was still alive.

Seeing someone often and then having him disappear felt like a death. Even though my mind knew he was still walking the earth, my heart didn't understand it. I wanted him with me, sitting here today with the rest of the family, but my wish won't come true—not today at least.

"I'm sure he'll call as often as he can, Ma," Joe interrupted, standing from the couch and heading toward the kitchen. "Thomas always calls," he said over his shoulder as he disappeared.

Sal turned toward me, a small smile on his face. "Maria, he'll be fine. Stop worrying about the man."

"I know, sweetheart. It's my job as his mother to worry." My nose tingled as my eyes started to fill with water. Damn it. I promised myself that I wouldn't get choked up today, but talking about him was just too much. Wiping away my tears lingering at the corner of my eyes, I smiled at Sal, shrugging my shoulders.

"Aww, love. Don't cry," he said as he stood, crouching down next to me as he wrapped his arms around me. "Thomas is a strong man. He has a good head on his shoulders. He'll be fine."

I drew in a shaky breath, trying to stop the onslaught of tears that were ready to break loose. "I want to believe that,

Sal." I rested my head on his shoulder, letting myself feel the protection and safety I always felt in his arms.

"I love you, Mar," he whispered in my ear, brushing his lips against my skin, causing a shiver to slide down my spine.

Even at our age, he still did it for me. I didn't see a man in his fifties, but the muscular, sexy man I met over thirty years ago.

He swept me off my feet during my senior year in high school. I hadn't caught his eye until he left for college and returned on Christmas break the following year. During that time, my chest filled out and my body took a more womanly form. We ran into each other at a party and spent the night dancing and laughing. From then on, we were inseparable. The Christmas break had flown by in a flash before he returned to college.

We didn't see each other again until summer rolled around and I was officially done with high school. I had a world of opportunities at my feet; living in Chicago in the early eighties, the world was my oyster. Spending time with Sal left me wanting more time with him. Unable to say goodbye in fall, I applied and was accepted to Notre Dame University, where he attended.

It wasn't like we had a fairy-tale romance. There were moments when our relationship was on the verge of collapse. His overprotective and jealous ways nearly had me running back to the city, looking for a reprieve. Every time I started to pull away, he sucked me back in. I saw that side of him in each of our boys, knowing now that it wasn't something he could control.

He wasn't the type of jealous that scared me, but he always reminded me that I was his. He was right, too. From the moment he put his lips on mine and wrapped me in his arms, I only had eyes for him. No other men existed for me.

Sal Gallo had me hook, line, and sinker. Listening to him tell the story of us, people would think it was the other way around.

"Love you too, Sal," I whispered back, turning my face and kissing his cheek.

Pulling away, he smiled, the small wrinkles around his blue eyes growing more visible. His jet-black hair was combed back, showing off his masculine good looks. The man had grown better looking with age, as was often the case. He looked like a man of the world, rugged and sexy, ready to take on anything that came his way

"You two are making my head hurt more," Mike chimed in, peeking underneath his arm with a smile. "Aren't you too old for that type of behavior yet?"

Sal turned, stalking toward Mike and slapping him on the arm. "Son, when you find the right woman, age will never matter. She'll always be the one you fell in love with."

"What's the secret, Pop?" Anthony asked, turning his attention away from the television. "After one night with someone, I can't stand to be in the same room with them."

Sal laughed at Anthony, rolling his eyes as he often did when Anthony spoke about his groupies. "You haven't met the right one, Anthony. When you do, she's going to knock you on your ass…*hard.*"

"I can't wait to see that," I added, the small smile on my face growing into a giant grin.

"Doesn't it get old? Being with the same person for over thirty years?" Anthony asked, ignoring my statement.

"Never. I love your mother more each day. I never thought a love like that was possible. Do you know the best part of my day?" Sal asked, looking at our children, including Joe, who had returned to his spot on the couch.

"Waking up?" Mike asked, trying to hold in his laughter. "Being old and all."

"Smartass," Sal said, whacking Mike on the head again.

"Ouch! Damn, stop that." Mike held his head, rubbing his temples with his thumbs.

"Stop being a jagoff. The best part of my day is when your mother and I crawl in bed and—"

"Don't you dare say it!" Izzy yelled, covering her ears and squeezing her eyes shut.

Sal laughed, tossing his head back as he held his stomach. The sound of his laughter, even after all these years, made my heart leap. "As I was saying, the best part of my day is when your mother crawls in bed with me and curls into my body. When she rests her head against my chest and I dig my fingers in her hair, I feel at peace."

"Way too much information, Pop," Joe stated, shaking his head and covering his eyes with one hand.

"When you find that—the one person who makes your day complete—that's the one you hold on to. Life can never be boring when you find your soul mate, like I found my Maria." He walked toward me, bent over, and placed a kiss on my lips.

The man still made my insides mushy. Butterflies would fill my stomach when he walked in a room. That's not to say we didn't have our fights, but they always ended the same—making love until everything was forgiven.

"So not happening for me. I hate anyone sleeping in my bed. I want to smack them if they even think about holding me. Makes my skin crawl." Izzy collapsed onto her back as she stared up at the ceiling, resting her hands across her stomach. "Never happening," she whispered.

"I'm with Izzy on this." Joe kicked his feet up on the coffee table, placing his hands behind his head. "I've never been one to want to hold someone. I like my space when I sleep. I get too hot to have someone else throwing off heat at me."

"Pfft," Sal stated, shaking his head. "You just wait. Shit is going to hit you like a ton of bricks. Find the one you want to hold at night, the person you *have* to touch, even in your sleep, and they're the one you can't live without."

My husband sounded like the world's biggest romantic. An outsider would never believe the soft side of my husband. He was much like Joe, steely exterior with a go-fuck-yourself attitude. But when it came to me, he was like putty in my hands. I liked to believe it was my softness and love that changed him, but I think that side of him was always buried inside, waiting for the right woman to make it blossom.

"Ma, what's for dessert?" Anthony asked, altering the course of the conversation. The boy had an insatiable appetite. How he stayed so thin without spending time in the gym was beyond me. He wasn't as big as his brothers; his body was lean and toned, and he was built more like my side of the family.

"Cassata cake." I pushed myself up from my chair, knowing that everyone would want a piece.

"I'll help, Ma," Izzy said, climbing to her feet and following me into the kitchen.

CHAPTER 2
MARIA

AS I REACHED in the fridge to pull out the cake, Izzy asked, "Do you think I'll find someone like Pop was talking about?"

I smiled with my face still hidden by the door. That was my hard-ass daughter, waiting until I was partially distracted and she was out of earshot of her brothers to ask a question like that.

"Yeah, baby girl. You'll find him someday." I picked up the cake, leaving the door open as I set it on the counter.

Izzy closed it, leaning against the fridge as she stared straight ahead, biting her lip. "I don't believe the fairy tales you told me as a child, Ma. I don't think I want someone to come charging into my life and changing who I am. I like myself. A lot. Too much to give myself freely to some man."

I chuckled, remembering thinking the same thing when I was just a few years younger than her. "The trick is to find someone who doesn't change you, but makes you better." I reached in the drawer, rifling through it for the cake server. Cassata cake could be tricky to serve, and I didn't like when it fell and turned into a pile of mush.

"Better how?"

Setting the knife and server on the counter, I turned to face her. "The person who makes you want to be better. They won't change who you are, but they'll bring out the good in you. Your father did that for me. Izzy, listen, I was scared when I met your father. I fell in love with him so fast it made me dizzy. He became my universe. Everything revolved around him, and it terrified me. You have to get beyond the fear to let in the love and allow the true Isabella Gallo to shine through."

"Are you sure you don't fucking work for Hallmark, Ma? I mean, Jesus, that was a bunch of lovely drivel, but I don't think I'm built for that kind of life. I don't think any of us have that ability like you and Pop. We're just too strong-willed." She pushed off the fridge and started to pull the plates out of the cabinet.

I touched her arm, stopping her. "Are you saying I'm weak, Isabella?"

She shook her head, her eyes dropping to the floor. "No, Ma. That's not what I meant."

"It sounded an awful lot like pity to me. When you fall in love someday, you'll have a different opinion." I touched her chin, bringing her eyes to mine. "It takes a strong woman to love a strong man. Strong women like us don't do well with a man who is less than us. You're going to find one who makes you want to run for the hills. It's in your nature to fight back, but if he's strong enough, he won't let you."

Izzy laughed, tilting her head as she looked at me. "We'll see, Ma. I haven't found one who has knocked my socks off. Do men ever grow up?"

Her question made me smile. It was valid and as old as time. "Eventually, baby girl. You're young, and the men your age are too much like children. Enjoy your youth and theirs.

It takes many years before they grow up. Case in point," I said, tipping my head toward the living room and the loud group of *men* talking. "Most of them haven't grown up, but their time is coming." I dropped my hand, reaching for the knife to cut the cake.

"Maybe I'm just surrounded by *them* so much that they taint my view of men." She leaned on the counter next to me, crossing her arms over her chest.

"Your brothers aren't very different than most men. They're stronger and more protective than others, but at their core they're all the same."

"Yeah," she whispered, releasing a deep sigh. "Doesn't matter. I'm having too much fun anyway."

"How's it going with Rob?" I asked, wondering why she hadn't mentioned him lately. Rob, Mike's trainer, was a cocky son of a bitch, and I didn't care for him too much. He wasn't right for Izzy. He didn't have the highest opinion of women, from what I could tell the few times I met him. He was a macho asshole and not the sexy type either.

"We're over."

"Why?" I asked, pretending to be sad.

"He made some dickhead comment, so I kneed him in the balls. It was a dirty way to end it, but swift." She snickered, wrinkling her nose and covering her mouth.

"That's my girl," I said, bumping her with my hip. She was exactly how I wanted her to be. Her brothers taught her the skills to protect herself, although sometimes she used them for other means, but in the end they were always necessary. Izzy was girly when she wanted to be and strong whenever possible. She was the rock of the family, the person who bound us together. "Go tell the boys that dessert is ready, please."

She cupped her hands in front of her mouth and yelled, "Dessert!"

"Jesus. I could've done that, Izzy." I balanced four plates in my hands, trying not to drop the china that was given to me as a wedding present. "Grab a couple since you're in the helpful mood."

She sighed, taking the rest of the cassata cake that was on the counter and following me into the dining room. The boys had beaten us and were already in their seats, waiting to be served.

"Lazy bastards," Izzy muttered under her breath as I set a dish in front of Sal.

I smiled, making eyes at him. "Here you go, sweetheart."

As he winked at me, one side of his mouth rose as a grin played on his lips. "Thanks, love," he whispered, rubbing his chin between his fingers and licking his lips. He was giving me the look I loved, the one that said I was getting lucky as soon as the kids left.

CHAPTER 3
SAL

GOD KNOWS I love my children, but right now, I wanted to wish them well and send them on their way. Right before they arrived, I had Maria pinned against the kitchen counter, kissing her neck as I ran my hand along her inner thigh. Just as I was about to pull out my cock and bury it deep inside her, the doorbell rang.

I swear to shit that kids are born with the ability to cock block. Ever since they were little, they'd walk in at the most inopportune time, putting an end to a very promising evening. Izzy was the worst. Maybe it was her being a female or needier than the others, but it seemed like every time I got Maria naked while still awake, Izzy would knock on the door. There's nothing that'll make your boner disappear along with your naked wife than a little girl crying over a nightmare.

I spent more nights sleeping in my bed with aching balls as my little girl slept in my wife's arms curled against her side. Even with that, Izzy was always my favorite. She's the one who wrapped her arms around my neck every day, giving me small kisses and calling me "Daddy." Her being so much like Maria didn't hurt either. Thomas, Joe, Mike, and

Anthony were more like me, but Izzy—Izzy was an exact replica of my wife.

"Daddy, do you want coffee?" Izzy asked as I dug my fork into the cake.

Even to this day, hearing her call me that made my heart melt. Her voice could turn a shit day into something magical. "Sure, baby girl. If you're getting yourself one." I smiled as I brought the fork to my mouth.

"What about me?" Mike asked as Izzy headed toward the kitchen.

"Get your own," she spat over her shoulder as she walked out of the room.

"Asshole," Mike mumbled, stabbing the cake.

Maria touched my hand, rubbing my wedding ring with her thumb. Her touch, no matter how innocent, made my pants feel a little bit tighter. Turning my wrist, I checked the time, calculating the minutes until the kids left and I could finish what I started earlier.

Locking eyes with Maria, I watched as she put a sliver of cake on her tongue, pulling the fork out slowly. She licked her lips, moaning quietly as a small smile spread across her face. I sucked in a breath, closing my eyes to break the contact.

As Izzy set a coffee cup in front of me, I opened my eyes and sighed. "So, do you kids have plans tonight?" If they did, they'd be gone sooner rather than later.

"Yeah," Joe said, wiping the whipped frosting from his lips. "We're all headed to Karma tonight to hang out with some friends."

"Didn't you go out last night?" Maria asked, looking down the table.

"Yeah, Ma, but it's ladies' night at the club," Anthony replied, shoveling a strawberry that had escaped from his cake in his mouth.

"It's my favorite night of the week at Karma," Mike said, rubbing his hands together and smiling.

Izzy placed a cup in front of Maria, pouring each of us coffee before she set the carafe on the table. "I get to drink for free, so I'm not missing that shit for the world."

I coughed, choking on a piece of cake. The thought of Izzy in a club filled with horny men made my stomach turn. "You're going to watch out for her, aren't you?" I asked, looking down the length of the table at each of my sons.

"Yes, Pop." Joe nodded, scraping the plate clean with his fork.

"We always do," Mike assured me, turning to look at Izzy. "If anyone gives her shit, we'll deal with them."

"That's the problem." Izzy rolled her eyes, crossing her arms over her chest. "They never let me have any fun. I swear to God if you douchebags do what you did last time, I'm going to lose my shit." She glared at Mike.

He shrugged, wiping his lips before placing his napkin on the table. "Yeah, I'm scared of that."

"I'm not a child," she hissed, uncrossing her arms before gripping the armrests on the chair.

"We know, or we wouldn't be so watchful," Joe replied, smiling at Izzy. "Too many assholes out there."

"That's for me to decide. You can't keep treating me like I'm fifteen anymore. I'm a woman, and it's for me to decide who I talk to or not."

"Sometimes it's our job to decide that, Izzy. We know everyone at the club. Some men aren't worthy of you, babe," Anthony stated, rubbing his eyes as he yawned.

"What did they do last time?" Maria asked, her thumb still stroking the skin of my hand.

"Mike kept coming over and pretending to be my

boyfriend. He chased off every guy who tried to talk to me. It was so embarrassing, Ma." She placed her face in her hands as she shook her head. "The men ran away from me. Word spread to leave me alone," she mumbled into her palms.

"Clever," I replied, proud of my sons for their quick thinking.

"Oh, honey. They just love you." Maria reached over, grabbing Izzy's forearm and giving it a quick squeeze.

Izzy dropped her hands, turning to face Maria with a frown. "I wish they'd love me a little less."

"It's almost six. Aren't you guys going to be late?" I asked, hoping they'd be running out the door at any minute.

"Nah, Pop, no one even shows up until after ten."

"Oh," I said, my voice betraying my unhappiness. "Good." I cleared my throat, trying to change my voice. "You won't be late then."

"We have plenty of time," Anthony said, licking the whipped cream off the back of his fork. "I could go for a nap, actually. I'm so damn full." He rubbed his stomach, yawning as he kicked back.

"You better go home and get a little rest, dear," Maria said quickly, her foot sliding underneath the bottom of my pants leg. Her soft toes slid across my skin, making the need I felt for her feel worse than it did the moment the doorbell rang.

"I can just sleep on the couch here."

"No," Maria and I said in unison, turning to look at each other with a smile.

"Do you want us to go?" Joe asked, eyeing us both with a suspicious look.

"No, sweetheart. We just don't want to keep you kids from a fun night." Maria smiled, and I wondered if the kids bought her load of crap.

"I think they want us to go," Mike chimed in, pushing

back from the table with his plate in his hand. "Maybe we should take a hint."

"What hint?" Anthony asked, scratching his forehead.

"They've been giving each other goo-goo eyes for hours now."

"Seriously?" Izzy asked with her mouth gaping open, looking between Maria and me.

Maria's cheeks turned a bright shade of pink as she covered her smile. "No, we love having you kids here. We were *not* making goo-goo eyes."

"Shit you not," Joe blurted out, standing and picking his plate up. "Let's head out and give the lovebirds some time alone."

"Really?" Izzy asked again, shaking her head. "Even after thirty years, you two want us to go so you can have…sex?" She made a face when she said sex, her body visibly heaving forward.

Maria laughed, the pink from her cheeks spreading across her face. "I love your dad."

"Aren't you two too old to have sex?" she asked as she too stood, pushing away from the table. "No. Don't answer that. I don't want to know. There are some things your children don't want to know."

I smiled at Maria, winking as she looked at me under her eyelashes. "Victory," I whispered, blowing her a kiss.

"I think we've scarred Izzy for life."

"She'll get over it, love."

Their muffled voices, mixed with the clanking of dishes, filled the house. I knew within minutes we'd have peace and quiet and be totally alone.

Joe walked back in the dining room and looked at us both with a smile. "We're out."

"Thanks," I said, smiling at my son. He knew. Men

always understood the unspoken truth about sex. Sometimes it was a necessity, the feeling of needing someone gnawing at you from the inside with only one way to make it go away.

He nodded, turning his head back toward the kitchen. "Let's go!" he yelled, walking to Maria and giving her a kiss on the cheek. "Pop," he said, holding out his hand to me. "Have some fun tonight, old man."

"You got it, son." I couldn't help but laugh. My poor wife probably wanted to crawl under the table, which gave me a thought—I wanted her under the table, taking my cock deep between her beautiful lips.

The kids left in a hurry. I assumed the thought of me having sex with their mother drove them out fast. "They're finally gone," I said, pulling her hand to my lips.

"Real smooth, Sal." She laughed, pulling her hand from my grip as she stood.

"Come here, love." I held out my hand to her, pushing back from the table a few inches.

Sliding her hand in mine, I pulled her into my lap, wrapping my arm around her and gripping her thigh with my other hand. Running my nose along her jaw, I could still smell the cake on her lips. I sank my teeth into her neck, stroking her skin with my tongue as she whimpered.

I fucking wanted her more than I had in a long time. Maybe having to wait and being unable to finish what we started this afternoon had amplified it. I would've never expected the want I felt for her to grow over the years, but it fucking did.

Gripping her thigh roughly, I nibbled on her neck, finding the one spot that had her quivering in my arms. Her body twitched as she gripped my arms, digging her nails into my flesh. I moaned, pushing her legs apart before sliding my hand in between.

My hard-on poked her in the ass, begging to be freed. I moaned as I ran my fingers along the side of her lace panties, feeling her wetness soaking through the thin material. Capturing her lips, I kissed her with passion, intertwining our tongues as I slipped my fingers under the lace.

Her legs fell open, inviting my touch, as she moaned into my mouth. I groaned in response, her ass pushing against my cock as she opened to me further.

"Fuck," I murmured against her mouth, thrusting my fingers inside her. She shuddered, her lips leaving mine as her head fell back. With her neck exposed, I kissed a trail across her skin, working my finger inside her pussy. Stroking her G-spot, I circled her clit with my thumb, feeling her pussy milking my fingers.

Maria loved to be finger-fucked. It was the quickest way to get her off. Her body had always been responsive to my touch, even more so as we aged. I turned her in my lap and she moved easily, knowing how I wanted her positioned. Her back to my front, her legs spread with her head on my shoulder, I dipped two fingers back inside her, using my palm to stroke her clit.

I bit her shoulder, digging my teeth into the tender muscle at the base of her neck as I continued to assault her pussy, bringing her closer to coming apart in my arms. Palming her breast, I held her in place, toying with her nipples through her dress.

"Oh, Sal," she moaned, spreading her legs wider in my lap.

"I fucking love your cunt," I whispered against her neck, pulling up with my fingers as I pushed against her G-spot and rubbed my palm harder against her clit.

Her thighs began to quake, and her head fell back on my shoulder as her eyes fluttered closed. My dick strained against my jeans, pushing against her ass as it throbbed for relief. Just as I felt her pussy contracting around my fingers, I dug my teeth deeper into her neck, moving my palm away from her skin and denying her the orgasm she so desperately sought.

"Not yet," I growled, withdrawing my fingers from her body as her bottom followed my hand, trying to get my fingers back inside her.

"Fuck," she muttered, lifting her head from my shoulder and squeezing her legs together.

Bringing my fingers to my lips, I licked them clean, tasting her on my tongue. "God, you taste so fuckin' good, love." I moaned, drawing them from my mouth. "I need to taste more."

"Oh." Maria turned, crushing her lips against mine, moaning as her tongue entered my mouth.

Grabbing her arms, I lifted her ass to the table. Moving the plates, I cleared a spot for her to lie back. "Lie down," I demanded, helping her recline on the dining room table.

Spreading her legs, I stared down at my wife. Her face was flushed, covered with a thin sheen of sweat, and absolutely stunning. Pushing up her dress, I reached for her panties, pulling them down her legs and tossing them to the floor. Reaching behind her knees, I pulled her down the table, letting her feet dangle and bringing her ass to the edge. I smiled at the sight of my wife spread-eagled and waiting.

Sitting back in my seat, I took a moment to look at her lying there with her dress hoisted up, legs open, and her pussy glistening. "Fucking beautiful," I muttered, resting my hands on each leg as I pushed her legs open wider.

"Sal," she whimpered, wiggling her ass against the table as she begged to be taken.

I pushed two fingers inside her, filling her as I latched on to her clit, flicking it with my tongue. Feeling her body shake with my touch, I thrust my fingers in deeper and sucked a little harder, bringing her back to the edge. Her legs clamped around my head, holding my face against her pussy, not letting me escape and leave her hanging.

"Don't stop. Oh my God. Yes!" she yelled, digging her fingers in my hair, pushing my face against her body. "Yes!"

Adding a third finger, I stretched her wide, sucking her clit deeper in my mouth as I caressed it with my tongue.

Her body seized as her head lifted from the table, her breath stuttering before she held it inside. There was nothing like watching a woman come as you ate her, tasting her orgasm against your lips.

Moaning, I chased her up the table as she tried to pull away while she rode the orgasm. Shaking and moaning, she wrapped her legs around my head, giving up on getting away. As her legs relaxed, her head fell back against the table while she sucked in a breath, her chest heaving as she tried to get air.

She rested her hand against her throat, swallowing hard as she grew limp in my arms. Withdrawing my fingers, I stood from the chair and undid my pants. Her eyes looked down her body, zeroing in on my crotch as I pulled out my throbbing cock. "It's my turn now, love."

"Oh God," she moaned, bringing her finger to her lip and biting down on it.

"I plan to make you say that a couple more times before I'm done with you." I smiled, sliding the tip against her wetness.

As I pushed my dick inside, her pussy was tight, still contracting from coming. I gripped her hips, pulling her body down to meet my thrusts as I grunted, chasing the release I so badly sought. Tonight I wouldn't last long; the teasing and waiting had had me on edge all day.

I pumped into her, feeling my balls tighten as my cock hardened inside her pussy. "Fuck," I hissed, gripping her thighs tighter as I held her in place. "Maria," I moaned, thrusting a couple more times before emptying myself inside her.

She locked her ankles around my ass, holding my body against hers as my body shook from pleasure. Tiny aftershocks overcame me, causing my body to collapse against her.

The top of her breast peeked out through her dress as I peppered it with small kisses, tasting the sweat on her skin. She moaned, digging her heels into my ass as she kept my dick inside her. Looking up, I trailed kisses up her chest, up her neck before capturing her lips. "I love you," I mumbled against her mouth as our breathing stayed heavy, both still trying to get enough air in our lungs. I opened my eyes with my lips still attached to hers.

"I love you too, sweetheart." She wrapped her arms around my neck, tangling her fingers in my hair. "Thanks for chasing the kids away."

"I'd do it again in a heartbeat." I laughed, giving her one last kiss before pushing off the table and pulling out. "That's the best dessert you could ever give me."

"Much easier than baking a cake too," she said, a small smile spreading across her face, still flushed from her orgasm.

I laughed as I helped her sit up, wrapping my arms around her body. She rested her head against my chest, returning the hug. "I thank God every day that you didn't let me get away."

"I couldn't," I declared with my face buried in her hair. "I was too in love with you not to spend eternity with you, Mar."

Whenever she told the story of how we met, she always made it seem like she fell first, but to be truthful, I knew I loved her the moment I laid eyes on her. It was like the world melted away, leaving only her and me.

Her senior year in high school was like torture. We couldn't see each other often, only when I had a break and could go back to Chicago for a few days. There weren't cell phones and Skype, just phone calls that were monitored by her parents and letters we wrote. Things were simpler then. Couples had time to miss each other, unlike today, constantly connected through technology.

I enjoyed the chase, trying to keep her as mine. She tried to run, pushing against what was inevitable from the moment we met. The way she blushed, pretending to be shy, she captured my attention. I couldn't think about anyone else, wanting only Maria and setting myself on a path to make it happen.

She was set to attend college close to home under the watchful eye of her parents. After some convincing and reassuring her family, she changed her mind and applied at Notre Dame. It was a Catholic college and got the nod from her parents, who were religious and figured she'd be safe. She was too, just not from me.

Before she joined me in Indiana, we'd only kissed, making it to second base. I never pushed her, happy with the small touches and kisses. I loved her, wanting to spend the rest of my life with her, and I would wait until she was ready.

Maria was innocent when I started dating her. Looking back at our beginning, I was selfish. I couldn't stand by and watch her date other men, playing the field like most college-age women. No, I made her mine and held on tight, not giving her any wiggle room.

My senior year at ND, I popped the question, making sure

I had her entirely. I couldn't bear the thought of leaving her in Indiana for a job in Chicago, choosing to stay and to find a lower-paying job just to be close to her.

As senior year ended, we found out she was pregnant. The wedding was already set and would take place before she started to show. By the time the family found out she was carrying my child, we were husband and wife, and there was nothing that could be said. Her parents were pissed but held their tongues, knowing we were in love.

From that day forward, I swore to love her, and I've spent my life making her happy.

CHAPTER 4
MARIA

LYING IN HIS ARMS, I listened to his snores as I thought about my life. I was truly blessed. I had five healthy children who grew up to be amazing adults. I still had the love of a good man, and there was nothing I wanted for. My life was made, filled with love and family.

I wanted our kids to experience a life filled with as much love as we had, finding happiness and peace. I feared it wouldn't happen anytime soon, most of them too content partying and womanizing to settle down. Kids today were different than when I was young. Things were simpler then.

I didn't worry about Isabella. She'd find her Prince Charming as soon as the right man entered her life. She was too much like me to give up on love. Even if she claimed her independence, wanting no man to weigh her down, she'd cave if *the one* walked into her life. I worried most about my boys, especially Anthony.

The rock-star lifestyle didn't lend itself to relationships. One-night stands, yes, but not companionship and love. Maybe he'd surprise me, settling down with a good woman first, but the likelihood of that happening was almost impossible. He loved the playboy lifestyle, living life by the seat of his pants as he jumped from one bed to another.

Maybe our children just hadn't found their match because of the love that Sal and I shared. We were deeply in love, openly showing our feelings for each other in front of the children. They grew up knowing how we felt for each other, and maybe that hindered their ability to settle. I looked at the ceiling, saying a prayer for my children before curling against Sal's body and drifting asleep.

I don't know if it was how he took me on the dining room table, but I dreamed of Sal in his youth. The way he touched me, commanding my body as he stole my heart.

In our youth, he was a wild man. In the dictionary, I swear there was a picture of him next to the word crazy. A stranger would have thought he was a good Italian Catholic man, attending college and working hard. It was the furthest thing from the truth. He did attend college and was hard-working, but he was also a die-hard partier, loved to drag race, and had a voracious sexual appetite.

I lost my virginity to him in college. Waiting for me to graduate, he was a gentleman and didn't force me into anything. Our first time wasn't in the back of a car or some seedy hotel room. That wasn't Sal's style. No, he whisked me away on a weekend trip, taking me to New York City and booking a room at the Waldorf Astoria. When we arrived, the room was filled with flowers, rose petals thrown about, and champagne chilling on the nightstand.

My mouth dropped open when we walked in the room. Soft music played as we sipped champagne and danced in front of the windows, watching the lights of NYC twinkle in the distance. It was one of the most romantic moments in my life. That night he made love to me, taking it slow and being tender. I cried when it was over, overcome with emotion.

After our first time, I wanted more. My appetite matched his as I tried to make up for lost time. We did it wherever we could—in his car, in a dance club, and in the dorms. The hunger I felt for him never died.

The man hadn't stopped romancing me, even now he'd come home with flowers or cook me a beautiful, candlelit dinner. When the kids were growing up, date night was a necessity. Needing to escape the five screaming kids, we'd go to dinner and sometimes a hotel just for some private time.

My life has been perfect. There wasn't one thing I'd change looking back on the years.

I dreamed of New York, the night in the hotel feeling so real I thought I was living it again. The feel of his lips on my skin and the way he touched my body had my skin tingling.

My eyes flew open, breaking the wonderful memory that my sleep brought me, as I heard his voice.

"You okay, Marie?" he asked, stroking my arm with his fingertips.

Turning to face him, I smiled and covered my mouth with the back of my hand as I yawned. "I'm perfect, sweetheart. I was having such a nice dream."

He kissed my forehead, lingering on my skin. "What was it about?"

I reached up, rubbing his cheek with my hand. "It was about you. Us. The first time we were together."

"Our first date?" he asked, a smile spreading across his face.

"No," I replied, feeling my cheeks heat at the memory.

"Oh," he whispered, his smile turning into a sly grin. "New York?"

"Yes," I admitted, closing my eyes as I tried to picture the room.

“I was slick, huh?” He laughed, kissing a path down my face, sucking my earlobe into his mouth.

“You were that, Sal.” I giggled as his scruff tickled my skin.

“It had to be romantic, Mar. I wanted to knock your knickers off.”

“You did that and more.” I opened my eyes, looking up at my amazing husband, the man to whom I’d given everything and received more in return.

“I wanted you to be mine forever. I didn’t want to leave any doubt in your mind that your heart belonged to me,” he whispered against my ear, sending small shivers across my skin.

“I always knew. That’s why it scared the shit out of me. You were too much for a girl like me.”

“A girl like you?” he asked, one eyebrow moving toward his hairline.

“An innocent.” I smiled, knowing it was a crock of complete shit.

“Mar, I was there. I know you weren’t an innocent. You may have been a virgin, but innocent? Not a fucking’ chance.” He laughed, running his lips down my neck, sucking my skin lightly.

“I was too,” I argued.

“Were not,” he reiterated. “You weren’t easy, but I didn’t corrupt you.”

“Sal,” I whispered as my eyes fluttered closed, feeling his tongue against my flesh.

“Yes?” he murmured against my neck.

“Once you touched me, I knew I could never get enough of you,” I confessed, tipping my head back to give him greater access.

“Mar, I *knew* you’d never get enough once I touched you.

I just needed to convince your mind what your heart already knew. I marked you, making you mine, and I've never regretted a moment of our life."

"Sal?" I asked, my voice breathy and full of want.

"Yes?"

"Mark me again and take me back to that night in NYC."

He laughed, his body shaking against mine as he continued the trail down my flesh with his mouth. "There's nothing I'd rather do this morning than make love to the woman of my dreams."

"Mmm," I mumbled as he captured my nipple in his mouth, sucking lightly as he nibbled with his teeth.

Sal made love to me, taking his time and touching me the way he did the first time so many years ago. I relished it, soaking in every moment and locking it away to look back on with the fondness with which I remembered our first night together. After we both collapsed, exhausted and realizing we weren't as young as were in NYC, we drifted back to sleep with our limbs tangled together.

An annoying ringing sound woke me. Taking a minute to realize what the noise was, I reached for the phone, checking the caller ID. Inked. One of the kids had interrupted a peaceful slumber.

"Who is it?" Sal asked as he rolled away from me with the sheets tangled around his waist.

"The kids," I replied, tapping ON to answer the call.

"Who else?" he muttered, throwing his arm over his face as he tried to block out the sunlight that streamed into the room.

"Hello." I tried to make my voice sound chipper, not like I'd just woken up.

"Ma?" Mike asked, his voice laced with concern.

"Yeah." I moved the phone, muffling my yawn with my hand against the receiver.

"Were you sleeping?"

"No, Michael."

"Are you sick?"

"No." Fuck, the kids knew our pattern. Typically when they called this late in the day, I was already buzzing from my multiple cups of coffee.

"You sound weird."

"I'm fine, baby. What's up?" I asked, trying to change the subject.

"Um, okay. We were wondering if you could stop by the shop today. I finished decorating the piercing room, and Izzy wants your opinion."

"Sure, Michael. I'll be there in a couple hours." I turned, looking at the clock and staring at it as it showed one in the afternoon.

"She'll be here in a couple hours!" Mike yelled before speaking to me again. "Okay, Ma. Bring Pop if you want to." Static filled my ear, and I could hear muffled voices. "Izzy wants to know what time?"

"Tell her I'll be there around three, and I'll see if your father wants to come too." I moved the phone above my head, yawning and trying to hide it.

"I don't know, Izzy. She said three. You fucking talk to her," Mike barked, his voice sounding distant.

"Ma, are you okay?" Izzy asked.

"I'm fine, Izzy. I'll be there at three." I closed my eyes, knowing she was going to start asking questions.

"Are you still in bed? You sound like you were sleeping."

"Baby girl, your father and I fell back to sleep. Everything is fine. I'll be there in two hours."

"You were sleeping? What the hell, Ma? It's afternoon."

"We were exhausted and fell back to sleep. It happens sometimes."

"I think they're sick, Mike. Maybe you should go check on them," Izzy said to Mike as the muffled voices in the shop were barely audible.

"No!" I yelled, sitting up in bed. "Izzy, do not come here. Jesus."

"I'm worried about you two."

"We had sex and fell back to sleep."

"Fuck, Ma. I didn't need to know that. Oh my God. My ears," she hissed, a loud clank causing me to jerk the phone away from my ear. "They were having sex," she said in the background.

"Ma?" Mike asked, returning to the phone.

"Yeah?" I puffed out air, waiting to hear his smartass remark.

"Way to go. See you at three."

Before I could respond, the line clicked dead.

"Freak her out?" Sal asked, knowing how much Izzy hated hearing about our sex life.

"Yep," I replied curtly, breaking out into laughter.

"Kids," he mumbled, stretching as he yawned.

"It's nice to drive them crazy for a change," I said, still laughing as I thought about Izzy dropping the phone in horror.

"What time is it?" Sal asked, turning on his side and resting his hand on my leg.

"One."

"Mm, just enough time for a quickie." He smiled up at me, sliding his hand between my legs.

"Sal," I warned, spreading my legs as I welcomed his touch.

"Let them wonder why we're late, Mar." His fingers raked through my wetness, my body still ready from earlier.

"You're bad," I whispered, lying back down.

"I'm going to show you just how bad I really am," he promised, kissing my hip as he slipped his fingers inside.

Fuck. We were going to be really late. Sal wasn't into quickies. It was against his nature. Inked and the kids would have to wait. It was adult time now, spending the day naked in bed with my husband, reliving our youth.

CHAPTER 5
SAL

STROLLING INTO INKED, THE KIDS' tattoo shop, we were about thirty minutes late. To my shock, Izzy wasn't prowling at the entrance waiting for us.

"Finally," Izzy moaned, standing from her chair as I let Maria walk in front of me when we entered the work area.

"Sorry," Maria said, holding up her hands to stop Izzy from continuing. "We were busy."

"Hey, Pop," Joe said, walking over to shake my hand and give his mother a kiss.

"Hey, son," I replied, looking around the shop. They'd done a ton of work. It looked nothing like it had when they purchased the store last year. Every time I visited, something would be changed, and I was truly in awe of their hard work. "It's looking damn good in here."

"Thanks. Just when we think we're done, Izzy has to change something. She's so damn picky." Joe rolled his eyes, taking a deep breath.

"She's a Gallo. Nothing is ever perfect."

"Fuck, I know it," he hissed, raking his fingers through his hair as he walked back to his station.

"So what was so important for me to see?" Maria asked, walking over to the wall and checking out some new artwork that had been hung. "These are stunning," she said, touching the glass.

"Thanks, Ma. I just hung them up the other day," Joe replied, sitting in his chair as he cleaned off his workspace.

"You made these?" she asked, staring at them in amazement.

"Yeah." He smiled, puffing out his chest as he took pride in his work.

"You're so talented, Joseph." She turned, smiling at him.

His face turned pink, showing a moment of embarrassment. Joe wasn't one to take a compliment. "Thanks, Ma."

"I'm so proud of each of you. The shop looks amazing." I beamed with pride, watching their faces light up. No matter how old they were, they still wanted our approval.

"Thanks, Daddy." Izzy gave me a peck on the cheek before grabbing Maria's hand. "I wanted you to see how I changed the piercing room, Ma. Come see," she said, pulling Maria toward the back of the shop.

"Does it matter, Izzy? Why someone would want another hole in their body, I'll never understand." Maria shook her head as she sighed.

"It's decoration, Ma, and makes a statement. It's about beauty, just like a tattoo," Izzy answered.

"A necklace is a hell of a lot easier and less painful than a piercing. Kids these days. Thank God you kids haven't scarred your bodies in that way." She looked around the room, watching their reactions.

Each one of them looked away, staring at the floor or in the opposite direction. They didn't have to admit it, but they all had a piercing. I hadn't known firsthand, but their reactions confirmed it.

"All of you?" Maria asked as she turned to look at each of them. "Damn. How do I not know these things?" She put her face in her hands, shaking her head.

"It wasn't important," Anthony replied, looking at Maria when no one else would.

"I think it's important to know that my children added holes to their bodies. Jesus," she hissed, moving toward Michael. "Did you do them all?"

He shook his head, still staring at the floor as he whistled. "Nope," he replied, not giving any more detail.

She sighed, shaking her head. "Nothing I can do now." She shrugged. "Show me the room, Izzy."

"I'm sorry, Ma," Izzy stated, leaning over and kissing Maria on the cheek. "Don't be mad."

"I'm not. You're all grown and can make your own decisions. Just don't hide anything from me again. Got it?" she asked.

"Yes," they each answered, nodding their heads as they looked at Maria.

"Good. Now let's see it." Izzy smiled, grabbing Maria's hand and taking her in the back room.

"How's business?" I asked, sitting down in Joe's customer chair.

"Busy. We're booked the entire evening. People are still hungover from New Year's," Joe answered, kicking back in his chair and placing his hands behind his head.

"I knew the shop would be successful. Is there anything I can help with?" They never asked for anything. Whether it was painting, picking out the location, or setting up a business, they handled everything and never asked for help.

"Nah, Pop. We got everything handled," Anthony replied with a giant smile on his face.

"I'm always here if you ever need anything or just want advice."

"We know. How about we take you and Ma to lunch? Have you eaten?" Joe asked, rubbing his stomach. "I'm starving."

"Sure, son. I worked up quite an appetite this morning."

"Jesus," Izzy groaned as she walked back in the room right as I made the statement. "I love you two, really, I do. But there are some things that aren't meant to be shared."

I laughed, knowing she was probably right, but it was too much fun watching her freak out. "Okay, baby girl. You're right."

"Did someone say lunch?" Maria asked, resting her hand on Izzy's shoulder and smiling at me.

"Yeah, Ma. We want to take you and Pop to lunch." Anthony stood from his chair, tossing garbage that was on his station in the trash. "Up for it?"

"I'm famished," she responded, walking toward me.

I slid my arm around her, tucking her under my arm. "How was the room, love?"

"It's beautiful. Way nicer than I'd expect for a room that inflicts so much pain."

"It's not painful, Ma," Mike stated, shaking his head as he locked up the register. "Some find it a turn-on actually."

Maria's body jerked as she turned toward Anthony. "You've got to be kidding me."

"Nope," Mike replied with a small smile.

"I finally understand when Izzy says it's too much information. I don't want to know anymore. Take me to lunch."

"Anything you want, my love." I smiled at her, holding her by the shoulder as we walked toward the door. "We'll wait for you outside while you lock up," I said, pushing opening the door and walking outside with Maria.

"I'm proud of them, Sal. They've done so well, you know?"

I stopped, moving her body in front of mine. Holding her face in my hands, I kissed her lips, inhaling her scent. "I do. They're great kids. You've blessed my life more than I can ever express, Maria. I'm eternally grateful for everything you've done for our family. My family."

"I couldn't have done it without such an amazing husband," she whispered, rubbing her nose against mine.

"I can't wait to get you home." I kissed her again, taking my time as I held the back of her neck, pulling her body against mine.

"You're insatiable," she murmured against my lips.

"Only for you."

I slid my hands down her back, groping her ass and grinding my cock against her. "This is only for you."

"Sal," she moaned, her body stiffening as the door opened behind us.

"Can't leave you two alone for five minutes," Anthony said, walking past us with a small smile on his face.

"How do you think you were all born?" I asked, releasing Maria from my grasp and holding her hand.

"I like to believe it was like the Immaculate Conception," Izzy stated, standing behind us as we walked into the parking lot.

"Someday you'll have someone you can't keep your hands off of, baby girl," Maria said, squeezing my hand as we approached the car.

"Shh," I whispered. "I don't want to hear that." I wrinkled my nose, unable to think of my daughter as anything but a little girl.

"Enough talking about love and all that mushy shit,"

Anthony said, opening the car doors for everyone to pile in. "One car?" he asked, turning to face me as I was about to open our car door for Maria.

"Where are we going?" I asked, opening the passenger door for my lovely wife.

"Let's hit the diner down the street. They have amazing burgers," Joe said, climbing in the passenger seat of Anthony's SUV.

"We'll meet you kids there. I want to be alone with your mother, and then we can head home from there."

"Okay, Pop," Anthony replied, jogging around to the driver's side as the rest of the gang piled into the vehicle.

I closed Maria's door, strolling to my side and climbing in. Starting the car, I placed my hand on the back of her seat, looking back before pulling out.

"We could've gone with the kids, Sal."

I shook my head, looking at my beautiful wife. "Not as long as I have a hard-on. I don't know what has gotten into me, Mar, but I feel like I did when I was twenty-five." I pulled out of my parking spot, following behind Anthony as we left the parking lot.

"They say we only get better when we age." Maria smiled, touching my cheek with her soft fingers.

"I can't wait to see what the next thirty years holds, love," I said, bringing her hand to my lips, kissing each finger tenderly as I drove.

"Me either, Sal. There's no one else I'd rather spend it with."

I don't know what I did to deserve such a blessed life. To have the love of a good woman, amazing children who have grown up to be spectacular adults, and health on our side—it was more than I could've ever dreamed for when I was young. I was a proud father and husband, the best thing in the world.

I had a feeling the best was yet to come.

THROTTLED

CHAPTER ONE

SUZY

THANKSGIVING

"Push," City barked as his face turned red.

"I am pushing, damn it." I could barely breathe.

"More, just a little bit more," he said through gritted teeth. "One more push, sugar."

I bore down and used my legs as leverage. My face felt prickly and I wanted to give up. It was too much for me to handle. I couldn't do this. Why did I ever think I could? City always made my mind crazy and had me agreeing to do things I didn't want. I knew I didn't have the physical strength to handle this.

I grunted, exhausted. "Fuck, I give up," I said, gasping for air but not letting go.

"You know your filthy mouth does wicked shit to me," he said, winking at me.

"I'm in no mood to talk about your dick right now, Joseph." I glared at him. Sweat broke out near my hairline as my legs began to tremble.

"As soon as we're done, I'm going to show you exactly how hard that mouth makes me."

I glared daggers at him. I didn't want to think about his beautiful cock. "Not happening," I said as I pushed with all my strength. "Are you even helping?" I bit out.

"What the fuck does it look like?"

"Looks like you're standing there getting a kick out of watching me push this damn thing by myself." I grunted, my knuckles turning white.

"If I could push and get this shit done, I sure as fuck would, sugar. You can do this."

I shook my head just as the bed slid into place. "I'm never helping you move furniture again. Shit's for the birds," I said as I collapsed on the bed.

The light streaming through the windows threw a shadow on the bed as City stood between my legs. "You were the one that said I shouldn't do it alone. Who am I to stop you when you put your foot down?"

He looked like an angel with the glowing sunlight behind him. His body was just as divine as it was the night I met him over a year ago. He had a chiseled jaw covered in short, dark hair, his fierce blue eyes shining as bright as the sun, his dark brown hair a mess. I wanted him just as much as I did the first time we touched.

I smiled at him as I admired his ruggedness. "You're still recovering, City. I didn't want you to get hurt. We didn't have to do it right this second, I just made a suggestion."

"Sugar, I know how you are. You don't do suggestions. You wanted it moved and now it is." He leaned forward, hovering over my lips. "I'm not breakable. I'm healed and got the okay to go back to full activity." He wiggled his eyebrows.

I giggled; the man made my heart skip a beat because I loved him so much. "I didn't know you were holding out on me." I wrapped my arms around his neck and kissed him.

"You couldn't have moved the bed by yourself anyway. It's too heavy."

"I could've, but it was more fun to watch you struggle." The deep vibrations of his laughter shook the bed.

I smacked his shoulder. "Could not." I grinned.

"Could too. Where was I?" He stared into my eyes. "Ah," he said, grinding his dick into my leg. "That filthy mouth of yours."

"You made me this way. I used to be sweet and pure. Now look at me," I said, digging my fingers into his thick hair.

"I'm looking, Suz, and I'm loving everything about you. I fell in love with the girl I found on the side of the road. You're mine forever now," he said as he pulled my arm down and placed a kiss on the diamond ring he gave me after his accident.

The happiness I felt was mixed with sorrow at the bitter memory of almost losing him. I would've been lost if he died that day. I never realized how full my life was and how much he meant to me until he was almost ripped from my grasp. "Always yours, City. Make love to me," I whispered against his lips.

"There's my cock-loving girl." He crushed his mouth to mine, his hands sliding up the side of my tank top. His touch gave me the shivers; the depth of his voice stole my breath even after a year. I couldn't get enough. I was his cock-loving whore, but only his. He had that effect on me.

Just as the rough tip of his finger touched my nipple, an alarm sounded from downstairs. "Fuck," he muttered, pulling back.

"Ugh, really?" I whined. "Can't we just let it go for a little while longer? Please?" I begged, grinding my panties against him, feeling the hard piercing press against my clit.

He leaned his forehead against mine, drawing in a shaky

breath. "We can't. You know how my family is. I can't ruin the turkey. I'll never hear the end of that shit, and neither will you."

I pouted, running my fingernails up and down the back of his neck. "Five more minutes won't matter."

"When have we ever taken five minutes?" he asked, sitting up. "Up ya go. We have cooking to do, woman. Everyone will be here in two hours." He grabbed my arms and pulled me forward.

"I don't know why we couldn't just get everything pre-cooked. I survived Thanksgiving without having made every-thing from scratch." I collided with his chest, peering into his baby blues with a smile.

"Gallos do not do already prepared. You watch and I'll cook." He kissed the top of my head, reaching under my ass and pulling me into his lap.

"How about," I whispered against his lips, rubbing the rough stubble on his face, "if I help and I get a little City appetizer before they get here."

He smirked, a small laugh escaping his lips. "You want to cook?" He raised an eyebrow.

"I want cock and for that I'll cook." I smiled, nipping his lips.

"You got yourself a deal, sugar," he said as he grabbed my sides and tossed me on the bed and ran. I giggled and kicked, hopping off to run after him.

CHAPTER TWO

CITY

"YOU LOOK FLUSHED, DEAR," Ma said to Suzy as she hugged her. "Are you feeling well?"

I covered my mouth, hiding the smile while Suzy blushed an even deeper shade of red.

"I'm just fine, Mrs. G." Suzy glared at me as she patted my ma's back.

"Are you sure?" Ma rested her hand on Suzy's stomach. "No bun in the oven yet?"

Oh, fuck. Suzy was about to pop her lid. I looked down, holding my face in my hand, unable to look Suzy in the eyes.

"Sorry to disappoint you, but no. No bun, Mrs. G."

"It's okay, love, and stop with the Mrs. G. Call me Ma. Soon it will be official."

"Yes, Ma."

I couldn't look up. Pissed-off Suzy was too damn cute and I knew I wouldn't be able to stop my laughter.

"Son." My ma rested her hand on my shoulder.

"Hey, Mama." I wrapped my arms around her and snuck a glance at my bride-to-be. She had my pop's full attention.

"Happy Thanksgiving, baby." She kissed my cheek, standing on her tiptoes.

"You too, Ma. Thanks for pissing Suzy off for me." I laughed.

"Just don't want anyone to forget about a grandbaby." She smiled innocently.

"We wouldn't forget, Ma. We watch you knit every Sunday."

"Crochet," she corrected me. "Is she really okay? I haven't seen her so red in a while."

I couldn't stop the laughter bubbling out. "She's just fine, Ma. She had her hands full before you got here." I looked over my ma's shoulder, winking at Suzy.

Her mouth dropped open as she realized what I said. Before my parents walked in the door, she was on her knees sucking me off. Her hand cupped my balls while the other stroked my shaft. Pure motherfucking heaven.

"I know Thanksgiving is a lot of work, Joseph. We appreciate all your hard efforts." She wrapped her hands around my back and turned toward Suzy. "It means a lot us."

"It was *hard*"—I coughed—"work, Ma, but Suzy took it like a champion." My body shook against my mother as I placed a kiss on her hair.

Suzy's eyes almost bugged out of her head. "Just a little thing, Ma," Suzy said, and then laughed.

I nodded to Suzy, impressed with her quickness. I'd get her later for that comment. "Hey, Pops." I couldn't take the double meaning anymore. I needed to change the direction of this conversation.

"The house looks amazing, son." He wrapped his arms around me, giving me a giant bear hug. I loved that my father wasn't afraid to show us how much he cared.

"We just finished everything last week. I don't ever want

to build another house again. What a pain in the ass!" I said as I smacked him on the back.

"The fireplace framed by the ceiling-to-floor windows is breathtaking," Ma said, as she walked to look out at the windows. There was a large pool with a waterfall on the lanai.

"I always thought you'd go with more of a classic Florida style of architecture, but I must say, I love the log cabin look. Reminds me of when your ma and I would take trips to the mountains before we had you kids." He walked next to Ma and placed his arm around her. He rubbed her shoulder, slowly stroking her skin while they rested their heads together.

Ma patted his hands and then turned. "Where's the nursery?" she asked with a large smile on her face.

"It's a spare bedroom, Ma," I said, trying not to laugh. The woman was relentless.

"Someday there will be a baby in there," she said, pointing at Suzy.

A change of subject was needed quickly. "Want a drink, Pop?" I asked, wrapping my arm around him, leading him into the kitchen.

"I'd love a stiff one," he replied, looking around the finished living room.

"Yeah, Suzy had one before you got here." I smiled, looking back at her over my shoulder.

"I'll get it for you, Mr. G," Suzy said as she walked by and elbowed me in the ribs. "Why don't you show your parents all the hard work we've done?"

I hunched over, feeling the sting of her bony elbow as I pretended to catch my breath. "Sure." I smiled at her.

Suzy was a vision. Skin slightly pink and pale, blonde hair flowing down her back with her knee-length white sundress. She looked like an angel, but I knew the truth. The girl came off as sweet and innocent, but she was a tiger and had developed quite a liking for curse words. I rubbed off on her. To say I was proud to call her mine was a complete understatement.

"The house is beautiful," Ma said as she grabbed my arm. "You trying to kill her?" she whispered as we walked into the great room.

"Ma, she gives as good as she gets."

"I'm sure, baby," she said as she patted my stomach. "Wow, the fireplace really turned out better than I thought."

I looked at it with pride. It took me days to get it just right, laying each stone one at a time. "Thanks, it was worth all the hours." The rounded river rock made it a challenge, but I sure as fuck wasn't going to let it beat me.

Ma touched the stones and ran her hand across the large wooden mantel. "I'm speechless. The entire place is…" She smiled, looking around.

"I know, Ma. It's perfect. Turned out better than I could've dreamed."

"Here's your drink Mr. G," Suzy said as she handed him a glass of whiskey on the rocks.

A loud pounding on the door made my mother jump. "I'll get it," I said.

Suzy nodded. "I'll show them around."

The banging continued. "Jesus," I yelled as I opened the door.

Mike's fist stopped in midair, as he was about to land another blow. "Sorry, didn't think you heard me."

"I think the dead heard you, brother." I opened the door, letting him inside. His large body hid Mia. "Hey, Doc. How the hell are ya?" I asked Mia as Michael walked inside.

She smiled, holding out her hand to me. I shook my head,

grabbing her, and pulled her to my chest. "I want a hug. We're beyond handshakes, Doc. You've seen me naked, for shit's sake." I laughed, feeling her tense in my arms.

She blushed, her cheeks turning red as she pulled away. "Well, um…"

"It's okay, Mia. I was dying and you saved me. I'm just harassing you."

She swallowed, looking at Mike before turning back to me. "You know how your brother gets." She chewed her lip as she looked around my body to Mike.

"Don't worry. He doesn't give a shit about me. He knows I have my girl. Come on in." I stepped aside, letting her pass. "How's the clinic?" I asked as I followed her toward the sound of Mike's voice.

"I promise I didn't look, by the way." She winked, with a small smile on her face. "It's so great, Joe. Your family has done so much." She smiled, stopping at the counter to watch everyone else in the great room.

"Mia," Ma said, holding out her arms.

I smiled as Suzy wrapped her arms around me, placing her head on my chest. Life couldn't get much better than this. Mike and Pop sat on the couch talking, Ma and Mia greeted each other, and Suzy was at my side.

The front door opened and I turned to see who it was. We were only missing Izzy and Anthony. "Smells damn good in here," Izzy said as she walked into the kitchen.

"Hey, sis," I said, walking over to hug her.

"I brought someone, I hope you don't mind." She smiled, looking up into my eyes. Izzy was never this sweet.

"Who?" I asked, looking up.

Anthony waved and stepped aside. Fuck. "Really?" I whispered in her ear, grabbing her by the shoulder.

"Come on, Joey. He didn't have anywhere else to be. He

was in town and I told him he could spend the day with us. I know you made enough food for an entire army." She batted her eyelashes at me.

"He's here now." I shook my head, looking down at her. "Next time ask, Izzy."

"Okay," she whispered in my chest, squeezing me before ducking under my arms.

I held out my hand to Sam as Anthony walked by and grimaced. He felt the same way I did about this fucker. "Nice to see you again, Sam."

He placed his hand in mine, gripping it roughly. "I go by Flash now."

"Whatever," I said, rolling my eyes. "Welcome to my home," I said, pulling him close as I crushed his fingers in my grip. "If you hurt my sister, I'll fucking bury you. Got me?"

"Easy now, City. I wouldn't dream of it. We're just friends." He stood toe to toe with me, gripping my shoulder.

"I don't care who the fuck you think you are or what MC you're in. You're still Sam to me and I can still whip your ass. Just so we're clear." I glared at him. Who the fuck did this punk think he was?

Suzy's arms slid around me as her tits crushed against my back. "Everything okay, baby?" she asked.

"Just perfect, sugar. This is Sam, Izzy's friend."

She released me and held out her hand to him. "Hi, Sam, I'm Suzy. Nice to meet you," she said, smiling, unaffected by his inability to dress up. He had on his MC cut and jeans—classy for the holidays.

"It's my pleasure, Suzy." He pulled her hand to his lips and kissed it gently. "You have a beautiful home."

"Thank you, Sam."

I growled, wanting to punch him in the face. His eyes

flickered to me, his lips turning up in a half-smirk before he looked back to Suzy.

"Joe's a very lucky man. I hope you don't mind me crashing the party." Sam's eyes flickered to me with a shitty grin before looking at Suzy. I wanted to rip his head off, the fucking weasel.

"Not at all. Come on in and make yourself at home," Suzy said with a smile.

As Sam walked past me, I glared at him but I knew I should be nice. Suzy stood on her tiptoes, rubbing my cheek and staring at me with her head tilted. "What's wrong, City?"

I looked down at her, giving her a half-smile. Her kind eyes and big heart always did a number on me. "Nothing, sugar. I just don't like him."

"I'm sure he's harmless. Let's enjoy our first Thanksgiving in our new home."

I kissed her hair, taking in the coconut sweetness on the silk strands. "Harmless isn't a word I'd use to describe Sam, but you're right, let's enjoy it."

"No more sex references either," she said as she pinched my ass.

"Sugar, I make no promises when it comes to you and that sweet pussy," I said as I crushed my lips to hers, stealing her breath.

CHAPTER THREE

SUZY

"WHAT STILL NEEDS to be done, dear?" Mrs. G asked as I sipped my white wine. "We're just over a week away." She smiled, her eyes soft. I knew she was happy and excited. The wedding was all we talked about anymore.

"I think everything is ready. I have a couple to-do lists, but it's last-minute stuff." I set my fork down, unable to take another bite. "Maybe you can look over the seating chart with me one more time while the boys watch football after dinner."

Her teeth sparkled as her smile grew wide. "I'd love to help."

"Me too," Izzy said from across the table. "Maybe we can have the boys do the dishes for once." She grinned, looking around the table.

"Oh, hell no," Anthony said. "That's women's work." He shook his head, shoveling another forkful of stuffing in his mouth.

Clinking from all the ladies dropping their forks on the table made me laugh. That wasn't the thing to say at this table.

"No shock why your ass is still single," Michael said, slapping Anthony on the back of the head.

"When have we ever done dishes on Thanksgiving? I'm just saying. It's our job to eat and watch football, and the ladies cook and clean. It's the Italian way." He smirked and his body jerked. "What the hell was that for?" He looked at Izzy.

"Being a dumbass," Izzy said as she rolled her eyes.

"Anthony, you boys can handle it this year. The ladies have wedding plans to finalize," Mrs. G said.

"But Ma," Anthony replied with wide eyes.

"No buts, mister. There are enough of you that you'll get it done quickly. Joseph and Suzy's wedding is more important than football this week." Her mouth was set in a firm line. Mrs. G was sweet as apple pie, but no one, and I mean no one, challenged her.

"Fine, Ma." He covered his mouth with his napkin and mumbled.

I bit my lips, stifling my giggle. "We never went around the room sharing what we're most thankful for."

"You're right, Suzy. The boys were so hungry, I didn't even think about it. Forks down," Mrs. G said, placing her fork and knife next to her plate.

A collective groan filled the room. The boys didn't like anyone getting between them and their food, or their women, for that matter. The two things were non-negotiable.

"I'll start," she said. "I'm thankful for my children and loving husband. I'm thankful for the new additions to the table and new members of the family, Suzy and Mia. I'm thankful that Thomas is safe even though he's missed another holiday. I've been blessed with each and every one of you being a part of my life." She smiled, wiping her eyes.

Mr. Gallo stood and cleared his throat. "I'm thankful to live another year to hopefully see the Cubs win the World Series." He laughed. "I'm thankful that I can be proud of each of my children, Mia and Suzy included. When I met and married your mother, I never dreamed that she would give me such wonderful children and a life filled with such joy. I can honestly say I have no regrets, and for that I thank my lucky stars each day." He tipped his head and winked at Mrs. G before sitting.

She blushed and blew him a kiss. I wanted that life. I wanted that love. The lifetime-enduring happiness that seemed out of reach for most.

"I'm thankful for my uncomplicated single life. No offense." Anthony looked at his mother. "I'm thankful for this meal and having you all part of my life. That's enough sappy shit for me to say in one day." He blew out a breath and smiled.

"Aw, you're so sweet, Anthony, you almost made my teeth hurt," Izzy said. "I'm thankful for having two wonderful parents. I'm thankful for having more women around the table. Being outnumbered sucks." She looked at Flash, and he shook his head before he turned to Michael.

Michael glared at him. "Fine, I'll go, you pansy ass." He cracked his knuckles and put his arm around Mia. "I'm thankful for all of you, but most of all for the woman at my side. I haven't been the same since the day I knocked her on her ass. I love ya, Mia, baby." He leaned forward, holding her chin, and kissed her gently.

All the love around the table made my eyes water. This family had become everything to me. City was the icing on the cake, but they were the silky-smooth filling.

"Pussy whipped," Anthony choked out.

"Shut the fuck up." Michael slapped Anthony on the head without looking, as his lips lingered over Mia's mouth.

City stood, looking down at me with a smile that made my stomach flutter. "On that note, I'll get the mushy shit out of the way. I'm thankful that Suzy has agreed to be my wife. I couldn't ask for a better person to share the rest of my life with. We had a rough beginning, but I knew I had her the moment I kissed her. I'm thankful to Mia for helping save my life after the accident." He smiled at Mia, and she blushed. "I'm thankful for my family…well, maybe not Anthony, but everyone else."

He wrapped his arm around my shoulder, pulling me forward before he kissed me. His lips were warm and sweet from the wine. My nose tickled from the facial hair he'd become so fond of. As he pulled away, I moved with him, wanting more of his mouth. He winked, giving me the cocky grin that always set my body on fire.

I swallowed, trying to regain my composure. "I'm thankful that City is still with me after all we've been through. I'm thankful that he survived and is healthier than ever. I'm thankful for each and every one of you for being around this table, even Anthony." I laughed as Anthony smiled, winking.

All the Gallo men were to die for—they were the panty-dropping variety. Women couldn't say no to them; that was how City stole my heart. Everyone dug back into their meal, scooping up the stuffing and dreaded green bean casserole, and chatter filled the large dining room. I set my napkin down, sat back in my chair, and let the joy I felt seep inside me.

There was something about a man that could cook. I hadn't gone hungry or worried about which brand of Ragu jarred sauce to use since I met City. He had so many skills, and every first impression I had about him was wrong. He was cocky, I hadn't been wrong about that, but City wasn't the overbearing brute I thought he was when we first met.

City was an artist, a romantic, a loving partner, a cook, and an amazing person. The most diverse and well-rounded person I knew. His artistry when it came to tattooing was beyond amazing, colorful and intricate; he spent hours in his studio upstairs creating designs for clients.

He wasn't easy or simple, but he was mine.

"Sugar, you okay?" City brushed the back of his knuckles against my cheek.

I turned to him, smiling, tears welling in my eyes. "Yeah, babe. I'm great." I wiped the corner of my eye, turning to him and taking in his rugged beauty.

"Why the tears?" he whispered in my ear, rubbing my cheek with the rough pad of his thumb.

"I'm just happy." I touched his hand, moving into his touch, and leaned to the side to kiss him.

He smiled, moving toward me and enveloping my lips in a loving kiss. "I can't wait to call you my wife." He searched my eyes, a small smile on his face. "You'll be mine legally."

"I've always been yours, City." I smiled, warmth flowing through my body. He'd never let me think otherwise. He'd laid claim to me early in the relationship and never let me too far out of reach. No matter how scared I was or how hard I tried to fight him, the pull he had over me was too great.

The cocky grin I could no longer live without spread across his face as he grunted. "There's no going back now, sugar." He crushed his lips to mine, stealing my breath, the familiar dull ache returning between my legs.

"You two are kinda nauseating," Anthony said, pretending to gag.

We both turned to glare at Anthony. City cleared his throat. "Someday you'll understand, brother."

"Not going to happen," Anthony said, grimacing before stuffing a piece of bread in his mouth. "I have too much to offer to be tied to just one woman," he said with a muffled voice and small pieces of bread falling from his mouth.

"Yeah, I can see that. Who couldn't resist such a specimen of a man?" I said, breaking out into laughter.

Mrs. G pushed back her chair to stand; the sound of the wooden chair scraping against the slate flooring sent a chill through my body, reminding me of fingernails on a chalkboard. "All right, boys, the ladies are done and we're going to work on the wedding plans. Get this place cleaned up." She raised an eyebrow and looked around the table. The boys, including Mr. G, nodded at her but grumbled under their breath. "Come on, ladies, we have work to do. We have eight days to make it perfect."

Mia, Izzy, and I rose from our chairs and followed Mrs. G out of the dining room. "I can't believe I'm going to have a sister," Izzy said, throwing her arms around me. "Finally, the tables are turning. We're so close to equalizing the cock in this family," she whispered in my ear, a small giggle escaping her lips.

"That's not possible," Mia said as she walked behind us. "All the vaginas in the world couldn't outnumber those boys. They're too…"

"Full of themselves," Mrs. G chimed in, turning to face us. All of us laughed as we walked up the stairs. Gallo men were unique, and we knew it. "It's my fault. I made them who they are, but never fear, ladies—we control everything, even though they think otherwise."

We sobered, hanging on her every word. "You control them, Ma. We sure as hell don't." Izzy rested her body against the wall outside the wedding war room I'd created.

"I'll share my secrets when we're inside and out of the

boys' earshot. They don't need to know who really holds the power. It may bruise their male egos," Mrs. G said, her body shaking with laughter.

"Come on, ladies. Be prepared, it's organized chaos inside." I smiled as I opened the door, standing back to let them walk in first.

"Wow," Mia said as she stepped inside and looked around with her mouth agape.

"Holy shit," Izzy said, stepping into the room with wide eyes as she spun around.

"I wouldn't expect anything less from you, dear," Mrs. G said as she put her arm around me and gave me a tight squeeze as we entered the bedroom.

I smiled at her, blushing. "We haven't made it into a bedroom yet. We're using it for the wedding only right now. It is pretty damn cool, isn't it?"

"Will it be a nursery?" Mrs. G looked at me with hopeful eyes.

"Maybe someday." I smiled, my stomach in knots.

We weren't ready for a baby, not just yet. I had too much City left to enjoy.

"No worries. I have all the faith in you, my sweet Suzy." She released me and walked toward the gown.

My body warmed from her sincerity and love as I took in the most important women in my life, all in one spot and without our testosterone-laden other halves.

"This is stunning," Mrs. G said, running her fingers across the lace skirt of my wedding gown.

"Joey is not allowed in this room anymore. I can't risk him seeing my dress." I shook my head. He begged me to wear it for him, he wanted to dirty it—his words, not mine—before I walked down the aisle. That wasn't going to happen.

"Good idea," Mrs. G said, smiling at me.

I watched them as they looked at every detail I'd laid out across the expansive space. I had a seating chart that looked more like an invasion plan for a war, tables and sticky notes everywhere in different colors to represent our two sides. Izzy eyed the party favors while Mia grabbed my wedding shoes and studied them.

"These shoes are amazing. Everything is going to be beautiful, almost magical." Mia placed the shoe back in the box. "You're so organized. I thought I was anal, but babe, you have me beat by a mile," she said with a small laugh.

"What needs to be done?" Mrs. G asked, staring at the seating chart.

I stood next to her, looking over my work. "I just need to make sure I have everyone seated correctly. I don't know most of the people on here. Joey said this person couldn't sit near that person. I'm so confused and don't want to mess it up."

She touched my hand, looking at me with a smile. "I'll inspect it, but from what I see so far, it's perfect."

"Thanks, Mrs. G."

She looked at me, her mouth set in a firm line.

I gulped, realizing my mistake. "*Mom.* Thanks, Mom," I quickly corrected.

She smiled, her face growing soft as she turned back to the poster board.

"Let's talk about the bachelorette party while Ma is busy." Izzy grabbed my arm, pulling me toward the small table on the other side of the room.

"Maybe she wants to come," I said, looking at Mrs. G.

"Nope, she's staying home with Daddy. I have everything planned out."

"Izzy," I warned, my eyes snapping to her face.

She smiled, looking overly pleased with herself. "Don't worry. I have it all under control," she said, winking at me.

"That's what I'm worried about." I said, leveling her with my stare.

"As a bridesmaid it's my duty to give you a kickass bachelorette party. Whatever happens, just blame it on me. I can take care of those boys."

"Give us the rundown," Mia said, not letting me respond to Izzy.

"Okay, well, we have a party bus picking up all the girls here on Friday night and the boys will have their own," Izzy said. "We'll be spending the evening at Shepard's Beach Resort. I reserved the top floor, where the suites are located, and we'll party our asses off. They have a dance club set up at night and we can drink till we puke and crawl to our rooms." She bounced up and down in her chair. "This shit is going to be so kickass."

I looked down, twisting my fingers in my hands. "No stripper, Izzy." I wasn't asking. I wanted to make it clear that I didn't want any half-naked men touching me.

"Don't worry," she said, her smile growing wider as my stomach turned over.

"Izzy, I'm serious." I stared at her, holding her with my gaze.

"Relax, Suz."

"I'm looking forward to a girls' night out," Mia said, squeezing my arm. "Michael doesn't let me out of his sight much. Well, really he doesn't let me out of his bed." She laughed, her face turning red.

Izzy winced. "My ears are going to bleed or my brain will explode with that image. Do not mention my brothers and sex. Ever. Ick," she said, sticking out her tongue like she was going to throw up.

"What about Flash?" Mia asked, smirking.

"He's just a friend." Izzy frowned, looking to her mother.

"He looks like he wants to be more than friends," I added. "You've never brought anyone around for family dinners, let alone a holiday, Izzy."

"Eh, he was in town and he doesn't have any family in the area. We hang out sometimes but it's nothing more than that." She drew in a breath. "He's not right for me, and the guys, well, they'd never allow him to be part of this family."

"What are you girls talking about?" Mrs. G asked as she sat down with us.

"The monsters that you've created," Izzy said quickly, changing the subject.

"Ah," Mrs. G said, turning to me. "Suzy, everything looks perfect. I wouldn't change a thing on that seating chart."

I smiled, happy that I hadn't messed it up. "So Ma," I said, the words still foreign on my tongue. "You were going to share your pearls of wisdom with us about how to handle our boys."

She laughed, her eyes twinkling. "Well, it's taken me many years to hone my skills and learn how to get what I want. It's a fine line, though, ladies. You can't let them know you're the one silently controlling the strings from the background. They like to think they're the puppet master, when in reality we hold all the strings."

"Still not giving me details," Mia said, shaking her head.

"Michael and Joseph are tough boys, and Izzy, any man that steals your heart will be just as tough as your brothers, if not more. This information will be for all of you to file away and use when necessary."

We leaned forward, waiting to hear her next words.

"Always remember to make them think they're in charge." She smiled and laughed. "That's the key. Don't ever make them think otherwise. Love them hard, ladies. Smother them with your love. Be fierce when necessary and never back down. Once you give in, they'll expect it always. When they won't give you what you want, well, that's when you deny them the thing they want most." She paused, wiggling her eyebrows.

"Oh my God, Ma. I don't even want to think about you and Pop having sex." Izzy stuck her finger in her mouth, pretending to gag.

Mia and I broke into a fit of laughter.

Mrs. G shook her head. "Deny them food, Izzy." She laughed. "Your mind is always in the gutter, child."

I couldn't control myself. I sagged into the chair, hysterical, with tears streaming down my face. Izzy glared at her mother, unconvinced by her pearls of wisdom. Mia put her head down on the table, her body shaking from the giggles we'd all developed.

I sobered, sitting up in my chair and leaning my elbows on the table. "That won't work for me, Ma. I don't do the cooking. It's hard to deny a man food when he does all the cooking."

"Well then, you only have one other weapon." She smiled, patting Izzy on the leg.

"For the love of God, Ma. Really. My ears are going to explode and I'll never be able to have sex again if you keep talking." Izzy closed her eyes, rubbing her fingers roughly against her skin. "No more. I can't listen."

"Izzy, dear. I was going to say that Suzy shouldn't snuggle with Joey. Snuggle, Izzy."

"Snuggle?" Izzy looked at her ma with wide eyes. "Really? Who the hell snuggles?"

My laughter returned, worse than before. Izzy and Mrs. G

were the cutest two people I knew. I could listen to them talk all day.

"All Gallo men snuggle, Izzy," Mrs. G stated calmly and matter-of-factly.

"Bullshit," Izzy coughed. "Suzy?" She looked at me for confirmation.

"I'm sorry to blow the image you have of your brother, but he loves to snuggle. He'll never use those words, but there's not a night that goes by that I'm not required to fall asleep in his arms."

"You've ruined the image I have of my brother being the big bad wolf." She shook her head, turning her attention to Mia. "Michael too?"

Mia nodded. "Yep, but there's no place I'd rather be. I feel so safe in his arms. He's like an overgrown security blanket. I don't think we've ever fallen asleep without our bodies being entangled."

Izzy rubbed her forehead, looking to the floor. "My mind is blown. Jesus. I know there's no way in hell Anthony is a snuggler. No goddamn way." She shook her head and looked at her ma. "You did this to these men, Ma."

"I snuggled them since the moment they were born, just like I did you. Even as little babies, their fingers would tangle in my hair, playing with the strands."

"I'm not a snuggler," Izzy interrupted, holding up her hand. "Never have been and never will be."

"You will, my dear. When you find the right man." Mrs. G swept her fingers across Izzy's cheek, tilting her head and smiling. There was so much love between the two women, it radiated off of them.

"Nope. I like my space. I'll never give in. Who knew I was really the one with the penis after all these years?" Izzy laughed, hitting the table.

"Don't let the boys hear you say that," I said, grinning at her.

"What are they going to do? Cuddle me to death?" she asked through her laughter, her body slipping from the chair in hysterics.

CHAPTER FOUR

CITY

"GET your ass up and help, Sam. We aren't done. You may think you're a guest, but you help like the rest of us. Earn your meal, *friend*," I bit out, trying to hide my obvious dislike of the man.

He sat at the table like a king, watching us as we cleared the table and started to clean up dinner. "Really? Izzy said I was a guest."

I walked over and leaned over the table so only he could hear. "I don't give a fuck what Izzy said. This is my house and you ate my food. Get your fuckin' ass up and help."

"I knew you were a prick," Sam said as he stood, grinning. "I don't remember your mother treating a guest like this in her home."

"I'm not my mother and I don't like you. Never have and sure as fuck never will." I leaned farther across the table, coming eye to eye with him.

"What the fuck did I ever do to you?" Sam glared, not breaking eye contact.

"I don't like you being with my sister. It's that simple."

"Izzy and I aren't together." He crossed his arms.

"I don't give a shit what you say. I don't like her even being near you. You're trouble, Sam."

"I'm not trouble, Joe. You know me. I've never done shit wrong." He walked around the table, coming to face me without a barrier.

"I know you're prospecting with the Sun Devils. They don't play games, Sam. They're the real deal. I don't want my sister involved in their bullshit." I snarled, fisting my hands at my side.

"They're good guys, Joe. I never take your sister around them. She and I spend time together when I come to town to see my parents or go on a run. Nothing more than that." His eyes softened as he stared at me; the glare had vanished. "I'd never hurt your sister. We've been friends since we were little kids. She'd kick my ass anyway. I mean, seriously, Joe, your sister doesn't take anyone's shit."

I shook my head as I laughed. "Good, Sam. Remember that. If she doesn't get ya, I sure as fuck will." I placed my hand on his shoulder, giving it a firm squeeze. "There's a whole line of Gallo men that have my back. Don't get her involved in that MC, you hear me?" I raised an eyebrow as my laughter vanished.

"I got ya, man. Your sister is the only girl that has ever earned my respect. I would never do anything to endanger her," he said as he held out his hand to me.

I stared at him, trying to judge his sincerity. "I'm going to hold you to your word, Sam." I gripped his hand, squeezing it between my fingers, letting him know that I could easily overpower him.

A hand landed on my shoulder as Michael said, "What's going on over here? While you two ladies chitchat, the real men are doing all the work." He looked at Sam before turning to me.

I smiled, increasing my grip on Sam's hand. "We're done, Mike. Just having a little heart-to-heart about Izzy."

Sam gritted his teeth and tried to pull his hand away. "I got it, guys. I'll treat your sister right."

"Damn right you will," Michael said, taking a step forward.

"What the fuck? I've never done anything to her."

"Keep it that way, Sam, and we won't have an issue," Michael said.

"Boys, get your asses over here and clean some shit. Football's on and I'm not going to miss the game. Move it," Pop yelled, causing us all to turn.

"Coming, Pop," Michael said over his shoulder. "Let's go. I think Sam has a clear enough picture of what's at stake."

"I do." He nodded, shaking out his hand after I released it.

I grabbed the remote, turning up the volume on the football game that was just about to kick off. We finished clearing the table, loaded the dishwasher, and polished off the pots and pans while we listened to the game.

Just as I put the last pot away, the girls walked back down the stairs. Their laughter filled the space, overpowering the sports announcer on the television. The guys had piled into the living room, making themselves at home on the couch.

I captured Suzy's wrist, pulling her against my chest. "What's so funny, sugar?" I asked, rubbing my nose against her temple.

"Just girl stuff. Did you boys have fun?" she asked, staring up at me, tears hanging in her eyes.

"You okay? You look like you've been crying." I swept my fingers underneath her eyes, catching a single tear.

"We were laughing so hard, City. I love them so much." She beamed.

"I don't think I want to know what you girls were talking

about. They love you just as much, Suzy. You're family now." I pulled her chin up, brushing my lips against her tender skin.

She closed her eyes, parting her mouth for me. My dick twitched, wanting to be inside of that pretty little mouth again. Grabbing the nape of her neck, I held her in place, claiming her mouth. The feel of her soft lips on mine drove me closer to the edge. I wanted to throw her over my shoulder and run upstairs for a quickie. She acquiesced, giving herself to me with her mouth as she snaked her arms around my body. My dick throbbed in my pants; the blowjob earlier wasn't enough to dull the constant ache I felt when near her.

Placing her hand on my chest, she pushed gently. "City," she said breathily against my lips. Her eyes opened slowly, blinking back the haze. "Later. Your family is here."

"I don't give a fuck. They won't notice if we disappear for a few minutes. I need to taste you, sugar. I need to sink my cock in you so deep that my balls slap against your clit until you scream." I held her in place, staring in her eyes, watching them dilate.

"Okay," she whispered, scrubbing her hands across my chest.

I looked over her head at my family sitting in front of the television. "Come on, let's sneak upstairs." I released her neck, putting her hand in mine, and pulled her toward the stairs.

"Shouldn't we say something?" she asked, looking back at them.

"No, they won't notice, I'll be fast." I winked at her as we walked up the stairs.

"We've gone over this. You're never fast."

I reached down, picking her up from under her arms and tossing her over my shoulder. She squealed and giggled.

"Everything okay in there?" Ma yelled.

"Perfect, Ma. Be right back," I yelled down the stairs.

"You've given us away."

I swatted Suzy's ass. "Now I *have* to be quick. Fuck."

She wiggled and laughed, grabbing my ass as I rounded the corner to our bedroom. Kicking the door closed, I released my grip, letting her body slide down mine. Her soft to my hard. I wasn't in the mood to take her gently. She wasn't my bride-to-be in this moment. She was mine, and mine to use.

"I don't think—" she started to say as I placed my finger against her lips.

"No talking." I shook my head, claiming her lips as I unzipped my jeans. As she walked backward, her hands found the top of my jeans. She pulled them down at the sides; my dick sprang free, slapping against her arm.

She moaned in my mouth. "Jesus, babe. You're so hard."

"You did this to me walking around in that hot-ass sundress shaking your ass." I reached under her dress, my eyes growing wide when I didn't feel any panties. "What the fuck, sugar? No panties? You never go without," I murmured against her lips, running my fingers through her wetness.

The silky smoothness of her cunt made my cock grow harder. The familiar ache that I'd been perpetually blessed with since meeting Suzy was almost too much to bear at times.

She rubbed her pussy against my palm. "Please, City. I need to feel you." Her eyes fluttered, her breathing turning harsh.

Grabbing her by the waist, I spun her around to face the bed. "On your stomach, hands on the bed, sugar."

She smiled over her shoulder, her cheeks turning pink. "City, everyone's downstairs. They may hear or come looking for us." She placed her palms against the crisp white down comforter.

"Then you better bend over so we can be quick." I smacked her ass and watched her jump.

She bent over as she rubbed her ass, bringing her sundress up her legs, showing me a hint of thigh. She planted her elbows flat against the mattress and stilled as my hand caressed her ass.

My dick twitched, screaming to sink into her. I grabbed it, stroking the length as I hiked up her dress. Running my cock through her wetness, I sighed, knowing I wouldn't be walking around with a hard-on for the rest of the night.

I pulled her hips up, lifting her slightly off the bed, my dick touching her opening.

"Wait." Her body stiffened as she planted her face in the mattress.

"What?" I asked, with my cock in my hand, ready to push inside.

"Condom?" Her voice muffled by the blankets.

"Sugar, you're on the pill. We're about to be man and wife. We've done it without before. Right now, I want to feel you with nothing between us. I want to feel your silky wetness as I fuck the shit out of you."

She sighed, relaxing her body. "Okay, but—"

"Enough talking. The only words I wanna hear out of you are 'yes' and 'give me more.'" I leaned over her, kissing her shoulder as I jammed my cock into her.

Her body jerked, accepting all I had to give as she melted into the mattress. The blankets were bunched in her hands as I stood, looking down at her.

I slid my hand up her back, tangling my fingers in her hair. Wrapping it around my palm, I grabbed it and pulled. She gasped, her eyes sealing shut as I thrust myself inside her. The flesh of her hip felt cool underneath my forceful grip.

Every time my dick slammed into her, my balls slapped her clit, causing her body to twitch and moans to escape her lips. I thrust harder, needing the release as I watched her body bounce off my shaft.

"You want me to stop?" I bit out, swiveling my hips to touch every inch of the inside of her pussy.

"No," she moaned.

"You love my cock?"

"Yes," she said as she bucked.

I pulled her down forcefully against my body. "This is my pussy." Pulling her hair harder, I wrapped it around my fist, holding it more securely. "I take it when I want, not when you want to give it."

"Yes, yes. Oh God, yes!" she yelled, her pussy convulsing against my dick. She drew her legs in closer together, almost crossing them, making her hold on my cock viselike.

I slid my finger from her hip to her abdomen and down to her clit. It was swollen, and she shuddered as I pinched it, rolling it between my fingertips.

Her face fell forward and she bore down, pulling the blanket between her teeth. She grunted, pounding herself against me as I worked her clit, bringing her to the brink of release.

"Say what I wanna hear." I stilled my hands as I pummeled her.

"It's your pussy," she moaned without hesitation.

I chuckled, biting my lip. Suzy went from saying "heck" to using the word "pussy" without hesitation since she met me. Hearing her say such dirty shit made my spine tingle. "Always, sugar. Come on my cock. Shows me who owns you."

Using two fingers, I covered her clit entirely, making small circles with the soft pads of my tips. Her grunts grew louder, her pussy milking me, as she tensed and stilled. My touch became more demanding, my thrusts rougher as I used my cock as my own personal battering ram. I wanted her to walk funny when she went back downstairs.

"Give it to me, sugar." I tweaked her clit, needing her to come before I did.

She sucked in a breath, not moving, as she came on my cock. As her body relaxed and she grew limp, I used it as an invitation to fuck her senseless. Her body bounced like a bowl of Jell-O underneath me.

The orgasm ripped through me, sending me collapsing on top of her, gasping for air. "Fuck," I moaned as I caught my breath, my knees feeling weak.

"Mm," she hummed as she lay underneath me, smiling.

Planting my palms on the bed, I trailed kisses across her exposed skin as I pushed myself up. Her ass was a light shade of pink from the relentless pounding I gave her. She lay there with her dress hiked up around her waist, her ass still in the air and her body bent over the bed. She looked how I felt: sated and happy.

I tucked my dick back in my pants, leaving the remnants of our mingled orgasm on my flesh. "Come on, let's get back downstairs before people come looking." I ran my fingers down her arm, stopping in her palm to make tiny circles.

"I don't want to," she whispered, her skin breaking out in goose bumps.

"No choice now, princess. Let's go." I grabbed her by the hips and pulled her upright.

She gasped as her eyes widened into saucers.

"What's wrong?" I searched her eyes, watching her face flush an even darker shade of pink.

"Everything just gushed out of me. Oh my God, it's running down my leg." She looked down. "I can't go down there like this." She glared at me.

My body shook from the laugh I couldn't hold in. "Sugar, go get cleaned up. I'll wait for you and we can go down together." I smiled, watching her move from one foot to the other.

"Ugh, this is so not sexy," she whispered, turning toward the bathroom. Her walk reminded me of the marshmallow man from Ghostbusters—her arms far from her side as she took large steps on spread legs. She stalked to the bathroom in the most ungraceful way, but that was my girl. I wouldn't change a thing about her.

As the bathroom door closed, I collapsed on the bed, placing my hands behind my head. She'd be feeling me in more ways than one for the rest of the night. She'd be my wife soon. *My wife.* It still felt foreign to think, let alone say, but there had been no other person in the world that had me the way Suzy did. I was hers completely, maybe more than she was mine.

I closed my eyes. I never knew life could be this fucking fantastic.

CHAPTER FIVE

SUZY

"IZZY, what did I tell you about tonight?" I looked at her as we entered the hotel suite. I couldn't pin it on her alone. She had help planning my bachelorette party. The girls in the wedding party plotted together to send me out of singledom in style. I knew that Izzy and Sophia would be a wicked combination.

The hotel suite was stunning. I'd never seen anything like it. It was larger than my first home and overlooked the ocean. The exterior walls were glass from floor to ceiling. The sunset made it look like an ever-changing picture hanging in a gallery. The red, purple, and orange shades reflected off the water as the sun kissed the horizon.

Izzy stepped in front of me, breaking me from my sunset trance. "I heard you, Suzy. We were good. Sophia helped me and you know that she always has your best interests at heart," Izzy said with a laugh.

Sophia was my best friend. She was my opposite, though, living life a little more carefree, taking chances, and was a little too much like Izzy for my liking. She may be a librarian, but the girl partied like a rock star. Fuck.

"What's wrong, Suzy?" Sophia asked, touching my arm.

"You two," I said, shaking my head.

Sophia's lips parted as she laid her hand against her chest. "What did we do?" Her innocent act wasn't convincing. Motherhood had softened her a little. She had more weight on her body and looked healthy. The happiness that had now filled her life was clearly evident when looking at her.

"I don't trust you and Izzy individually, and I sure as hell don't trust you together." I glared at her, watching a small smile creep across her face. My stomach filled with knots. The two of them didn't follow any of the normal rules, let alone mine.

"Suzy, would I do anything to upset you?" Her brown eyes twinkled as a large smile spread across her face. Crossing her arms, she tilted her head and waited.

I studied the look on her face. "Yes, yes you would. Just the girls tonight, right?" I asked, watching her reaction very closely.

She nodded, her brown hair bobbing against her breasts that peeked out from her V-neck dress. "I only invited the girls. I swear."

The knot in my stomach loosened a bit with her statement. "I just don't want there to be any trouble tonight."

"Oh, there won't be." She shook her head and wrapped her arms around me, drawing me against her body. "I'm so happy for you, Suzy. Do you think I would do anything bad and have to deal with Kayden's bullshit?"

"No," I whispered as I hugged her.

Kayden was her man and the father of her son, Jett. Their love was complicated. The road they traveled to happiness had been filled with bumps, but they made it through and never looked back. Kayden was a man I could rely on, a friend that would lay down his life for me. Sophia had told me that he could be "wicked jealous." Her words for him, not mine.

"Okay then, let's grab a drink. The girls are all about to arrive." She held me at arm's length, smiling and squeezing my hands. "We're here to celebrate before you become Mrs. Joseph Gallo."

"I don't want to drink too much, Sophia," I mumbled as we walked toward the already prepped bar area.

Izzy was pouring herself a hefty glass of Jack Daniel's as we approached. "What'll it be, ladies?" she asked as she set the bottle on the counter.

"Just a glass of wine," I said, looking at the dozens of bottles on display.

"No wine tonight, Suzy. Pick your poison." Izzy smiled, waving her hands over the liquor.

"Bahama Mama." I winced, my stomach rolling at the thought of getting drunk. "Light on the liquor, though."

"Honey, it's your bachelorette party and if you don't get shit-faced drunk and party your ass off then I haven't done my job as a bridesmaid." She smiled as she started pouring the rum in the glass.

I watched, my eyes growing wide as she poured and poured. "That's enough, Izzy," I said, placing my hand on her arm. "I want to make it until at least ten."

She burst into laughter as she set the rum down. "We'll get ya there. We have the whole night planned out. It's going to be one for the record books. When we're old and pissing our pants with dentures in our mouths, we'll be telling stories about tonight." She smiled, pouring the juices and rum in the cup before handing it to me.

I shook my head and grabbed the Bahama Mama from her hand. "That's what I'm afraid of," I muttered as I brought the glass to my lips. The rum didn't smell overpowering; maybe I'd misjudged the amount of alcohol she poured.

The fruity concoction of pineapple and orange danced across my tongue as the liquid slid down my throat, causing a slow burn. I closed my eyes, enjoying the taste, although it was a bit stronger than I wanted.

Izzy tipped my cup. "Drink up, girl. We have a big night ahead of us."

I batted her hand away, pulling the cup from my lips. "Last time I drank too much I ended up in your brother's bed." I smiled, my body warming at the memory.

If I hadn't been tipsy that night, I would've been a total mess the first time I saw him naked. The man had a kickass body, and don't even get me started on his piercing. If I had been stone-cold sober, I probably would've run out of the room screaming once that caught my eye. Even to this day, I get a thrill looking at him naked.

"You're a dirty whore and we all know it." Sophia nudged me, cackling like a loon.

"Am not," I said, my cheeks heating as I glared at her.

"Suzy," Izzy interrupted, "you're with us, your girls. You can drop the good-girl bullshit. We know you're a closet freak. If you weren't, you wouldn't be with my brother." She laughed.

A knock on the door saved me from the conversation. One by one, Izzy and Sophia's friends and mine from work poured into the door. My sister wouldn't be here tonight. She said that she couldn't get off work to be here in time for the bachelorette party. She'd make it for the rehearsal dinner. The girls in this room were more like family to me than my own flesh and blood anyway.

I stood at the window, watching the sun kiss the horizon as I sipped my drink. I felt blessed, surrounded by loving women, marrying the man of my dreams, and officially becoming a member of the Gallo family. The ladies chatted and drank, their laughter filling the room.

"Hey, you okay?" Sophia asked, standing at my side.

"I'm just so happy, Soph. I never thought I could be this happy." I turned to her, a sad smile on my face.

"What's the sad face for?" Her eyebrows drew together as she looked at me.

"I'm not sad. I'm just thinking about what City and I have been through. I almost shut him out of my life by judging him. I would've never known the love I do now. Then the accident happened and he was almost ripped from my life forever." I shook my head, trying to force the sad memories from my mind. "I'm so happy right now…happier than I've ever been before. Is this as good as it gets?" I asked, grabbing her hand and squeezing.

"Nah, there's more good things to come." She smiled, squeezing my hand. "Wait until you hold your firstborn in your arms. There's nothing like it." She smiled, releasing my hand. "I'm proud of you."

My eyebrows shot up at her words. "For what?"

She giggled, covering her mouth. "For staying with City. I know he scared the hell out of you. I know how OCD you are with your lists—even that fucking list of your husband requirements. You threw them out the window and took a chance for once. You listened to your heart and not your head. When I met him, I knew he was right for you." She wrapped her arms around me. "Now, let's stop talking sad shit and party our asses off. I have a night without Jett and Kayden. I want to get drunk and enjoy a night without baby food on my clothes."

I chuckled and squeezed her. "I love you, Sophia. For you, I'll party like it's 1999."

"God, you're such a dork," she said as she laughed, holding me by the arms, shaking her head. "But I love you. I don't know why, but I do."

"Bitches, I better see you two drinking a little quicker," Izzy said as she grabbed my glass and looked inside. "Let me refill this. Sophia, want more?"

Sophia held her cup out, shaking it. "Feels a bit light to me. Another Jack and Coke, please." She handed the cup to Izzy.

"And I'll—" I started to say as Izzy started to walk away.

"Got it, light on the alcohol," Izzy yelled over her shoulder.

"Gifts! Let's do gifts," Sophia said, pulling on my arm.

I loved presents. It's not that I was materialistic; I just never had the type of family where the gifts were piled higher than me. I always received a couple of small gifts for my birthday or Christmas. My family decided to draw names for Christmas that year. Just when I thought it couldn't be more depressing, bam, wrong again.

"Okay," I said, nodding, trying to hide my excitement.

Sophia clapped, drawing everyone's attention. "It's time for presents!" she yelled, pulling me toward the couch.

I sat down on the large U-shaped sectional in the middle of the living room that faced the windows. Everyone fit snugly on the couch as I opened each gift. I felt slightly uncomfortable being the center of attention. I liked to blend in to the background, but I knew the entire weekend would be filled with uncomfortable moments. I was the bride, and as such, I'd definitely be the center of attention.

"Open mine next," Sophia said, holding out a pretty pink box with a giant white bow. I'd opened six presents so far and they'd all been lingerie and nighties to wear for City. He'd love them, but I knew most likely one or two would get ripped. The man was a brute.

Pulling it from her grasp, I smiled nervously, unsure of what was inside. With Sophia, it could be romantic or downright dirty. "I don't trust you," I said, placing the box on my lap and pulling on the ribbon.

She chuckled, covering her mouth. "I wouldn't either."

I stilled my hand, looking up at her with a glare. "Do I want to open this in public?"

She nodded, her smile growing larger. "You do. Don't be a baby and open it already," she said, putting her hands on her hips.

I pulled the ribbon, letting the white material fall away from the present before tearing into the shiny pink paper. When I opened the box, I gasped and put the lid back on. "Sophia," I said, trying not to laugh.

"You have to show us," Izzy said as she stood. She grabbed her phone from her pocket and held it up to take a picture. "Come on, Suzy. We're all girls here. Don't be a pussy."

I sighed, realizing I wouldn't win the battle. "Fine," I said, opening the lid and grabbing the first object. Fuckin' Sophia. I held it up and listened to the whistles and giggles.

"What the fuck is that?" Mia asked.

"That, my dear," Izzy said, snapping a photo, "when assembled, is a spreader bar." Izzy giggled and snapped another picture.

My face grew flushed, but I couldn't help but laugh. "I've never had a problem keeping them open for City." I winked at Sophia. She and I always swapped stories about sex. Before City came into my life, sex had always been bland and boring. I'd lived vicariously through her and always went to her for advice.

"Oh, I know. You've turned into quite the little sex kitten since meeting City. This gift may seem like it's for you, but it's really for him." Sophia smiled and looked very pleased with herself. "Next."

"Whore," I mumbled as I pulled out a pair of nipple clamps.

"I don't want to think of you using any of this shit with my brother. I can never look at you two in the eye again. I know too much. Too much, I tell you." Izzy snapped another photo before taking a seat at the end of the couch.

I quickly pulled out the other objects, crotchless panties and a crop, and held them up before dropping them back in the box. The crop was the one I'd always wanted and admired. It had a heart made of leather on the end. I just loved the look of it, but it had to sting like a mother when hit with it.

Knock. Knock.

"Oh," Izzy said, jumping from the couch. "There's my gift. I had to have it delivered."

I looked at Sophia and she shrugged. Motherfuckers. I knew they wouldn't listen when I said no strippers. I hung my head, rubbing my face, as I heard the door open.

"Why, hello there, officer," Izzy said. She giggled and backed away from the door.

For the love of God—I wanted to kill her right then.

"I heard there's a disturbance up here. I'm here to investigate," the man, who obviously wasn't a cop, said as he looked around the room.

I thought for a moment that I was in a movie. Cop stripper comes to the door and then the real party starts. The last thing I wanted in the world was someone other than my fiancé touching me.

"She's right over there—the blonde in the middle. She's a real handful." Izzy looked at me with a smile, and winked.

I blushed, all eyes turning on me as he started the little CD player he had in his hand. The girls started to scream, scrambling from the couch.

I sat alone, leaning back, and crossed my arms over my chest. He handed the CD player to Sophia as he approached me. He stalked toward me, untucking his shirt and shaking his hips. Izzy held her phone in our direction.

"Don't you fucking dare take a photo of this," I warned. The last thing I needed was this getting into City's hands. He wasn't a jealous man, he knew I was his, but still, there would be a sting.

"You're such a killjoy," Izzy said as she shoved the phone in her pocket.

"Bad Ass" by Kid Ink played as the stripper tried his best to seduce me. He wasn't bad looking—blond hair, thin but muscular, and beautiful brown eyes. He ripped his shirt open, exposing a hairless chest. He turned, shaking his ass in my face as he ripped off his pants. Was he twerking?

I wanted to laugh, but I didn't want to be rude. He was trying hard to impress me, but he wasn't my City. I uncrossed my arms, letting them fall into my lap, as I watched him shake his ass. He turned and I came face to face with his cock, thankful it was tucked neatly in a G-string. Wouldn't work for City and his well-endowed package.

"Smile, for shit's sake. At least pretend to have a good time," Sophia whispered in my ear. "As soon as he's done with you, the rest of the girls will get their shot at him."

I turned to her and glared, but did as she said. I smiled and pretended to enjoy myself. My stomach flipped when he sat on my lap and started rubbing against my chest. He nuzzled his face in my hair as he scooted forward, and all I could think about was City, and how he loved being wrapped in my gold locks.

His small, semi-erect dick touched my stomach, and I cringed. I closed my eyes, thinking about something other than what was happening.

"Hey," he whispered in my ear. "Don't worry, the song is almost over."

I opened my eyes and blew out a breath. I couldn't be the only ambushed bride in this uncomfortable situation.

"Thanks," I whispered, and smiled. His words put me at ease and helped settle my nerves, knowing the torture was almost done.

When the song ended, he grabbed my chin, kissing me on the cheek. My eyes grew wide as I pulled my head back, letting his fingers fall from my chin. He smiled sweetly and turned his attention to Mia sitting next to me. I sighed, happy that it was over and I could relax.

I stood on wobbly legs and approached Izzy. She couldn't stop laughing. "Happy with yourself?" I asked, my hands on my hips.

"Very." She laughed louder. "You're done now, Suzy Q. Drink up. Let the other girls enjoy him for a while. We'll head down to the party around the pool in a bit."

"I need the entire bottle of rum to forget the feel of him against my body." My body shook as I remembered foreign skin against mine.

"Well, good thing for you I brought extra. Help yourself," she said with a grin, motioning toward the temporary bar with her head and wiggling her eyebrows.

"I'm still pissed at you," I said as I pointed at her and glared.

"You love me, don't bullshit yourself." She kissed my

cheek and walked toward the gaggle of girls stuffing ones in the strippers G-string.

Grabbing my phone off the table, I checked my messages. Nothing. City and I hadn't spent much time apart since the motorcycle accident, and I missed him. I didn't want to be the clingy, annoying fiancée, but I couldn't help myself, I sent him a text.

Me: Having fun?

I set my phone down and grabbed the bottle of rum and poured half a glass. I didn't know how much to put in a Bahama Mama, but it looked like the same amount Izzy poured earlier. I added the juices and watched the color change to a salmon pink after the grenadine splash. It was as pretty as it was tasty. I sipped it, sat down at the dining room table, and waited for his reply.

City: Miss you, sugar.

That was a vague and cagey reply. He didn't say if he was or was not having fun. I didn't want to know what the boys had planned for him tonight. No one would tell me anyway, or any of the girls, for that matter. I sent him a quick message as I watched the bump-and-grind show taking place on the sectional.

Me: Miss you too.

Sophia sat down next to me and frowned. "Why are you over here and not over there with the rest of the party?" She tilted her head and chewed on her bottom lip.

"Just rather watch that hot mess than participate. I could ask you the same thing. Why aren't you copping a feel?" I raised my eyebrow and challenged her. I didn't need an answer. She felt the same way I did.

"Hell no. I don't need someone pawing at me. I'm here to have a girls' night, not stare at his tiny junk."

I choked on my drink, and wiped the liquid off my chin. "You noticed that too, huh?" I asked.

She laughed, throwing her head back and relaxing in the chair. "Gotta be blind not to. You ready to be Mrs. Joseph Gallo?"

"Yeah, I'm excited, but you know I don't like too much attention."

"Well, you're going to be the center of attention here and there this weekend. Might as well get used to it." She grabbed her Solo cup, downing the last remnants of her drink.

"At least City will be by my side." I checked my phone, but there wasn't a new message.

Izzy ripped the phone from my hand. "Oh, no. This is a man-free night. This is all about us celebrating and partying our asses off. No phones, no Joe. Got it?"

"You're a bitch," I said as she shoved my phone in her back pocket. "If this is your idea of celebration then you're not who I thought you were, Izzy." I stuck my tongue out.

"This is the pre-party. The real fun starts downstairs. The nightclub opened an hour ago. No good club starts until eleven. Keep your granny panties on. We'll be going shortly. Keep drinking." She gave me a cocky grin and walked away.

"I love her," Sophia said, getting up to refill her cup.

"You would," I mumbled before downing the last of my Bahama Mama, a slow burn sliding down my throat and spreading throughout my body.

Mia sat in the chair Sophia had been in. "It's nice to finally get a night away from the guys, isn't it?" she asked, smiling before she took a sip of her drink.

"I guess so. I love City, but I love my girls too."

"There's nothing wrong with that, Suzy. It's good to have some time apart. I've spent as much time with anyone as I do with Michael. I mean, I love him—fuck, most days I can't get enough of him—but I needed tonight," Mia said as she leaned back in the chair, resting her head against the high chair back.

"Are things okay with you two?" I asked, concerned about them. I loved Mike and adored Mia. I wanted them around and loved any time we were all able to hang out. With all of our work schedules, it wasn't easy.

"Yeah, things are great. Sometimes we get in arguments, but that's when he wants to pull his man bullshit, and I eventually put him in his place." She laughed, bringing the cup to her lips. "Gallo men are a breed of their own."

"Yeah, no truer words have ever been spoken."

"Are you ready for the wedding?" she asked me, tilting her head and twirling the cup in her hand.

"Ready as I'll ever be."

"You have that need for control, like Mike. It'll go off without a hitch, Suzy. Every Gallo will make sure it does. I'll help too. I'll do anything you need that day."

"Thanks so much, Mia. I just want it to be perfect."

"Perfection is overrated," she said, smiling at me.

"On my wedding day, I don't think it is," I said, my stomach turning at the thought of anything going wrong.

"Suzy, it's life's imperfections that stand out and make memories. They're what great stories are made of, and we'll tell them over and over again. Imperfections make the world more interesting. Think about your relationship with City, how you began. Was it perfect?"

I shook my head, the power of her words calming my rumbling stomach. "Hardly. We hit some bumps along the road."

"Does it make your love story less worthy or the journey less sweet?" Mia asked.

"No, it makes me hold on tighter, thinking of what I could've lost."

“Perfection isn’t all it’s cracked up to be. Just enjoy the day. All that matters is that you’re husband and wife at the end of it all. Not if the cake was perfect or if the seating chart was right. Just Joe and you becoming one.”

I leaned forward, wrapping my arms around her. “You’re right, Mia. Everything else is trivial. Thank you for your kind words. I couldn’t have picked a more perfect person for Mike.”

“There’s that ‘perfect’ word again. I’m far from it, but we’re a good fit,” she said, hugging me back. “Now, I’m ready to party my ass off with the girls and worry about the men and wedding later. You in?” she asked, releasing me.

“All in. Let’s do it,” I said, standing to find Izzy and Sophia. I was ready to dance. Clearly, I’d had too much to drink.

CHAPTER SIX

CITY

"I CAN'T BELIEVE that shit can even be done," Anthony said, holding his stomach as he laughed.

"She has mad skills." Mike shook his head, all of us still stunned.

"When she shot that thing out of her pussy, I almost shit a brick." Anthony scrubbed his hand across his face, shaking his head.

"A ping-pong ball. Jesus Christ, I'll never be able to see anyone play that fucking game again." Mike grabbed the beer from the cup holder and downed it.

We were safely on the limo bus after a rather interesting trip to some shit-ass dive strip club in Tampa. It wasn't my idea of a good time, but since Mike and Anthony planned the entire night, I sat back and tried to enjoy the ride. I felt guilty watching strippers, knowing that Suzy was off enjoying a peaceful night with the girls. Izzy promised me that they were just going for drinks and maybe dancing and that they'd be staying in a hotel room so they wouldn't drink and drive.

"Why the fuck aren't you talking?" Bear said as he nudged Tank.

I shook my head, laughing at the mix of guys on this bus. For some unknown reason, Mike and Anthony decided to invite Bear, Tank, and a few other guys from the Neon Cowboy. They knew each other from Inked since they were not only friends but also clients.

"I'm talking. Just listening about the pussy show." I glared at Bear and then looked at Tank, tilting my head while I studied his face. "What the fuck is that smirk for?"

"You're so pussy whipped." Tank tipped his glass, his smirk turning into a smile. The corners of his eyes wrinkled as he chuckled and took a swig of beer.

"Fuck off," I growled. "I'm not pussy whipped. Why look at ground meat when I have grade-A platinum pussy at home? I know you boys don't know the difference." I smirked, looking to Mike. "Not you, brother, you get the good shit too. You know what I mean."

He smiled, nodding. "I do, but I am still in disbelief. Mia better never shoot anything out of that pussy. Shit's too good to ruin with a ping-pong ball or anything other than my dick, fingers, and tongue," Michael said, making a V with his fingers and tonguing the void.

"Clearly you've had too much to drink," I said, looking at him, unable to contain my laughter.

"Two fuckin' pussy-whipped bastards. You sure you two still have your balls attached?" Bear slapped his knee.

"Why don't you suck my dick and find out, motherfucker?" I smirked as Bear stilled and gagged. "You're just jealous, plain and simple."

He mumbled, bringing the bottle to his lips. "You know I've always been fond of Sunshine. Couldn't be pussy whipped over a better girl."

"We're here," the driver called out as the limo-bus stopped in front of a beachside hotel.

"What the fuck are we doing here?" I looked out the tinted windows, confused by the destination. I didn't think we'd end the evening at a hotel. We'd already seen the strippers, so I didn't think that awaited us inside.

"Shepard's has the best fuckin' nightclub in the St. Pete. Get your old grumpy ass up and let's dance." Anthony stood, taking the glass from my hand.

"One, I don't fuckin' dance without my woman. Two, don't ever touch my beer. Three, this wasn't supposed to be a night for you to find a piece of ass," I said as I climbed off the limo bus.

"Fine, you drink and stew in your moodiness while the rest of us enjoy the ladies, right, men?" Anthony pumped his fist, his body shaking with excitement. "Right?"

Michael cleared his throat, looking away from Anthony. "I'm with Joe. I'd rather drink and bullshit than look at any other women. Mia would have my balls in a sling if I even thought about looking at another woman. I'll hang with my brother while you bastards find your next victims." He laughed as he walked by, and slapped me on the shoulder. "I got your back," he said softly so only I could hear.

"More for us," Tank said, heading toward the door.

"Yeah, this looks like your type of place, Tank." I shook my head. "The girls are going to run away screaming from your ass." The warm air of the Florida night felt good against my skin. The salty smell of the air and the gentle breeze of the ocean were soothing.

"I'll show them what a real man looks like," Tank said. "They're too used to these pansy-ass boys that pluck their eyebrows and wax their body hair. They need a little Tank in their life. What the fuck are those douchebags called again?"

I rolled my eyes. The man was clearly full of himself.

"Yeah, I'm sure they do. How the fuck am I supposed to know what they're called?"

"Metrosexuals," Bear said, giving a weak smile.

"What the fuck?" I said, totally in shock. I never ever in a million years though Bear would know that fucking term. A big, burly biker like him should not know that term. "You reading *Vogue* magazine or some shit?" I raised an eyebrow, studying his face.

His cheeks turned pink as he looked at the ground. "I have sisters, asshole. Their boyfriends are metrosexuals. Beats the fuck outta me. They throw the term around like it's the most glorious thing. Someday they'll figure out what they're missing being with such a pussy."

I laughed along with the rest of the guys. "Had us worried there for a second," Tank said, smacking Bear in the back of the head. "I was about to do a dick check."

"I know you've always wanted to get your hands on my cock, Tank. I don't swing that way. Sorry, buddy."

I smiled as we walked through the lobby. I had the best friends and brothers in the whole fucking world. Before Anthony pushed open the doors to the pool, the glass panes started to shake from the bass of the music on the other side.

"Ready, boys?" Anthony asked, looking like he was about to enter a little piece of heaven.

"Just open the fuckin' doors already," I growled.

He nodded, pushing open both doors at once. We took two steps and stopped dead to take in the sight before us. Girls in bikinis, skimpy dresses, and various other kinds of tiny, barely there clothing writhed and danced to the beat of the techno music.

"Wow, I've been missing out at that hick bar," Tank said, his voice filled with disbelief.

"Neon Cowboy women do not look like that." Bear held

his hand out, moving it up and down, motioning toward the crowd, and licked his lips.

"There is sure as fuck is something to be said for city girls." Tank headed toward the crowd, winding his way through the ladies.

At least Tank and Bear didn't come in their camo or some other redneck attire. They wore clean denim jeans, black t-shirts, and boots. We looked like the redneck biker version of the Rat Pack. Our tats were clearly visible on our arms—metrosexuals we most definitely were not.

"Bar," I growled, pulling Tank off the back of some chick. He had her by the hips and she was pushing back against him with a big smile on her face.

"What the fuck, man? I was enjoying myself."

"She had a ring on her finger, dumbass," I yelled over the loud music.

"Who cares? I was looking to hit it and quit it." He laughed, making a smacking motion while thrusting his hips.

"Shots. We need them in mass quantities." Bear threw a fifty on the bar.

"That won't get you far here, Bear." Michael threw an extra fifty on top. "This isn't the Podunk bar you're used to. This is the city, and everything is three times as much."

We leaned against the bar, studying the dance floor like a scene from *Saturday Night Fever* as we waited for our tequila shots and beers. I reached in my pocket for my phone as panic started to set in. Fuck.

"What's wrong, Joe?" Michael asked, resting his hand on my shoulder.

"I don't have my phone. Suzy's going to be pissed if I don't text her back."

"I got it in my pocket. You'll get it back tomorrow. Tonight it's all about us and not our ladies. She'll be fine. It's her party night too. Trust me, those girls have her too busy to even bother looking at their phones. So chill the fuck out and drink." Mike shoved the tequila shot under my nose as a smile crept across his face.

"You're right." I grabbed the drink from his hand and turned toward the guys. "What are we drinking to?" I asked, raising the glass.

"Platinum pussy and unlimited blowjobs." Anthony clinked his glass to mine as all the guys joined in with a laugh.

I grimaced as I downed the liquid. Tequila and I were never friends. We slammed the shot glasses on the bar, grabbing our beers to wash it down.

"Another," Tank said, motioning to the bartender. "Same," he yelled as the man approached.

"Gonna be one of those nights, huh?" I said, sipping my beer as I looked around.

The setting was amazing. Suzy would love it here. She didn't like to dance when I met her, but when we were on the dance floor together, our bodies moved as if they'd known each other a lifetime. She knew how to move, but being with me gave her the confidence to feel uninhibited in the sack and in a club.

"Earth to Joe." Bear tapped me in the head, annoying the shit out of me.

I swatted his hand, ready to tear his finger off, and turned toward him. "You wanna lose that finger?" I smirked, moving into his personal space.

"Shut the fuck up and drink, shithead." Bear pushed my chest, knocking me back a step.

Grabbing the drink off the bar, I slammed it back, enjoying the warmth. "Ahh, another," I said as I put the glass down, turning to see everyone's mouths agape. "What?"

"Jesus, you're going to be shitfaced. Pace yourself, brother." Michael threw back his drink, calling the bartender over.

We spent the next hour laughing and drinking. We talked about women. Michael and I spoke of our girls while Tank, Bear, and Anthony talked about their plethora of pussy. The stark contrast of the caliber of pussy the three of them enjoyed was astounding. I knew the club bitches Tank and Bear spent their nights with, and I wasn't too impressed. They could do better, and hell, they deserved more. They may be rough around the edges, but they were good, honest men.

Anthony was just Anthony. He was a manwhore to the nth degree, enjoying life a little too loosely. I couldn't blame the guy, but at some point, you have to give up the chase and enter the adult world.

"Here," Anthony said, nudging me. "You look a little lost in thought, or you're already shitfaced." He laughed, pushing the glass of amber liquid in front of me.

"I'm not even close to being shitfaced."

"I want to do a special toast," Michael said, holding up his glass, waiting for us to follow suit. As we raised our glasses, holding them together, he spoke. "To Thomas. He couldn't be here again, but this one's for him." He frowned, his eyes glistening a little in the club light. "To the best goddamn brother out there. May he stay safe and come back to us in one piece." A weak smile formed on his face as he brought the glass to his lips.

My chest felt tight as I thought about Thomas. I wanted him to be here to celebrate this weekend with us, but he had gone too far under at this point. We were on a no-contact basis the last few months. We could check in with his superior, but beyond that, we hadn't heard from him. "Way to bring a party down," I said, shaking my head. "To Thomas." I downed the tequila before wiping my mouth with the back of my hand.

I looked at Anthony, and his eyes were the size of saucers. He wasn't moving, the shot in front of his lips, frozen in place. "What the fuck, man?" I asked, turning to see what caught his attention.

What the fuck? My heart started to hammer, my mind racing as I fisted my hands at my side. *There's no fucking way.* I shook my head, trying to get rid of the image, hoping it was an optical illusion. Fuck, it wasn't.

Across the pool danced *my* bride-to-be with some motherfucker doing the bump-n-grind. I moved forward, but a hand stopped me, clamping down on my arm.

"Don't cause a scene, City," Bear said, gripping me tightly.

I looked down at his hand, a growl starting deep in my throat. "That's my woman. No one, and I mean no one, puts their hands on her." Pulling my arm from his grip, I stalked across the pool, cracking my neck and preparing for the shitstorm that was about to happen.

Sophia stopped dancing, her mouth hanging open as she nudged Izzy, motioning to me with her head.

"Fuck," Izzy mouthed, shaking her head, her eyes growing wide.

With Suzy's back to me, I grabbed the asshole groping Suzy's collar, removing him from my fiancée. Suzy turned slowly, all the color draining from her face as her eyes found mine.

"Fuck off," I growled, pushing him away as I tried to restrain myself.

"You fuck off, asshole. I'm dancing with the beautiful blonde. She ain't yours." He moved forward, standing toe to toe with me.

I snarled, moving closer to his face. "She's my motherfucking fiancée. You had your shitty-ass hands all over her."

"City," Suzy said, grabbing my arm. "Baby."

I pushed her away, not looking in her direction. "You need to back the fuck off and go find some other pussy. This one is *mine*," I roared, grabbing his shirt and pulling him closer to my face.

"I didn't hear her say no when I started dancing with her, motherfucker." His words were slightly slurred as tiny droplets of his spit hit my face when he spoke. "Her ass felt so good in my hands."

"City," Bear said, touching my shoulder. "Not here, man."

"What did you just say?" I asked, tightening my grip.

"Her ass…you can bounce a quarter off that shit." His mouth slowly turned up into a cocky-ass grin.

As I released him, I pushed him back and swung. I connected with his jaw, the bones crunching under my knuckles. His arms flailed as he fell to the ground and I grasped his face.

"Keep your fucking hands to yourself, dickhead." I spat on the ground next to him. "Worthless piece of shit."

He dragged his hand across his lips, wiping the blood that had trickled out of his mouth. I fisted my hands at my side, waiting to see if he'd retaliate, but he stood slowly and walked away. Pussy.

Bear patted me on the back. "Can't say the asshole didn't deserve it."

"He deserved more. If we were at the Neon Cowboy I would have beat him unconscious, but here it's like a damn show."

I looked around the crowd that had gathered. People were smiling and laughing and looked impressed. Such is city life at a club. They just wanted to see someone get their ass kicked. I closed my eyes, trying to calm my breath before turning to see Suzy.

Her arms were crossed and her head cocked as she glared at me. "You're such a caveman. Does everything require violence?" She snarled.

I'd never seen Suzy so pissed off. She had no fucking right to be pissed. I was defending her honor, *my* soon-to-be bride. "You're pissed at me?" I asked. "Why the fuck are you pissed off at me? You're the one letting him manhandle you."

Her glare turned ice cold as she walked toward me. Her hands dropped to her side as she stopped in front of me. "You knock a guy on his ass and you want to know why I'm pissed off?" She poked me in the chest, her nail digging into my skin. "It's my bachelorette party and I was having some harmless fun. What the fuck is wrong with you?" She smacked me in the chest, trying to push me backward.

I grabbed her wrist, pulling her closer. "Some asswad has his hands on my woman and I'm just supposed to, what? Tap him on the fucking shoulder and say may I cut in? No, I'm going to confront that shithead and do what I have to do. I'm the one that's pissed, and rightfully so. You *let* him touch you. What the fuck happened to faithfulness?" I released her arm as her eyes flickered to the ground.

Her eyes returned to mine filled with anger and hurt. "I was being faithful, you big, dumb oaf. It's a bachelorette party and I'm here with your sister. I wasn't doing anything wrong. You're just being your difficult, overprotective self." She shook her head. "You always want to solve things with your fists. We're not twelve anymore, City."

"Sugar, I'll protect you until my last breath. I don't share, not now and not ever. You're mine and only mine. No one is allowed to put their hands on you, no matter the situation." I grabbed her by the waist, drawing her to my body. "Maybe

I'm being harsh, but the thought of someone else touching you just pisses me off. I tried to control myself, but the prick had to keep running his mouth." I touched her cheek, holding her face in my hand.

Her face softened as she leaned into my touch. "He did. I'm sorry. I'm drunk and we're just having some harmless fun."

I leaned in, hovering just above her lips. Her eyes fluttered closed as I inhaled the smell of Suzy. The scent wasn't right. "What the fuck?" I sniffed her cheek and neck. She had a sweaty, musky scent on her skin. "Why do you smell like a man?"

Her eyes flew open and grew wide. "What are you talking about?" she whispered.

"You smell like another man's been pawing you. That jagoff didn't touch your face. Why the hell does your face and neck smell like someone else?" My heart started to pound sporadically; my chest felt hollow except for the flutter of my heart.

"I don't know what you're talking about. I haven't touched anyone." She grabbed my shirt, holding me to her.

"Like fuck you haven't. I can smell him." Nausea overcame me as the realization that Suzy had been that close to another man. Maybe she wasn't the woman I always thought she was.

"City, I haven't touched anyone. You're making shit up."

I backed away, dropping my hand from her cheek. "I find you with some guy with his hands all over you and now I can smell someone all over your skin. Don't you have anything to say for yourself, or are you just going to deny it?"

She looked to the sky and back to me, her eyes glistening in the light. "I didn't do anything wrong," she yelled, her hands fisted at her side.

I shook my head, feeling my heart shattering into a million tiny pieces. The thought of her cheating on me made me feel like death would be preferable. I didn't want to look at her anymore. I couldn't take the lies or the dull ache in my chest. "I don't believe you," I whispered, looking over her. I couldn't stomach looking in her eyes anymore.

"City," she pleaded, reaching for my arm.

I recoiled, moving my body out of reach. "No, not this time, sugar. I need some time to myself," I said as I turned my back to her.

I didn't want to see the hurt on her face. I didn't have to look at her to know it was there, but I was too pissed off to stick around and talk about it. I needed to get away and cool off.

"Bro, where ya going?" Michael said, stepping in front of me.

"I need to be alone, brother. I'm taking a cab home," I said, trying to control my breathing. I closed my eyes and breathed out through my mouth before looking him in the eyes.

"Come on. We have the party bus. We can go somewhere else." Michael gave me a fake smile.

"Fuck that. I'm going home. Take the party bus and enjoy the night. Tell Suzy to stay here with the girls. I need to be alone tonight."

I walked around him, leaving them behind. I found a cab and headed home. I tried to process how the night went so terribly wrong. Did I overreact? Probably. Did someone touch my fiancée? Most definitely. Could we be fixed? Only time would tell.

I closed my eyes; the blur of palm trees made my head hurt more than it already did. I thought about everything we'd been through in the last year. Suzy lost her good-girl image and stole my heart. I wrecked on my bike and almost died. The woman nursed me back to health and waited on me hand and foot.

It may have been a bachelorette party, but the shit still stung. My overactive imagination and the words the cocksucker spoke were like a punch to the gut. I knew my Suzy. She wouldn't cheat, but the thought of someone else touching her made my stomach hurt and my heart ache. I literally pushed Suzy away and turned my back on her. I let my anger rule instead of using my head. I reacted without thinking and would have to deal with it tomorrow.

I rubbed my face, wishing I could wash it all away and go back in time. I'd been a total dumb fuck, and there would be a heavy price to pay and most likely groveling. I wasn't one to grovel and beg, but this was my sugar. I'd do anything for her, to keep her, and make her mine. The closer I got to the house, our house, the more I knew I fucked up.

After paying the cab driver and walking up the driveway, I pulled out my phone and checked my messages. Not a message since I'd left her.

Me: I'm sorry. I love you.

The house was eerily quiet. It had been quiet before, but tonight it was deafening. Suzy was missing. Her joy and laughter usually filled the space. The girl was a damn chatterbox at times, and as I walked to the bedroom I realized how much I missed it—how much I missed her. The stillness of our house made me feel uneasy. I wanted my woman in our bed with me. I wanted to hear her giggle as I whispered in her ear before she fell asleep. She was the sunshine in my day; she softened me and filled my life with happiness.

I emptied my pockets, placing my wallet and keys on my nightstand. I removed my clothes, the stench of the clubs clinging to the fabric as I tossed them to the floor. No reply from Suzy as I crawled in bed, laying the cell phone next to me. I didn't want to miss her message. I stared at the ceiling, watching the fan create moving shadows in the darkness. For the first time in months, I felt completely alone.

Fuck, maybe I *was* pussy whipped.

CHAPTER SEVEN

SUZY

FUMING. It's the only word I could use to describe what I felt. City had always been a little on the impulsive side, but tonight put the fucking icing on the cake. How could he think I had been unfaithful? I told Izzy no strippers, but did she listen? Of course not, when does she ever listen to anyone?

I'd had too much to drink, but I was still in control. I wasn't sloppy drunk, just at that point where everything was wonderful and nothing got me down. Well, nothing until Mr. "She's Mine" Caveman killed the party. When the guy that City laid out tried to dance with me, I said no and pushed him away. Izzy intervened. Fucking Izzy, said it was my last night and every girl had the right to dance with whomever they wanted before they're officially off the market.

I didn't see any harm in it. It was just a dance and nothing more. My girls surrounded me and they would never let anything happen to me. Furthermore, I don't cheat. It's not in my nature. I'm madly in love with City. I don't mean just that type of comfortable love. I'm talking that "take my breath away, make my stomach flip" type of love that I couldn't imagine being without.

But, and this is a huge but, could I deal with his testosterone-laced, fist-throwing macho bullshit for the rest of my life?

If I answered the questions based solely on the amount and way I loved him, the answer would be yes. If I used my brain and really thought about City and his quickness to stake his claim and scare anyone with a cock away from me, the answer would be, "I honestly don't know." He said that's his way of protecting me, and it's how he's built.

The night I was attacked at the Neon Cowboy, his level of protection increased and became almost stifling at times. Somehow I managed to survive the first twenty-something years of my life without his watchful eye and brute fists. The trauma we endured during our relationship didn't help matters. My assault and then almost losing him in the motorcycle accident—they were events that put a strain on our emotions but brought us closer together.

The night we sat in the hospital waiting to hear if he would survive was the longest night of my life. I couldn't form a coherent thought until Mia told us that he'd survive. I felt like my world was ending. I didn't have control and I hated it. Control was something I strived to maintain. I made my lists and planned everything out. Having City's life hanging in the balance and relying on someone else to make him better was maddening.

I didn't think I could ever get mad at him again, but here we were. City walked off and left without talking to me. He didn't want to believe anything I had to say. He jumped to his crazy-ass conclusions and stalked off.

My mind was hazy as I sat on the barstool and watched the club moving to music that was muffled in my ears. I couldn't process anything but my thoughts of City and what the fuck just happened.

"Suzy, let's go upstairs, babe." Sophia grabbed my elbow, trying to get me to stand.

"No," I whispered, not ready to move.

"Come on, I'll go with you. Let's get out of here so we can talk," she said as she brushed my hair off my shoulder.

I looked at her with blurred vision; a line of tears sitting in my eyes hadn't yet fallen. "What's there to talk about? He walked out on me."

"Now listen to me, woman. He loves you and you love him. You both have been drinking and the scene went south quick. You know that isn't how City is, babe."

I blinked, letting the tears cascade down my cheeks. "That's exactly how he is, Sophia. I don't know if I can deal with that forever." My voice cracked as I wiped my cheeks.

"Up ya go, sugarplum, upstairs for you. You've obviously had more to drink than I thought if you're questioning your future with this man." She grabbed me around the waist, helping me stand on steady feet.

"Fine, Soph, but only because I could use a little peace and quiet. There's no one else I can talk to about him and get an honest opinion but you. They're all related or partial to the Gallo family." My legs felt rubbery as we walked past the dance floor and made our way to the outside elevators. "Thanks, Sophia." I smiled at her. She was my best friend, the only person in the world that knew everything about me. We'd been through too much together to not be able to read each other like an open book.

She smiled back at me but didn't say a word as we entered the elevator. I sagged against the wall, trying to keep my balance as it was ascending to the top floor. As soon as we walked into the suite, I kicked off my shoes and threw myself on the couch. Wrapping paper, boxes, sex toys, and lingerie were strewn around the room. Partially empty glasses, bottles of liquor, and champagne sat on the coffee table. The night had started with so much promise.

"All right, beautiful. Spill your guts," Sophia said as she sat down next to me and put my feet in her lap. God, I missed times like these. Sophia and I used to stay up late at night having talks about men and our problems. Life had changed so dramatically for both of us over the last two years. Being here with her, like this, made my broken heart long for the olden days.

"Did you hear what he said to me?" I asked, nestling my head into the soft throw pillow.

"I did. He was drunker than I've ever seen him."

"So what, are you saying I should give him a pass?"

Shaking her head, she rested her hand on my chin. "Never. Fuck that. I've learned you can never give someone a free pass, but don't throw it all away. Look, I fell in love with Kayden, and Lord help me, that man has been a whole heap of trouble. I should've been tougher on him and called him on his bullshit more. I paid the price, but I've learned and now we're in a better place. You need to talk to City and tell him how you feel."

"He hurt me tonight, Sophia." I closed my eyes, remembering how my stomach fell when he pushed me away.

"Physically?" Her eyebrows turned downward as her eyes snapped to my face.

"No, he hurt my feelings. He basically said I cheated on him. The accusations stung." The tears started to flow easier. His words finally sank in, and I processed the entire scene as if watching a bad movie. "He's never been mean to me. Tonight he was just a plain asshole."

Sophia chuckled, covering her hand with her mouth.

"What's so funny?" I squinted at her, not understanding the humor of the situation. "I'm sitting here pouring out my soul and crying, and you're laughing. What the hell, Sophia?"

"You said asshole like it was a word you used every day. Not so long ago you were using terms like 'get the heck out of here' and 'you big b.' The shit just rolls off your lips like it's been part of your vernacular for years." She rubbed my leg, running her nails over my skin. "He's a man, Suzy. They do not like to see their woman near other men. That guy said some nasty shit too. I'm surprised City didn't beat the fuck out of him until he was unconscious."

I sighed, putting my arm over my eyes. "City changed me. I can't deny it. He made it sound like I was a piece of property. I mean, why doesn't he just piss on me like a dog marking his territory?" My eyes were heavy and burning. The tears and alcohol made it hard to keep them open.

"Now you're just being overdramatic. Let's get you tucked into bed and see how you feel in the morning." Sophia moved my legs to the couch and pulled me up by my arms. "A little help would be nice," she said, as she tried to hold me in a sitting position.

"I'm just so tired. Just leave me here." I opened my eyes to look at her, and quickly closed them after seeing she wasn't amused.

"Get your ass in that bed. All the drunk bitches will be back and they'll wake you up."

I stood, using Sophia for leverage, and wobbled. "Yes, Mom. You're so damn bossy." I smiled, leaning forward to kiss her on the cheek. "I've missed you, Soph. I don't know what I'd do without you."

She wrapped her arms around me, embracing me in a tender hug. "You'd be at home making lists about lists." She chuckled, releasing me and helping me toward the main bedroom.

"You're probably right. I was such a boring human being." My voice had become quiet, almost mouse-like as sleep started to overcome me.

"In you go, princess," Sophia said as she pulled back the covers.

I didn't bother to get undressed. I just wanted to sleep. I wanted tonight to be over and to deal with everything tomorrow. Grabbing an extra pillow, I turned on my side, tucking it into my body. I'd grown used to snuggling against City. I needed something to fill the void, and the pillow was my only option.

The lights turned off before I heard the click of the door as I drifted off into a restful sleep. All thoughts and worries disappeared as I dreamed about my City. His deep voice, ice-blue eyes, and the feel of his arms wrapped around me. I could feel the love he had for me even in my dreams. He invaded every part of my life, became ingrained in my entire being.

I loved him even subconsciously.

CHAPTER EIGHT

CITY

I ROLLED OVER, feeling for my phone, but didn't find it where I left it. Somehow, during the night, I had pushed it under Suzy's pillow. I tossed and turned, waking up feeling like I hadn't slept a fucking wink. There were no new messages or calls on my phone, and no word from Suzy or any of the girls.

Bits and pieces started coming back to me as I lay in bed staring at the ceiling. I'd fucked up, and managed to do it royally. I left Suzy behind without so much as an "I love you," just an accusation and shitty words. I had to fix it. I fucked up and I had to man up and say I was sorry.

I grabbed my head, the throbbing almost blinding as I climbed out of bed. The quiet from the night before that felt deafening now became overwhelming. I couldn't sit around the house today and idly wait for Suzy to come home so that I could ask for her forgiveness. I had to go to her, find her, and mend the shattered pieces of our relationship.

Leaning over the sink, I stared at myself in the mirror, and was disgusted by the person looking back. I was better than this. The man that acted out last night wasn't me. He was a jealous asshole and I'm a lovesick fool. I quickly showered and brushed my teeth before throwing on my jeans and t-shirt. I didn't give a fuck what I looked like; I just had to get to Suzy.

I barreled down the highway, making my way to the hotel. Izzy hadn't replied to a text I sent her before I left. I kept the phone in my pocket on vibrate, but it remained still. I weaved in and out of traffic, needing to not waste another minute away from Suzy.

The closer I came to the hotel, the more butterflies filled my stomach. What if she didn't forgive me? I knew I'd hurt her, and I prayed that our love for each other could overcome the words of the previous night. As I shut off the bike, sitting in the parking lot of the Shepard's Hotel, I texted the only person that may be awake at this hour — Sophia. It was only eight a.m., but I was banking on her above anyone else.

Me: Sophia, it's City. I'm at the hotel and need to see Suzy.

I walked toward the door, waiting for a reply, with the phone gripped tightly in my hand. A lump formed in my throat, worry hanging in the air so thick I could almost taste it.

Sophia: Room 1215. She's still passed out but I'll let you in. You have a lot of sucking up to do.

Sophia wasn't a bullshitter, and she was Suzy's best friend. I knew no truer words were ever spoken.

Me: I plan to do a lot of sucking up. I'll do anything.

Sophia: Anything?

Me: Just open the damn door, woman.

Sophia: You better make it good. I'm waiting.

The elevator ride seemed to take forever, stopping on every other floor to let off guests. Everyone had been downstairs enjoying the complimentary breakfast. When the bell chimed and the twelfth floor was illuminated, I thought my heart literally stopped in my chest.

Fisting my hands at my sides, I squeezed them, trying to release some tension. I lightly knocked, waiting for Sophia to answer, and swallowed hard. My mouth felt dry, my stomach ready to expel the last ounce of alcohol, and my heart was ready to burst from the rapid pounding in my chest.

"Quiet," Sophia said after she opened the door. "Follow me." She motioned and led me through the suite.

Izzy lay on the couch, passed out and oblivious to my presence. Someone else I didn't recognize, mostly because they were facedown, lay on the floor next to her. The hotel suite was a mess. Wrapping paper, boxes, clothes, and glasses were everywhere. The girls had partied harder than I would've thought, but then again, this was Izzy's doing, and she didn't do anything half-assed.

Sophia stopped in front of the door to a bedroom and crossed her arms over her chest. "Now listen here, mister," she said, poking me in the chest.

I looked down at her bony finger digging into my flesh, and smiled. The girl had balls, and big ones at that. I loved Sophia for the simple fact that she was Suzy's friend, but she and I could've been friends if we had met first. She had the piss and vinegar that reminded me of my sister. She was fierce, loyal, and cared deeply.

"She's crushed, and I haven't seen her since I put her to bed last night. She loves you, City, and you better get down on your knees and beg for her forgiveness. Do whatever it takes."

"Yes, ma'am." I nodded. She hadn't told me anything I didn't already know.

"Don't be a smartass," she said, slapping me on the shoulder. "You made her feel trashy and like shit. You need to make her feel like the princess she deserves to be treated as. You've always done that for her. Made her feel good about herself. I was always your cheerleader, even when she wasn't sure about you. So don't fuck this shit up."

"I got this." Fuck, I really hoped I did.

"You better, but I want to tell you a few things first. The guy she was dancing with, she didn't want to dance with him. Not at all, but your sister told her it would be her last dance as a single girl and she couldn't turn him down. She said some bullshit about bachelorette etiquette. Your sister can be very persuasive." She paused, tapping her lip with her finger.

"Fuck, she's a pain in the ass." I sighed, looking toward my sister passed out and dead to the world.

"Second, the smell on her last night was the weirdo stripper your sister hired. Suzy told her more than once that she did not want a stripper under any circumstances. The guy came in and did a quick dance, but Suzy was totally uncomfortable. As soon as he realized that, he broke contact and gave her a sweet kiss on the cheek when he was finished. She didn't touch him at all and he didn't do anything inappropriate." She straightened her back, looking me straight in the eyes. "City, if you would've seen him you would've laughed. You're like an Adonis compared to this man. You're the only thing that has Suzy's eyes and heart. Grovel, my friend, grovel." She leaned over, kissing my cheek before she left me to enter the room.

I stood there staring at the door, and closed my eyes. I'd been a complete tool. How in the fuck did I even think Suzy would allow someone to touch her or that she'd been unfaithful? I knew Suzy inside and out, but I let my territorial bullshit get in the way. My heart ached at the thought that maybe I made our relationship fubar. Was it fucked up beyond repair? Had I crossed the line that she wouldn't forgive? I'd listen to Sophia's advice and beg for her forgiveness. Not as a sign of weakness, but because of the love I had for her. It was the only way I could fight for what I wanted most—Suzy.

I opened the door slowly, trying not to startle Suzy. Sunlight streamed through the sheer drapes along the wall behind her bed. The rays cascaded across the floor, framing the bed and my bride-to-be. I stood at the foot of the bed, staring at her. Her long blonde hair was fanned out across the pillow, making a halo and giving her an angelic look. My heart ached at the thought that I could possibly lose her. Maybe I fucked up so badly that she wouldn't forgive me. Sometimes words are more painful than any physical harm inflicted by another person. Pain evaporates, but words last a lifetime, replaying in our memories and feeding on our insecurities.

Her soft snores and heavy breathing mingled with the sound of the waves crashing on the shore below. She clung to a pillow, holding it against her chest, her arms tightly wound around it.

Sitting on the bed, I tried to keep my movement to a minimum, not wanting to wake her just yet. She was mine, and had been the only person I'd ever used that term with. No one else had a chance to capture my heart, but Suzy and all her sweetness bored into my heart like a cavity from too much sugar.

I kicked off my shoes, needing to touch her, to hold her in my arms. My body ached for her. I didn't feel comfortable in my skin without contact from her. I couldn't explain it, and I'd never voice it in front of the guys. They already thought I was a pussy-whipped asshole.

Grabbing the pillow, I pulled it from her arms, making sure she remained asleep. She didn't move or twitch as her arms fell against her body. I threw the pillow on the floor, crawling under the covers next to her, and pulled her against my chest. Her breathing changed as she snuggled against me, burying her face against my shirt. I closed my eyes, enjoying the quiet moment and the feel of her in my arms. As soon as she realized I was here, there'd be hell to pay.

I peppered kisses against her temple, brushing back the hair on her forehead as I inhaled the smell of the woman that had stolen my heart over a year ago. It wasn't a pure scent; the alcohol she'd consumed the night before permeated her skin. If we had both been sober, last night wouldn't have happened. Really, if I hadn't consumed a few too many shots and seen someone touching what was mine, then it wouldn't have happened.

Her body stiffened in my arms, and I closed my eyes, knowing the moment had been broken. "Suzy," I whispered, trying to hide the fear in my voice.

"What are you doing?" she asked, her voice laced with anger as she pushed against my chest.

"Sugar, don't push me away. I'm sorry." I tightened my grip, holding her head against my chest.

"I don't want to talk to you." She didn't touch me or return my embrace.

"Don't talk, then. Just let me talk while I hold you." I held her tighter, resting my chin on top of her head as I wrapped my legs around hers. I caged her in; there was no escape and I had a captive audience. "I'm sorry I was an asshole last night." I sighed, knowing my words weren't enough to make up for my behavior.

"More like a giant dickhead," she interrupted, not sagging into my embrace like she normally did.

"Call me what you want. All the terms fit. I'm sorry I didn't listen to you last night. I had too much to drink, but I'm in no way blaming the alcohol. I'm solely responsible for my actions. I fucked up, sugar. I didn't mean to imply that you had been unfaithful to me. Seeing you with that guy and then smelling someone on you pushed me over the edge." I inhaled, winded from the words that I had said without stopping. I was too worried to break in the middle of my speech.

"I would never do anything to risk our relationship, City," she said, digging her fingernails into my bicep.

"I know, sugar, I know." I kissed the top of her head and rested my cheek against her silky, golden hair. "Please forgive me. I have no other excuse except for the love I have for you. You've scrambled my brains. I've never felt as territorial or protective over someone like I do with you. When I see someone touching you, I want to rip their hands off and shove them down their throat. I control it most times."

"No you don't." Her laughter broke the tension, making *me* laugh.

"Trust me, sugar, I do. I wasn't going to hit the guy last night but he wouldn't shut his fucking mouth. He kept talking shit and I couldn't hold back anymore. I couldn't stop myself from knocking him on his ass."

"City," she said as she adjusted her body, looking into my eyes. Her lip trembled as she spoke. "I'm not upset about you hitting him. He deserved it. You hurt me by questioning my faithfulness. You made me feel dirty." A single tear formed in the corner of her eye and slid along the bridge of her nose.

I wiped the tear with the pad of my thumb, cradling her face in my palm. "I never want to make you feel that way. You're the most pure and honest person I know, Suzette. I know you're faithful and I never meant for it to sound otherwise. I'm sorry. You consume me and became a part of me. Your love is as vital to me as the air I breathe. The thought of losing you terrifies me." To admit the last sentence scared the shit out of me. I'd never felt so vulnerable in my life. My heart and happiness lay in her hands.

"Promise me you'll never make me feel that way again, City." She blinked, causing more tears to trickle down her cheek. The redness in her eyes made the blue even more breathtaking. "You're the one person in the world that I thought would always have my back. I never expected you to treat me that way, and I won't stand for it. I refuse to be married to a man that treats me like that. If you do it again, I may not be so easy to find."

"I promise, Suzy. I will never act like that again. I love you more than anything in the world. I'd kill for you and give my life to save yours." I enveloped her in my arms, squeezing her tightly against my body. "You're everything to me and I will do everything in my power to show you how much you mean to me. I will spend every day showing you all the love I have for you and profess my love to you on my deathbed."

"Jesus, you're so morbid. 'I promise' and 'I'm sorry' would've been enough." She laughed, wrapping her arms around my body.

"It takes more than two words to explain the amount of love I have for you, but right now, I'd rather show you." I smirked, grabbing her chin and bringing her lips to mine.

"Oh, how are you going to do that?" she asked with garbled words as she spoke against my lips.

Breaking the kiss, I looked in her eyes. "I'm going to make love to my fiancée the day before our wedding." Her breath hitched as her eyes searched mine. "Tomorrow you officially become Mrs. Joseph Gallo."

"Why can't you become Mr. Suzy McCarthy?" She giggled, rubbing her nose against my cheek.

"Not how it works, sugar. I'm the man and you're the

woman, but you can call me whatever the hell you want when we're in private." I smirked, nipping her nose with my teeth.

"Mmm, I like the sound of that." A warm smile spread across her lips as her body melted into mine.

I kissed her lips, gently prodding, trying to find her tongue. I wanted to taste her. "Suzy, why won't you kiss me back?" Maybe her heart hadn't caught up to her words. I prayed to fuck that was the case. When someone won't kiss you and show you the love you want to convey, it's like a stake to the heart.

She covered her mouth with her hand. "I didn't brush my teeth yet. I think a small furry animal died inside my mouth last night." The corners of her mouth peeked out the sides of her hand, the smile touching her eyes.

Laughter bubbled out of me, slow at first, until my entire body was shaking as her words hit me. "Baby, I don't care if you have bad breath. I won't breathe through my nose." I leaned my forehead against hers.

She shook her head, moving her face farther away from mine with her hand still covering her mouth. "Not happening. Either I get up and brush my teeth or you don't get a kiss until after."

"You feel this?" I asked, pushing my erection into her stomach. "I'm not waiting until you find your toothbrush and get lost in the bathroom. I need to feel you from the inside. I don't give a fuck about your breath."

"I'm not going to kiss you," she said firmly, her mouth set in a firm line.

"Didn't say anything about kissing you, sugar. I want to fuck you, and I only care about your pussy right now." I was done discussing the topic. I needed to be inside her and I needed it now. My body craved her and my heart needed her; I wasn't in the mood to be patient.

CHAPTER NINE

SUZY

"I LOVE when you talk dirty to me. You just want to mark your territory." I smirked, watching him hop off the bed and unbutton his jeans.

"You bet that sweet ass I'm marking it. I'm going to crawl so far up that pretty little pussy that I'll ruin you for life." He shucked his pants, kicking them to the side as he pulled his t-shirt over his head.

What the man didn't understand is that he had already ruined me. I was destroyed, damaged goods, and no one would ever compare to him. As hard and sexy as he was, the soft and loving side of City was what ultimately stole my heart. The man loved me so fiercely that no one could ever come close. The small looks he stole when he thought I wasn't looking, the loving touches as I fell asleep, and the sweet nothings he whispered in my ear when he thought I was dreaming—those were the things I loved most about him.

I yawned, pretending to be unimpressed by his words and sexy-as-hell naked body. "Well, you can try anyway. I'll let you know if your words ring true."

He grabbed the comforter, yanking it off my body before

pulling me down the bed by my feet. I squealed; the quickness of his movements caught me off guard. Pulling me off the bed in a standing position, he quickly stripped me of my clothes.

"So far, a C for effort. You can do better." I smiled, watching the corner of his lip twitch.

He placed his hands under my arms, firmly gripping my waist before throwing me on the bed. He pounced on me, not giving me a moment to catch my breath before smothering me with a perfect closed-mouth kiss. My stomach fluttered like it did the first time he kissed me. The nerves and emotion of the last twelve hours poured out through our lips.

I dug my fingers into his dark locks, fisting the hair in between my fingers as I held his mouth to mine. I wished I had brushed my damn teeth. I wanted to taste him. He pulled away, breaking the connection we had, and looked down at me. The heat of his chest seared my skin and the thump of his heart matched mine. He was just as nervous as me, both of us on edge from last night.

"This will be the last time I'll make love to you before you become my wife." He smiled; his teeth sparkled in the sunlight.

"What about tonight?" I asked, totally confused.

"Sugar, I can't see the bride the night before the wedding. We've talked about this before. I'm going to stay at my parents'."

"I don't like that idea. That's two nights not sleeping in your arms." I sighed, rubbing my thumb across his unshaven cheek. The roughness matched the man more perfectly than the silky skin I felt some days.

"Me either, but it's only for one night. We can't break tradition."

"Make it good, then, handsome. Make me still feel you

when I walk down the aisle tomorrow." I always felt him for hours afterward. The days when he was insatiable, I could feel him for days, often sore the next time he wanted to fool around. Knowing that this was the last time before we were married warmed me and turned me into a puddle of goo.

Growling, he brought his mouth down on mine. I moaned, the regret about brushing my teeth growing. His tongue darted out, sliding across my lips before traveling down my jaw to the sweet spot on my neck. Goose bumps and shivers racked my body as the warmth of his mouth and coolness from his breath skidded across my skin.

When he captured my nipple in his mouth, nibbling on it with his teeth, my entire body convulsed. The rough stubble of his face, the sharp pinch from his hold, and the silky smoothness of his tongue flicking the hardened tip had me seeing stars and moaning his name. I held him to me, fingers wound in his hair as he sucked and flicked until I begged.

"Please, City. I want to feel you," I said.

Grunting as he held my nipple between his lips, he lifted his hips and fisted his cock. The cool metal rubbing against my clit made me twitch before he rubbed the tip through my wetness. As he thrust my hips forward, trying to force him to put his dick inside me, I could feel the deep, low laugh in his chest.

"So ready, sugar. You're always ready for my cock," he whispered against my breast.

"Yes! Yes," I chanted, growing impatient with his lack of thrust.

Swiping it through my wetness again, he placed the piercing against my clit and made tiny circles, capturing my clit with the motion. The combination of the hard metal and smooth tip drove me closer to the edge, but I didn't want to come like this. I closed my eyes, sealing them tightly, trying to stave off the orgasm that was about to rip through me.

"No," I whispered, "not like this."

"You want to come on my cock? You want to feel me thrusting in and out of you as your pussy squeezes me like a vise?" he asked, his voice low and husky.

"Don't make me beg," I said, keeping my eyes closed, moving my hips, trying to escape his cock circling my clit.

Without warning, he rammed his cock inside me in one quick thrust. My eyes sprang open; I felt completely filled as a tiny spark of pain shot throughout my body. He pulled out slightly and stilled, staring down at me with a cocky grin on his face.

"Is that how you want it, sugar?"

"Don't stop. I'm so close." I pulled back and pushed myself forward, fucking him. I couldn't take the lack of motion.

Slipping his arms under my back, he held my shoulders, as he began to rock into me. Each lash of his cock against my G-spot sent tiny shock waves through my system, making my toes curl. I grabbed his hips, relishing the feel of his muscles constricting as he moved inside of me. Our bodies worked in unison, driving me toward an orgasm I knew would leave me breathless and with blurred vision.

His hips started to rotate as he pulled out and rammed back into me straight. The movement intensified the pressure building inside of me. His breathing became ragged as he maintained the momentum, driving into me without mercy.

Colors dotted my vision, the light almost blinding, as everything in my body coiled and released at once. I felt like a slingshot pulled to the max and then let go, flying forward with no escape or ability to control the outcome.

I screamed, "City," as my body became rigid and my

breathing halted. My head flew off the pillow, my body grounded by his hold on my shoulders as my curled toes started to cramp.

My core convulsed around him, the hardness of his cock giving nothing as he continued in the pursuit of his orgasm. His moans turned to growls as he stiffened above me, emptying himself inside me. Gulping for air, he collapsed on top of me, his body twitching with aftershocks.

I closed my eyes, listening to our mingled breaths as I enjoyed the afterglow. The feel of his weight crushing me made me feel encapsulated, as my body grew limp underneath him.

His breathing slowed as his breath skidded across my ear; the low growls of pleasure bringing a smile to my face. As he pulled out, everything he'd just worked to achieve slid down my body, forming a pool on the bed. I still hadn't gotten used to the feel of a man coming inside of me. I felt like I wet myself and couldn't stop it.

"Let me grab a washcloth," he said as he pushed off the bed.

I grabbed his arm, stopping him. "Let me. I'm dying to brush my teeth. I want a proper kiss." I smiled at him, trying not to run my tongue across my dirty teeth.

He collapsed against the mattress, staring up at the ceiling as he rested his hand on his chest. "I'll be waiting." He grabbed my arm with his free hand, sliding his palm down my arm. "Make it quick," he said with a crooked, happy smile.

I groaned as my feet touched the floor. The aftereffects of an evening of overindulgence and wicked high heels hit me. I swayed, grabbing the mattress to steady myself.

"You okay, sugar?" City asked as he sat up and touched my hand.

"Fine, baby. Just not as young as I used to be. Can't party all night and bounce right back."

"I doubt you partied all night too much even in your college years." He laughed, covering his mouth with his hand.

"I didn't sit in my dorm room and study all the time," I said sarcastically. It was all bullshit. I rarely partied. The number of times I had been drunk in college I could count on one hand, but sometimes I didn't like to be reminded of just how much of a good girl I had been.

"Uh, huh," he said, resting his head on his hand as he watched me walk away.

I flipped him off, a small chuckle escaping my lips. He knew me too well. Knew I could never escape my good-girl qualities even though I liked to pretend I had a badass side. I knew I was a cream puff, and I accepted it, though I did so begrudgingly.

My mascara was smeared down my cheeks, the result of my crying last night over City. I looked as bad as I felt. My hair was a tangled mess, makeup half on but not in the right places, and my eyes were swollen. Thank God the wedding wasn't today. I'd have to live with horrible wedding pictures for the rest of my life.

Grabbing the tube of toothpaste out of my toiletry bag, I stood on my tiptoes and leaned into the mirror. Shit, I looked horrible. I quickly backed up, not needing the up-close reminder of last night. After washing him from my body, I covered my toothbrush with paste. I needed to clear the funk out of my mouth. My mouth felt drier than the Mojave Desert on a blistering summer day. Just as I stuck the toothbrush in my mouth and started scrubbing, I heard my phone chirp.

"Suzy, your mother sent you a text," City yelled from the bedroom.

Fucking great. I loved my mom, but she added an extra bit of pressure and stress to an already nerve-racking situation. Weddings are supposed to be blissful, but no one seems to tell you about all the turmoil and decisions that need to be made. My mother could be judgmental at times, and I often felt like my decisions weren't good enough.

I pulled the toothbrush out of my mouth, balancing the paste remnants on my tongue as I yelled, "What's it say?"

I scrubbed my teeth, my motions more feverish at the thought of my parents being in town. She always watched City with a suspicious eye when she didn't know I was looking. She was happy that he had money, although it wasn't the reason I fell in love with the man. I would've been with him even if he were only a tattoo artist. It's a good job, and he's talented. She couldn't get beyond his looks. He had a roughness about him, and the tattoos didn't exactly win him any points in her mind. She'd bust a cork if she knew about the piercing that decorated his lower extremity, or if she ever found out that I had my nipple pierced.

"She just wants to know if she should be at the rehearsal dinner early to help."

I spat the toothpaste into the sink, cupping water in my hand and swishing. The last thing I wanted was my mother there for her type of help. Everything was ready and all we needed to do was show up, including her and my father.

I washed my face quickly, erasing the nightmarish mess from the smudged makeup before returning to the bedroom.

"She's become such a pain the last few months," I said as I crawled in bed.

"She's still your mom and she loves you," he said, grabbing my hand and planting soft kisses across the top.

"You grew up with a different type of mother, City. Your mom has made me feel more like a daughter than my mother ever did. Don't get me wrong, I love her, but she doesn't know how to make me feel loved." I closed my eyes when they watered as I thought about what it would've been like to grow up calling Mrs. Gallo Mom. I always felt like my parents had to fit me into their schedule, and often there wasn't a slot for me unless I had called in advance.

"Let's just get through the next thirty-six hours and everything will go back to normal. You have the Gallo family now, and they're not letting you go."

I'd felt like a member of the family since that first Sunday dinner so long ago. They made me feel like I belonged and had always been there. My sister and I had never even really been close. I didn't ask her to be a part of my wedding party. Izzy had become more of a sister to me than she ever had. We don't get to choose our family, but we do choose those people we let into our life, and with whom we spend time with going forward. For me, the people I wanted nearest were the Gallos. They were a loving and diehard-loyal group. Above all else, they had each other's backs and no one could tear them apart. They accepted each other for their flaws, embraced the bad with the good, and loved unconditionally.

"We should go soon. I have a ton to do before the rehearsal dinner tonight." I snuggled into his side, enjoying the last moment of peace.

He pulled me tighter against his chest, rubbing the tender skin on my upper arm as he kissed my hair. "It'll all work out. Somehow it will all fall into place."

"I'm sure you're right." That statement was a total lie. I couldn't give up my incessant need to be in control and plan every last detail.

"You can't control everything in life, but I know you try like hell. It's one of the things I love about you."

"Tell me five other things you love, City." I swiped my

fingers across his chest, stopping on his nipple to tug on his piercing.

"Where do I start?" he said before rattling off a list that left me feeling more loved than I had ever felt before. The list wasn't filled with vain things like my beauty, which would fade over time, but the things that made me as a person. My success, education, kind heart, and silliness were just a few things he listed without much thought.

"I love you, City," I said, moving my body to plant a wet, sloppy kiss on his lips.

Breaking our connection slightly, he whispered, "I love you too, sugar." He kissed me with as much fervor and passion as he did the first night we met.

We made love one more time before dragging ourselves from the hotel room and heading home to prep for the chaos that awaited us. Wedding weekend was in full swing and there was no turning back.

CHAPTER TEN

CITY

NEVER IN A MILLION fucking years did I think I'd be standing in a church dressed in a tuxedo—not as a groom, at least. I wasn't a cynic. I'd just never found anyone worthy of my time or commitment until Suzy walked into my life. Sometimes when we least expect it and stop looking, fate has a way of playing its hand. Mine came in the form of a drop-dead gorgeous girl broken down on a deserted street. I thanked my lucky stars each goddamn day that her car was a piece of shit.

"You look a little nervous, son," Pop said, slapping me on the back, pulling me from my thoughts.

I rubbed my hands together; they slid easy from the sheen of sweat that had formed over my entire body. I wiped my brow, feeling more nervous than I had ever felt in my life. "I am, Pop. Just never thought I'd be standing here."

"Amazing the place hasn't burst into flames," Anthony said, and laughed. "We surely aren't the churchgoing crowd, and Lord knows we've broken more than one commandment." He fidgeted with his bowtie, pulling it away from his neck.

I laughed. His words were true, but that wasn't why I was nervous. I turned to my Pop, who had a smile on his face. "Did you feel this way when you married Ma?"

He nodded, his smile growing larger. "I was scared as hell, son. It's a big step to take in one's life. It's a serious commitment, but times are different now. I didn't live with your mother before we got married like you've lived with Suzy. It was a leap of faith." He grabbed my shoulder, squeezing it gently. "Do you love her, son? The type of love you can't be without for even a day?"

"I do, Pop. I know she's the one. She makes me a better person, and I want to be surrounded by her and make a family. I want to be in your shoes one day. Suzy is more than I deserve."

"She isn't more than you deserve. You two were made for each other. Just like your mother and me. She brings peace and tranquility to my life, and gave me an amazing family. My life would've been meaningless without her."

I didn't doubt that marrying Suzy was the right decision. The events of Friday night scared the shit out of me. The thought of losing her drove me half insane. I'd never wanted to need someone in that way, but I did with her. I needed her in my life, needed her to be mine, and wanted to spend the rest of my days on Earth with her.

The door creaked open as Ma poked her head inside. "Where's my baby boy?" she asked, opening the door with tears in her eyes.

"Why ya crying, Ma?" I asked, as she wiped the tears.

"Damn, I'm going to mess up my makeup." She pulled a tissue from her bra and blotted the skin under her eyes. "I just saw Suzy and she looks stunning. I'm the happiest woman in the world today. They're tears of joy."

"How is she, Ma? Is she okay?" My heart pounded, my throat feeling constricted by the button-up shirt.

"She's better than okay; she's glowing and ready for the ceremony to start." Ma wrapped her arms around me, holding me against her as she spoke. "You've made me a happy woman, Joseph. I couldn't love Suzy any more than I do if I had given birth to her myself." She rubbed my back as she kissed my cheek.

"You just have baby Gallos in your mind, Ma," Michael said as he kicked back in a chair against the wall. He looked so put together and calm.

"So what?" she asked as she placed her hands on her hips and turned toward Michael. "I'm old, boy and all I want is a baby…just one damn baby. Is that too much to ask?"

"Not really, Ma, but it'll happen when it happens. We're still young and enjoying our life," Michael said, leaning forward, resting his elbows on his knees.

"By the time I was your age, I had four children. I enjoyed every bit of my life, and maybe more so since it was filled with such love. Children don't end your life, Michael, they add to it."

"Bullshit," Anthony muttered, covering his mouth and coughing.

Ma narrowed her eyes at him. "Anthony, you better stop acting like a playboy and living your hollow existence. You have to settle down sometime, and when you do, you'll regret all the years you spent alone."

"I'm rarely alone, Ma." He smiled, his hair flopping over his forehead.

"I mean emotionally alone." She stared at him, waiting for him to respond, but he didn't. "Okay, I want a picture with my son on his wedding day. Where's that damn photographer?"

Pop walked toward the door, pausing as he opened it. "I'll go get him."

As the door clicked shut, my ma turned to me. "Nerves are normal, son. Once you see how breathtaking Suzy is in her dress, everything else will fade away." She rested her head on my chest as she held my hand.

"I know, Ma. I'm just ready to get this started. I hate waiting; I've never been a patient man." I kissed the top of her head, getting lost in the strawberry scent from my childhood.

"You don't say." She laughed, squeezing my hand. "Just like your father." She sighed, drawing her body closer to mine. "I wish Thomas could've been here. I'm more worried about him than I've ever been, Joseph."

"I know, Ma. I haven't spoken to him in a while. He's too deep undercover now. I don't like it, not one fucking bit."

"Y'all are going to burst into flames with the language in this room. We are in a church," Izzy said as she entered the room with Pop and the photographer.

"If you haven't, then no one will, Izzy," Anthony said with a laugh.

"Enough. Let's take some photos. We have five minutes until you boys need to be at the altar."

Five minutes felt like an eternity as we took more pictures than I wanted to count. My line of sight would have a perpetual dot from the camera flash. By the end of the night, I'd have dozens of tiny blobs in my eyes and possibly be partially blind. We took photos as a group, the Gallo family minus Thomas. We took turns taking pictures with our parents; it wasn't often that we were all dressed up and in one place together.

I was thankful when there was a knock on the door and a voice said, "It's time."

Cracking my neck, I straightened my back and headed for

the door. Ma grabbed my arm, stopping me. "I'm proud of you, baby." She smiled and released me.

I nodded, leaving the tiny room and heading toward the church. Anthony and Michael filed in behind me as we stood in our designated spot at the top of the altar in front of the crowd. The church was packed with people, many faces I didn't know. Ma and Suzy went overboard on the invites, but my mother insisted that her friends be invited, besides our gigantic family that had flown in from all parts of the world. The Gallos didn't know how to do anything small.

As the music started, the doors in the back of the church swung open and the entire church stood and turned. The attention no longer on me, I squinted down the aisle, catching a glimpse of Suzy. She looked like an angel dressed in off white.

The tulle straps created a V, encasing her breasts. The fact that I knew the word tulle disturbed me slightly, but Suzy had educated me about bridal fashion…whether I wanted to know it or not. The bodice was form fitting; a wide ribbon around her waist held a large fabric flower just below her left breast. The bottom of the dress was loose with layers of tulle that flowed and shifted as she walked. It wasn't over the top of puffy shit, it was perfect and totally Suzy—classy and sweet. I couldn't wait to rip the fucking thing off her. A veil covered her face, more traditional than I thought she'd be. I desperately wanted to see her.

She walked arm and arm with her father, slowly moving down the aisle, facing forward. I rubbed my hands together, the last bit of nerves leaving my body, replaced by excitement and a calm that I hadn't expected. When she stopped in front of the first step, our eyes connected. Through the thin veil, I could see the smile on her face as the priest approached her and her father.

The priest stepped down and said, "Who gives this bride away today?"

"I do," her father said, releasing her hand and lifting her veil. He placed a chaste kiss on her cheek before stepping back.

Suzy ascended the stairs, stopping in front of me with teary eyes.

"I love you," I whispered, trying not to become misty-eyed myself.

With a smile on her face, she tilted her head and said, "I love you too."

Sophia reached around and grabbed the flowers from her. Suzy held her hands out to me, and I grasped them with both of mine and squeezed. With one last smile, we turned toward the priest and waited.

We stole glances at each other as he spoke; his words were lost on us. With our hands in each other's, we faced forward and tried to pay attention, but it was impossible. I leaned over, close enough for only her to hear. "You look beautiful, sugar."

She blushed, squeezing my hand. The priest cleared his throat; clearly, we had missed something, as we were so lost in each other.

"The rings," the priest repeated.

I turned to Michael, my best man and brother, and held out my hand. He placed the two platinum bands in my palm and I closed my fingers around them. I had hers engraved with *You're mine, sugar.* A simple statement, and she was from the moment she walked into my life. I handed him the rings and we watched him bless the metal, saying a prayer over them before returning his attention to us.

"Suzette, repeat after me," he stated, turning toward her.

"I, Suzette McCarthy, take you, Joseph Gallo…" She

repeated his words, never breaking eye contact with me. She slid the ring on my finger, a smile on her face, as we both felt the power in the moment. Her voice never wavered as she finished with "Until death do us part." She wiped a tear from her eye as she finished. I had to fight every urge I had to wrap my arms around her and kiss her.

"Joseph, repeat after me," the priest said, holding her ring in his hand.

I repeated the words, without missing a single one, letting the power behind the statement seep into my veins. We were connected, a single soul in front of the eyes of God, joined in holy matrimony. We never broke eye contact, keeping each other grounded in the moment.

As I slipped the ring on her finger, I held her hand in mine, running my fingertips against her dampened flesh. We stood there for a few more minutes after I finished my part of the vows and stared at each other. He could've said the church was on fire and we wouldn't have known. I always looked at Suzy, usually watched her sleep, but to stand here and just look into each other's eyes was some heady shit. I loved this woman, more than I loved anyone or anything in my life, including myself.

"I give you Mr. and Mrs. Joseph Gallo," the priest said as we both turned to him. "You may now kiss the bride."

Without needing another word, I grabbed her by the waist and pulled her to my body. Stopping briefly above her lips, I searched her eyes and could see only joy. I crushed my lips to hers as the crowd began to whistle and holler in the background. Their voices faded away as I kissed her, my wife and bride.

When we backed away from each other, we both had watery eyes. As we turned toward the people, now on their feet, I grabbed her around the waist and held her to my side.

Our friends and family clapped and cheered as we made our way down the aisle and out of the church doors to the small bridal suite.

As soon as I closed the door, I pulled her into a kiss. Not the small kiss I gave her in front of the family, but one that left us both breathless and needing more.

"We did it, sugar. You're mine forever," I said, as I swiped my fingers against her cheek.

"No, baby, you're mine." She smirked, a devilish expression on her face as she leaned in and captured my lips.

CHAPTER ELEVEN

SUZY

AFTER WE GREETED the guests at the door, my feet were on fire. The shoes I had picked were beautiful and made me feel almost the same height as City, but the damn things were like torture devices. I loved how the satin ribbon of the high heels intertwined and laced up my feet, stopping around my ankle with a bow. It was too bad the dress was so long that no one could see them. I grabbed City's arm, leaning over to rub my ankles.

"You want to go change your shoes?" City asked, watching me with a concerned look.

"You think we can sneak away for a minute upstairs? I'll never be able to dance in these."

"It's our wedding, sugar. We can do anything we want." He smiled and winked at me. He turned toward his mother and said, "Hey, Ma, we're going to run upstairs and get different shoes for Suzy."

She smirked, not believing the reason for our hasty exit. "Sure, just don't be too long, son. We have a wedding to celebrate."

City nodded, holding my hand and pulling me from the

line. As we walked out into the hotel hallway, he grabbed me by the waist and scooped me up into his muscular arms. I squealed from the sudden movement and sighed as I rested my head on his chest. The intense pain in my feet turned into a dull throb as he carried me to the elevator.

"It's great that we had the reception in a hotel. Makes life so much easier," he said.

Reaching up, I touched his cheek, still not believing we were married. "We really did it, huh?" I asked.

"We did, sugar. Now comes the fun part," he said as the doors to the elevator opened.

"Dancing?"

"Fucking my wife," he said, a deep growl low in his chest.

He quickly adjusted me as the doors to the elevator closed. Pushing my back against the wall, he pressed the STOP button on the elevator as soon as it moved. Holding me against the wall, with one arm supporting my weight, he quickly undid his zipper and reached under my dress.

His eyes twinkled as a naughty grin decorated his face. "No panties again. It must be my lucky day."

"I wanted to give you a surprise when you put your head under my gown for the garter."

"Don't give a shit about that right now. I want to fuck my wife, right here, right now."

I didn't speak, just threw my head back as he thrust inside of me. I wrapped my legs around his waist, holding him to me as he moved. He nibbled on my neck and kissed my lips as he pulled out and slammed back into me. The building tension from the day quickly drove me to the edge as his body slammed into my clit.

I panted, so close to the edge as he rocked his cock into my core. Within minutes, our bodies shook and we both came on bated breath. Our bodies were dotted with perspiration, and our breathing was ragged as he rested his forehead against mine. He must have pressed the STOP button, because the elevator began to move again as he pulled out and zipped back up.

As he cradled me in his arms, I felt utterly loved, completely content, and totally sated. He carried me to our suite, placing me on the couch as we entered. He knelt down and undid the cloth straps on my heels. Grasping my feet in his large hands, he massaged the ache out of them.

I moaned, throwing my head back against the couch cushions. "That feels so gooood."

"I should feel insulted that you're moaning more now than when you were in the elevator." He laughed, pushing harder on the tender flesh.

I giggled, kicking my feet out of his hands. "I'm okay now. Let me grab my shoes before they send out the search party." He backed away, grabbing my hand and helping me stand. "Fuck," I said as his come dripped down my leg.

"What?"

"I feel like I just peed myself, damn it." I sighed. "I can't go down there like this." I lifted up my dress, touching the wetness with my fingers.

"You grab your shoes," he said as he stood, "and I'll grab a washcloth."

"Okay, but you get to do the honors," I said as I walked to the bedroom with my legs as bowed out as possible. I didn't want it to get on my dress any more than it already had.

City entered the bedroom behind me, disappearing into the bathroom for a moment. I grabbed the pair of white tennis shoes I had brought just in case I needed some relief, and waited for him.

"Just stand there and let me do it all, sugar," he said as he knelt down and disappeared under my dress. He wiped my legs gently before taking great care, and probably joy, in wiping his come from between my legs.

"Don't get any ideas," I said, feeling a tingling from the warm washcloth.

"I can control myself only for so long." He laughed as his head popped out from under the layers of lace. "Give me your shoes."

I handed him my shoes and stood still looking down at the man I loved. I held his shoulder, trying to maintain my balance as he placed each shoe carefully on my feet and laced them up tight. They felt like tiny pillows, relieving the pressure in the muscles of my feet.

"Better?" he asked, running his hands up my legs.

"So much better. Thank you, City."

"It's my job to take care of you," he said as he stood and grabbed my chin. "I plan to spend my lifetime doing just that, sugar."

"Mmm," I mumbled as he leaned forward and kissed me.

I could've collapsed in his arms and fallen into a peaceful slumber, but there was a party going on downstairs and we were the main event. We couldn't miss it even if we were exhausted. As we entered the ballroom, the party was in full swing. The DJ was playing instrumental music before dinner, and many of the party guests surrounded the bar in conversation.

"Hey, sister," Izzy said as she walked toward me. "I'm so excited to be able to say that and it be true. I've always wanted a sister." She wrapped her arms around me, squeezing me a little too tight.

"Can't breathe," I whispered.

"Man up," she said as she released me.

"I'll be back, ladies; I'm going to grab a drink at the bar

with my boys," City said as he kissed my cheek and left us alone.

"Where's your sister?" Izzy asked, looking around the crowd.

"Don't know, and don't give a shit either."

"You know you've turned into a badass with a potty mouth, Suz." She smiled, shaking her head.

"City. It's all his fault."

"I'd like to think I played a part in it too." She laughed.

"You're always getting me in trouble, Izzy."

"Me?" she asked, holding her hand to her chest.

"Always."

A man cleared his throat next to us and we both turned in his direction. "Excuse me, ladies, I don't mean to interrupt."

"Well then don't," Izzy said, looking the stranger up and down.

He was big and handsome as hell. He reminded me of an Italian version of the Rock. Muscles bulged from his suit, and he had close-shaven black hair, shimmering green eyes, and knockout lips. They were the puffy kind that fit his strong jaw line perfectly and called the name of countless women.

"Don't be rude, Izzy," I said, turning to face him. "How can I help you?"

"I'm a friend of Thomas' and he asked me to drop off a gift on his behalf." The man held out an envelope and waited for me to take it.

"Is he okay?" Izzy asked before I could thank the gentleman.

"He is, and he's very sorry he couldn't make it," he said, looking down at Izzy as if he was not sure of how to take her change in attitude.

"Don't mind her," I said to him, my eyes flickering between the two. "Thomas is her brother."

"Ah, you're *that* Izzy," he said, his lips turning up into a smile. "I've heard a lot about you."

She snarled, not entirely liking the shitty grin on his face. "And you are?" she said, holding out her hand for him to take.

"James." He grabbed her hand and stilled. "James Caldo."

"Never heard of you, Jimmy," she said with a twinkle in her eye.

"Perfect," he said as he brought her hand to his lips and placed a kiss just below her knuckles.

I could feel the electricity between the two of them. Izzy basically eye-fucked him as he kissed her hand. As soon as he looked up, her face went back to a pissed-off sneer. The girl could play a good game, but as an observer, I could see the lust.

I coughed, breaking the moment of awkwardness for myself. "Thanks, James. I'll give this to Joseph for you. Why don't you stay and enjoy the wedding?" I said, smiling at the man. He'd taken the time to get dressed up and I wanted to see Izzy squirm, in all honesty.

"What?" Izzy asked, turning toward me.

"We have plenty of food and I'm sure the Gallos would love to talk with you about their Thomas." Izzy gave me the death glare. "You can keep James company tonight, Izzy. You didn't bring a date." I smiled, and I could almost see the venom dripping from her fangs.

"I'd love to stay. Thank you. Izzy, would you like a drink?" he asked, still holding her hand in his.

"Only because Suzy would want me to be a gracious host," she said, looking at me out of the corner of her eye.

"I don't want to put you out or anything. I'm a *big* boy and can handle myself. I just thought you could use a drink to unwind a bit. You feel a little tense, and that mouth of yours could get you into trouble."

"I don't need a babysitter, Jimmy, but I'll take the drink."

"It's James," he said, squeezing her hand.

I'd been around Izzy enough to see when she was attracted to someone, and she was to James. She may not want to admit it—Izzy often picked guys that she could push around—but I had a feeling James could give her a run for her money.

"You two kids play nice," I said as I waved and walked toward my husband. I curled my arms around his waist, leaning my head on his back as he stood talking to Michael. "Hey, baby. Someone dropped this off for us."

"What is it?" he asked as he grabbed the envelop from my fingers.

"A card from Thomas."

I could feel his chest tighten before he tore the envelope open. His eyes scanned the card, his eyebrows drawing together as he read the message from Thomas.

"What does it say?" I asked, dying to know what Thomas wrote.

City sighed, pinching the bridge of his nose before handing the card to me. "Read it for yourself, sugar."

"Are you sure?" I asked as I opened the card. He nodded and closed his eyes. Inside was a brief message from Thomas.

Joe,

Sorry I couldn't be there for your wedding. I'm in deep... too deep to get away, even for your wedding.

I'm safe, my cover still intact. Shit's worse than we thought and I'm trying to bring them down as soon as possible. I couldn't take the chance of blowing my cover and risking the lives of our family. This is the path I've chosen, and I refuse to risk anyone's life but my own.

Please know I love you and can't wait to meet Suzy. Give my love to everyone.

Love Always,

Thomas

I closed the card and handed it back to City.

He shoved it in the inside pocket of his suit. "Who gave it to you?"

"The man over there." I pointed down the bar where James and Izzy stood with shots in their hands. "The one with your sister."

"Who is he and why is he having a drink with my sister?"

"He's Thomas' friend and I invited him to stay and enjoy himself. Izzy will take care of him."

He rubbed his face. "That's what I'm afraid of," he said, his chest expanding before he exhaled.

"Don't worry, City. They're like oil and water," I lied. "You don't have to worry about him. He knows all about your sister from Thomas."

"That may not be a good thing either. I'm going to go introduce myself," he said, trying to break free of my grip.

"Oh no you don't. Give them some time to talk."

"I want to talk to him about Thomas," he said, turning to face me with no smile on his face.

"Come on, kids," Mrs. Gallo interrupted. "It's time to be seated for dinner."

I smiled at him, happy that he couldn't barge into the conversation his sister was having with James. It looked heated and made me giddy inside.

"I would say you're both in cahoots if I didn't know any better," he said before kissing my lips.

"You're going to need some fuel for our wedding night." I laughed, burying my face in his chest.

"Sugar, I could live off you alone."

"Pfft," I said, pulling him toward the table at the front of the dance floor. "I wasn't born yesterday, City. You do need to eat."

He leaned down, his hot breath against my ear. "The only thing I need to eat is your pussy."

My core convulsed; the sated feeling I felt before evaporated and was replaced with lust and an ache between my legs. "Don't you start," I said as I took my seat.

"I've only just begun," he whispered in my ear as he pushed in my chair.

I smiled, looking at the crowd, wishing I could run out of here and back to the suite with him. It would be hours before we could escape this place. I figured I'd use the time to torture him as much as he tortured me.

Our guests started clinking their glasses as the rest of the wedding party was seated. I leaned over, placing my lips on his and inhaling the scent that was distinctly him—musky and male and pure sex. I ran my hand up his leg, resting it against his cock and squeezing. His body twitched as he sucked in a breath. He broke the kiss, looking at me with a mischievous grin.

"Do it again and I'll take you in the bathroom and fuck you. I don't care who's in there."

I bit my lip, trying to hide my laughter. He wouldn't dare. I loved this man, caveman attitude and all.

I played nicely as we tried to eat our food, constantly interrupted by the clinking of the wine glasses. It was cute at first, but then it just became annoying. I was starving, and eating had become impossible. After ten minutes of trying to choke down the steak, we both gave up and headed into the crowd to greet the guests we missed earlier.

The rest of the evening was fantastic. It was amazing being surrounded by so much love. Everyone I cared for was there. Sophia and Kayden, minus the little bundle of boy. My friends from work, the boys from the Neon Cowboy, and everyone else that played a role in our life. My parents and sister were there too, but they mainly stayed with my side of the family and stuck to themselves. Pity, really. The two sides would probably never mingle, but then again, I could choose whom I spent my time with.

The most memorable part of the evening was our first dance as husband and wife. We picked "All of Me" by John Legend as our song. It was City's choice; I loved it and couldn't deny him his request. It was perfect. It was our story tied up in one song. It was written for us, or at least it felt like it had been.

City sang it in my ear as he held me against his body and we danced. Tears formed in my eyes. The man could be romantic, and I believed every word of the song. Hearing his deep voice in my ear professing his love through lyrics made me melt. I buried my face in his chest, wiping my tears against his jacket as the song came to a close.

He grabbed my face, looking into my eyes before he kissed me. The love I felt in this moment was almost overwhelming. Sometimes his touch made me feel weak in the knees, like a teenage girl that was lovesick.

I was blessed to spend an eternity with this man.

CHAPTER TWELVE

CITY

WE SPENT two weeks in Italy, touring my homeland, and I showed her the vineyard my family owned. It had been her first time outside of the US and I wanted her to experience the beauty that Italy had to offer. Suzy fell in love with the people of Italy. The culture is so different than in America. Life was slower; people enjoyed the simple things and didn't move through their day at breakneck speed.

Although neither of us wanted to say goodbye to Italy and head back to reality, the moment we walked into our home, everything felt right. I carried her over the threshold, not wanting to break tradition and also being told by Suzy that it was a requirement. I laughed when she refused to walk into the house until I picked her up and carried her inside.

Waking up in our bed made me feel more rested than I had in over a month. Suzy slept peacefully at my side with the sheet covering half her body. Her breasts were exposed, her hair flowing around her head, as she softly snored.

I kissed her neck, feeling her pulse under my lips. She stirred, a small moan coming from her lips.

"Morning, sugar," I said against her skin.

"Morning, husband." She stretched, the sheet cascading down, exposing her entire body.

"I love the sound of that," I said as I partially covered her body with mine.

I slid my hand up her side, stopping on her breast, feeling the fullness in my hand. I rubbed my palm against her nipple, feeling her twitch. I grabbed it with my fingers, giving it a slight tug.

"Ouch," she said, her face contorting.

"Sensitive today. Is it time for your period?" Typically that was the only time she complained that my touch was too tough or abrasive.

"I haven't been keeping track. It must be," she said with a yawn as I cupped her tit in my palm.

"They feel fuller than usual," I said, squeezing them lightly.

"I probably gained ten pounds in Italy. The food was so amazing."

I looked down at her. I knew her body like I knew my own. I'd spent hours worshiping it. "Suzy, are you…?" I sucked in a breath. Suzy's body hadn't changed in the year since we met. No amount of pasta or Gallo family meals had added a curve to her hourglass perfection. Missing her period and her overly sensitive nipples had my mind spinning.

"Oh no," she said, sitting up quickly, grabbing her breasts. "I can't be."

"I'm greedy and want you all to myself, but when it happens I'll be the happiest man alive, sugar." I touched her stomach, resting my hand against her skin and smiling.

"I'm on the pill, but I missed a couple days with traveling. I can't be," she said, blowing out a puff of air, resting her hand against mine. "I'm sorry I forgot my pill, baby."

"I fucked you so much there should be quadruplets in

there." I laughed, moving to rest my head against her abdomen. She snaked her fingers in my hair, massaging my scalp. "There's no greater honor than for a woman to carry a man's child. Don't ever say you're sorry. When it happens it happens, but let's try to not have it happen so soon." I kissed her stomach, making a ring around her belly button.

"Your mom would be so damn excited," she said, pulling my face up.

"You'll make her the happiest woman in the world someday, Suzy." I kissed her lips, enjoying the feel of her against me. "But would you be happy, sugar?" I asked, looking into her eyes.

"I'm not ready to give *us* up yet," she whispered. Suzy swallowed hard and rubbed her forehead. "City, what if I am?"

"If you are," I said, rubbing her cheek with my thumb, "I won't be pissed off. You'll be carrying a part of us and we'd still have nine months to ourselves before our world would be rocked."

"I'm not ready," she whispered, her eyes closing as she frowned.

"Sugar," I said, touching her chin and forced her to look into my eyes. "You can handle anything. You're stronger than you think, and I'll be here with you when it happens. Let's not worry about something that we can't control. We'll find out soon enough if you are or aren't. You worry too much. I'm sure it's just the stress of the travel. Let me help you forget." I smiled as I watched her gnaw on her lip.

"You're right. I'm sure it's from the stress of the wedding and travel. How are you going to make me forget?" she asked, and wiggled her eyebrows.

I crushed my lips to her mouth, devouring her lips. She

melted into my touch, her mind occupied by the feel of my rough hands gliding across her soft skin. I made love to Suzy in our bed for the first time as husband and wife. Life couldn't get any better.

CHAPTER THIRTEEN

CITY

CHRISTMAS

Suzy and I decided that we'd wait until Christmas day to share the news with the Gallo family. My parents had everything they could ever want, and buying a gift for them was a bitch. The one thing we could give them that they couldn't get anywhere else was the news of their first grandchild.

"You ready for this?" I whispered to Suzy as we sat down on the couch.

"Who's going first this year?" Anthony asked, sitting next to Izzy on the floor.

"I'll go last," Izzy said, leaning back, looking uninterested.

"That's total bullshit, Izzy. You always want to be first," Michael said, sitting down next to Mia on the love seat.

She placed her hands on her chest as she spoke. "Being the baby earns me the right to always go first. I was left out of everything growing up. Christmas day was mine, all mine."

"Please, you were so far up our asses, you were never left out of anything," Michael said, laughing and wrapping his arm around Mia.

Suzy leaned over, whispering in my ear. "I'm kind of nervous. Everything is about to change." Suzy turned her attention back toward the family.

I nodded, leaning over so only she could hear. The shit was about to hit the fan, but for once, it would be a great thing. "Just be ready to have your eardrums shattered." I laughed. God, the Gallos could be loud, but I imagined my mother's happy screams would be near window-cracking volume.

"Why don't we start oldest to youngest," Anthony said.

"That's not necessary; your father and I don't need presents," Ma said, sitting in her chair next to the Christmas tree.

My parents had outdone themselves this year. The Christmas tree almost touched the ceiling. They never went with an artificial tree. My pop had to cut down a tree each year. My parents spent days finding just the right one on their property before cutting and hauling it inside. Thank God they had boys, because it took all of us to help him carry it inside and set it up. Ma spent days decorating it, adding ornaments that dated back to our childhood. The woman kept every decoration we ever made, and they lined the tree.

"Ma, stop. You and Pop deserve presents. You've always spoiled us and now it's our turn to give back," Izzy said, turning toward Ma. "Not really happy about the oldest-to-youngest thing, but I can wait."

"You're a sweet dear," Ma said, leaning forward, stroking Izzy's cheek.

I rolled my eyes. The sugarplum fairy must've invaded my sister's body.

"Open my present first, Ma," Izzy said, reaching under the tree and pulling out a small box wrapped in red glitter paper and a silver bow, which she handed to Ma.

Ma shook it, putting it next to her ear. "Hmm, I wonder what it is."

"Just open it," Izzy said, bouncing on her knees.

"Patience, Isabella. It's a virtue," Ma said, pulling the ribbon and removing the bow.

"Virtues and me don't get along," Izzy said, her laughter growing loud.

"You're a Gallo, none of us do," Pop said as he smiled at Izzy and chuckled.

Ma opened the box, a giant smile spreading across her face. "Oh, Isabella, it's beautiful." She pulled a bracelet lined with rubies and diamonds from the box.

"It's our birthstones together, Ma," Izzy said, crawling closer to her. "Can I put it on you?"

"Yes, I'd love that." Ma handed the bracelet to Izzy. "It's beautiful. I love you, baby girl." Ma leaned forward, kissing Izzy on the head as she snapped the bracelet around Ma's wrist.

"Love you too, Mama." Izzy moved the bracelet so the stones sat on top and were visible, before crawling back to her spot next to Anthony.

"City, why don't you go next," Michael said, winking at me.

"Did you tell him?" Suzy mouthed at me with wide eyes.

I shook my head, because I hadn't said a word to anyone. "No, brother, you go ahead," I said, trying not to spoil their gifts by going before them.

"I can't follow up Izzy's gift. You always give strange things to Ma, so I'd rather go after you," Michael said as he slapped his knee.

Everyone laughed, and Mia elbowed him. I always bought Ma something special and meaningful. The woman didn't care about price; she only wanted something that was heartfelt and meaningful.

"I hadn't planned on giving Ma our gift so soon, but we'll go now just to make you happy," I said with a smirk. He'd shit a brick in a moment…it served his ass right for his shitty comment.

"I want to give it to her," Suzy said, placing her hand on mine before pushing off the couch.

We'd spent hours talking about the best way to break the news. Suzy decided to have a shirt made that said "World's Greatest Nana," along with the first ultrasound photo tucked underneath. Damn kid looked like a jellybean, but I knew it was enough to make my ma squeal.

"Izzy, can you give me the big box with the snowman paper, please," Suzy said as she approached the tree.

Izzy grabbed the box, shaking it as she handed it to Suzy. "Is it an ugly Christmas sweater? You know a girl can never have too many of those." Izzy smiled as Suzy ripped it from her hands.

"Shush it, you. I'm still mad at you," Suzy said, sticking out her tongue at Izzy. She turned toward my parents, sitting in their favorite chairs next to the tree, side by side. "We had something made for you this year, Mom." Suzy handed her the box and came back to sit at my side.

"That's so sweet of you, dear," Ma said, tearing the paper slowly.

"It's for both of you," I said, grabbing Suzy's hand, giving it a squeeze.

"Thanks, son," Pop said, watching Ma open the box.

As she pulled the shirt from the box, Izzy said, "I knew it. Ugly Christmas clothes. Nice, brother."

"Izzy," I warned.

My ma's eyes grew wide, her lip trembling as my pop

grabbed her arm. Her mouth dropped open as she read the shirt. "Really?" she whispered.

Pop reached in the box, pulling out the ultrasound photo and bringing it close to his eyes.

"What the hell is it?" Michael asked.

Ma turned the shirt around, a giant smile on her face. "Promise me you two aren't joking?" she asked, holding the shirt in the air.

"We would never joke about that, Ma," Suzy said, squeezing my hand and leaning into my side.

The shrill scream from my ma had me covering my ears. She hopped from her seat, coming at us quickly.

"Fuck," Michael said, clearly understanding the error of his previous statement.

My ma was so lost in her baby haze that she didn't even flinch at his statement. She stopped in front of us, tears just starting to stream down her cheeks. "When?" she asked, clutching the shirt in her hand.

Suzy laughed, hopping to her feet. "August," she said, wrapping her arms around my ma.

"Oh my God, August is so far away, but there's so much to do," Ma said, grabbing Suzy and squeezing her tightly.

I stood, walking toward my pop, holding out my hand. "Congrats, Grandpa," I said, waiting for his response.

He placed his hand in mine, pulling me toward him, embracing me. "I'm proud of you, son. Damn proud. There will finally be someone to carry on the family name…about damn time." He laughed, patting me on the back.

"Only if it's a boy, Pop," I said, sighing and feeling completely content.

"Look around; boys are genetic. Girls are an anomaly in this family."

Ma grabbed me, pulling me from his arms. "And you, how could you keep this from me?"

"We wanted to be sure, Ma. Don't be mad," I said, kissing her cheek.

"I'm not mad. I don't know if I've ever been as happy as I am right now," she said, resting her head on my chest. "A baby, finally a baby," she whispered, her tears soaking through my shirt.

Over my shoulder, I could see everyone surrounding Suzy. She beamed, a giant smile on her face and her cheeks slightly pink. She didn't like attention, but she'd better get used to it. She'd be the center of attention until the baby arrived.

Anthony touched her stomach. "Wow, it's going to be like the movie *Alien*. That's some scary shit, Suzy." He smiled, patting it before moving like the creature that busted out of John Hurt.

Mike batted his hands away from Suzy. "Stop it, you dumbass. You're scaring her. Congrats, doll. I'm so excited to finally be an uncle." He smiled at her, wrapping her into his arms, but holding her like she was breakable.

"Maybe someday Mia can be an aunt?" she asked as she pulled away to see his face.

Mike laughed, nervously looking at Mia. "We'll see. I'm still trying to figure out if she's 'the one,'" he said, and laughed.

Mia smacked his ass, causing a loud crack to fill the air. "You could only be so lucky," Mia said. "Come here, Suzy, give me a hug, Mama. Are you ready for this?"

I watched my family as they showered her with love. We weren't the main attraction anymore; the world would now revolve around the baby.

Suzy huffed out a breath. "Ready as I'll ever be." She shrugged before hugging Mia.

"Congrats, Suzy," Izzy said, pulling Mia off Suzy. "Remember, that baby better have a vagina." Izzy poked her in the stomach and bent down next to her belly. "Hey, little girl, Auntie Izzy will teach you everything you need to know about life," Izzy said, rubbing her hand over Suzy's stomach.

The color drained from Suzy's face, as her eyes grew wide. "Izzy, we don't know the sex yet, but boy or girl, they'll be lucky to have you as an aunt." Suzy looked at me with her eyes bulging like she was scared to death of Izzy getting her hands on our baby. There were worse things than having Izzy teaching a girl how to be strong. Izzy could be a pain in the ass, but she was a tough cookie. The man that could tame her would have to be a beast, if it was possible at all.

RESISTING

CHAPTER ONE

IZZY

I'M A SIMPLE WOMAN. I grew up in a house with four brothers and loving parents who have remained married even after more than thirty years together. They showered us with love and affection. I'm the youngest of their children.

I have four very annoying older brothers. They're overprotective, and even though I'm an adult, that's never changed. They chased every man I ever liked (fuck the L-word) away as they screamed bloody murder and ran for their lives. Some would call the Gallo men alphas, but not me. I call them pains in my ass.

They helped mold me into the woman I am today. I don't take shit from anyone. I know how to throw an amazing right hook, just the right angle to knee a guy in the balls so he'll never have children, and how to keep my mouth shut.

A couple years ago, we opened a tattoo shop together. We simply named it Inked. Our family has money, but we were raised to not sit on our asses like spoiled brats. We get up each day and go to work. It's our goal to stand on our own two feet. So far, we've been successful. Even though we fight like cats and dogs, we love each other fiercely and are very careful whom we let into our little Gallo Family Club.

Thomas, my eldest brother and an undercover DEA agent, is the only one who doesn't work in the shop. He's a silent partner, and we pray that, one day, he'll get sick of his undercover work and settle down. He's been working inside the Sun Devils MC for some time. Moving up the ranks, he's made his mark and is on the verge of bringing the entire club to its knees.

Joe is one badass motherfucker. He's kinda my favorite, but I'll never tell him that. Shit, I'm not stupid. He's an amazing artist and tattooist, and will be an amazing father. A while back, he rescued a little hot blond named Suzy. She's sweet as pie and used to be innocent. His badass biker ways ruined her, but naturally, I rubbed off on her, too. Some of his friends call him City because he was born in Chicago. The name fits him, but he'll always still be my Joey.

Mike is our shop's piercer, and he's built like a brick shithouse. He trained for years to be an MMA fighter. He was moving up the ranks and making a name for himself. That was until he literally knocked the woman of his dreams on her ass. He traded in his fighting days to help the love of his life, Mia, with her medical clinic. I'd almost say that he lost his balls somewhere along the way, but that would just be my jaded, fucked-up perception of love talking.

Anthony. What can I say about him? He's my partner in crime most of the time. He and I are the single ones out of the group. Thomas doesn't count, because we never know anything about his life. Anthony wants to be a rock god. He wants ladies falling at his feet, professing their love, and freely offering their pussies to him with no strings attached. It makes me laugh, because honestly, he's already arrived if those are his criteria. He's stunning. One day, someone is going to steal him from me and I'll end up being a lonely ol' biddy.

Then there's me—youngest child who still uses the word *daddy.* I'm not talking about some sick fuckin' fetish shit either. I melt into a puddle of goo when my father's around. I've always been a daddy's girl. I don't think that'll ever change.

I live by no one's rules—well, maybe my daddy's at times—and I try to cram as much fun as I possibly can in my one shot at this life. I don't make apologies for my behavior. I shoot straight and tell it like it is. I never want to be tied down. Fuck convention. I don't need a husband to complete me a la Tom Cruise in *Jerry Maguire*.

Men are only good for a few things. One—they're handy when you have a flat tire or some other thing that requires heavy lifting. Two—their cocks are beautiful. Three—did I mention cock? Four—fucking. Wait… that's still cock-related.

I take it back. They're only good for two things in life: lifting heavy shit and fucking. Walks of shame are for pansy asses. I proudly leave them hanging, walking out the door, and I make no apologies for it. I'm not looking for a prince charming or knight in shining armor. I want to be fucked and then left the hell alone.

That is where my life was headed. I was blissfully happy and unencumbered. Life was grand—one big fucking party and I was the guest of honor.

Ever have a man walk into your life and alter your entire universe?

I'm not talking about the small shit. I'm talking about the "big fuckin' bang." You're minding your own business, enjoying yourself, and then *WHAM.* Everything you think is right suddenly spins on its axis and bitch-slaps you in the face.

The party came to a screeching halt the night of my brother's wedding.

He changed everything. He fucked it all up.

World altered. Party over.

James Caldo became something bigger.

I couldn't resist him.

CHAPTER TWO

IZZY

"EVERYONE'S ASS better be at my house tomorrow at two," Joe said as he finished cleaning his station.

"Yeah, yeah." Anthony kicked back and sipped a beer.

"Don't give me that shit. Be there on time."

"Is Suzy cooking?" Mike emptied the trashcan, not turning around to look at Joe as he waited for an answer.

"Fuck no," Joe said, breaking out into laughter.

We all knew that Suzy couldn't cook. God love her, and Lord knows she'd tried, but it wasn't in her DNA.

"Thank fuck," I huffed out, walking to the backroom to grab a cold one.

"Dude, someday you have to teach her to cook," Mike said, shaking his head.

"Fuck that. She doesn't need to learn how to cook. It's not why I love her."

"We all fucking know that," Anthony said, rolling his eyes as he rolled the beer bottle between his hands.

"Shut your fucking mouth. You're talking about my fiancée."

"Uh huh," Anthony muttered, wiping the drops of beer from his mouth.

Moments like this I loved. Sitting around, shooting the shit, and just laughing made me happy. I loved my brothers and their women, but I liked having them all to myself.

"I couldn't give a shit about Thanksgiving dinner, Joe. I'm waiting for the bachelorette party," I said, smiling as I walked toward my station. Then I kicked my feet up, leaned back, and took a sip.

"Izzy," Joe warned, glaring at me from his chair.

"Oh, shove it, mister. It's a girls' night and we're going to have fun. Don't tell me you boys are just going to sit around and watch sports all night. I know what the fuck happens at bachelor parties. What's good for the goose is good for the gander."

"What the fuck does that shit even mean?" Mike snorted.

"Dumb fuck," I mumbled against the rim of my Corona.

"What the hell did you just say?" His voice boomed as he turned to stare at me.

I gave him an innocent smile. "Love you."

"Dude, I can't believe you're getting married in a week. What the fuck? I never thought you'd be the first to be tied down," Anthony said, getting up from his chair. "I'm grabbing a beer. Anyone else want one while I'm up?"

I picked up my phone to scroll through my Facebook newsfeed. "Nope," I said.

To my delight, there was a message from Flash. We grew up together and I think I've known him forever. We used to play doctor when we were alone. It was the first time I ever saw a penis. As we grew up, the quick peeks turned into touching—then fucking when we hit high school.

Flash and I had an understanding. Neither of us wanted to be tied down, and we weren't exclusive. He was my booty call when I had an itch that needed to be scratched. He moved away a couple of years ago, and since then, every time he was in town, I would get the call offering a quick fuck and an even quicker goodbye. It was a match made in heaven.

Flash: Whatcha doin' baby?

He was the only person in the world I let call me baby. It was patronizing and I fucking hated it. Typically, it would earn a man a punch to his junk, but when Flash said it, I let it slide.

Me: Getting ready to head home. U?

"Izzy, are you listening to me?" Joe asked, casting a shadow on me as his big body blocked out the light.

I shook my head as I looked up at him. "What?"

"Do not have naked men at the bachelorette party."

"What's a little peen between friends?" I asked, laughing in his face.

"You know I love you, Izzy. I never judge you, but do not have *peen* at my soon-to-be wife's party." He put his hands on his hips and tapped his foot.

"Pfft," I said, standing up. "You having pussy at yours?" I asked.

"No."

"Fucking liar!" I shouted, hitting him in the chest with my finger.

He looked down, watching me as I poked him. "I mean it, sister. I don't want any nasty-ass stripper touching my woman."

I kept poking him. "Do you hear yourself?"

"I ain't fuckin' deaf and neither are you. I never ask for much, but this is non-negotiable. I believe Suzy told you she didn't want one."

"Suzy doesn't know how to have fun." I waved him off as I tossed the empty bottle in the trash.

"Suzy does. She just prefers my dick. She doesn't need some greasy male dancer touching her."

"Joe," I said, sliding my arm around his waist, "the stripper is only there for the other girls, not for Suzy."

"Bullshit," he mumbled, kissing the top of my head. "Please, Iz. For me."

I puffed out a breath, moving the hair that had fallen in my eyes. "Fine, Joe. As long as you're happy," I lied.

There was no way in hell I'd throw a bachelorette party for my soon-to-be sister-in-law and not have a stripper. If the boys got to see snatch, then fuck yeah, we were seeing peen.

"Thanks, baby girl," he said, squeezing me tight.

"Any time." I looked up and smiled. Releasing him, I stuck out my tongue at Anthony as I sat.

He winked, knowing I was full of shit, and started talking with Mike about the big Thanksgiving football matchups. I tuned out, picking up my phone as I waited for us to close the shop.

Flash: Interested in a little company tonight?

I tapped my phone as I thought about his offer. Did I want to see Flash? I didn't have to be up early the next day, but then again, I never had to be up early. I hadn't had sex since the last time he'd dropped by, and that was over a month ago. I could use a good fuck.

Me: Hell yeah. Get your sexy ass to my place. Meet ya there?

Flash: On my way. Be there in 30.

I stood, shoving the phone in my pocket. "I gotta go, boys."

"Where the hell you runnin' off to?" Mike asked, stretching out and looking comfortable.

"None of your business. I got shit to do," I said as I grabbed my purse out of the backroom.

"Two o'clock tomorrow, Izzy," Joe said as I reached for the door handle.

"Got it!" I yelled over my shoulder, leaving my brothers behind, and headed home.

"Yo!" Flash bellowed as I heard the door slam shut.

"Back here," I replied, before spitting out my toothpaste.

He walked into the room and said, "Get your sweet ass over here and gimme a kiss, baby."

I turned toward him, glaring as I wiped the leftover paste from my lips. "You must have me confused with someone else." I winked at him and laughed.

He smiled, leaning against the doorframe with his arms crossed. "I know exactly who I'm talking to." Then he closed his eyes and puckered his lips.

I threw the washcloth at him, hitting him square in the face.

His eyes flew open as the cloth fell to the floor. "What the fuck was that for?"

"You're not the boss of me, Flash," I said, putting my hands on my hips as I stared at him.

His eyes softened as he pushed off the doorframe. "I've missed you," he whispered, trying to wrap his arms around me.

"Flash," I warned, pushing him away. "I'm not your girlfriend."

"A guy can dream, can't he?" He brushed his lips against my temples, finally gaining a firm grasp around my body.

He felt nice. I'd never admit it, but I did like Flash. I loved him, but no way in hell was I *in* love with him.

"Might as well shoot for the stars." I giggled, snuggling

my face into his chest and inhaling. My nose tickled. His normal smell was missing and seemed to have been replaced by something offensive and stinky as fuck. "Flash, you smell like shit," I said, pushing him away.

He lifted his arms, sniffing his pit as he wrinkled his nose. "Fuck," he muttered, pulling off his shirt. "Let me grab a shower and I'm yours." He kicked off his shoes and unzipped his pants. Bending over, he pushed down the jeans and tossed them to the side.

"You're mighty comfy here, aren't you?" I asked, taking my turn to lean in the doorway and stare at him. He was rough around the edges but beautiful. His smile was killer, but he wasn't the boy I'd had a crush on when I was a kid.

As he reached in the shower, turning on the water, he turned to me and smiled. "I can fuck you smelling like shit." His back stiffened as he stood straight, cracking his knuckles. "As long as I get some pussy, I don't give a fuck what I smell like."

"Get your dirty ass in the shower," I groaned, ready to rip my hair out but itching to touch him.

He laughed, climbing in the shower. Flash was always cute, but as he'd aged, he'd turned into a ruggedly handsome man. Less and less of his skin was visible, replaced by tattoos that decorated his body like a storyboard—most of the work I'd done over the years. He'd been my best test subject when I was learning my craft. Stupid fucker, if you ask me. I wouldn't let some newbie put ink that soap couldn't wash off on my body. He was tall, a couple of inches taller than I was, and lean. He wasn't overly muscular or bulky, but he fit between my thighs like a glove.

"You starin', baby?" he asked, his voice muffled by the water.

I blinked, pulling my eyes away. "Fuck no. Hurry your ass up," I said, stomping out of the bathroom.

I pulled back the blankets as I waited for Flash. His whistling filled the room, along with the plops of water that cascaded off his body, hitting the shower floor. I stripped off my clothes, fell on the bed, sprawled out, and stared at the ceiling.

I used to get so excited when he said that he was dropping by for a little while. Not so much anymore. I kept telling myself, "It'll pass," but it never did. He'd grown more loving and tender, and both of those freaked me the hell out. It ain't my bag.

Years ago, I'd be jumping up and down on the bed, waiting for the big, bad Sam, a.k.a. Flash, to come toss my apples. Now, it was—

"Ready or not, here I come!" he yelled from the bathroom, interrupting my thoughts.

"Yippee," I muttered, rolling my eyes as I leaned up on my elbows.

He strode into the room stark naked and dripping wet. "You look edible." He stopped at the foot of my bed and stared down at me. "I think you need to come, Izzy. You're wound tight tonight. Let me help you out." He grabbed my feet and yanked my body to the edge of the bed.

"Up for the challenge?" I asked, raising an eyebrow as I placed the bottom of my feet on his chest.

"Babe, really?" he asked, holding my ankles.

"You think you're that good at eating pussy?" I laughed, trying not to hurt his male ego.

"I munch like no other."

I knew the man tried to be sexy, but ew. He wasn't. "Show me whatcha got. If you're a good boy, I'll give ya some pussy."

He rubbed his hands together before placing my foot on his shoulder. "I'm going to eat it like it's my last fucking meal."

I melted into the bed, feeling his hot breath on me as he inhaled.

"Better than fresh-baked apple pie."

"Less talking, more eating, Flash." I threw my arm over my face, blocking out all light as he placed his mouth on me.

Moaning, he sucked my clit into his mouth, making my eyes roll back into my head.

"Fuck," I hissed, drawing in a sharp breath.

He mumbled, the vibration penetrating my skin, as he drew me deeper into his mouth. Sinking into the bed, I reached down and grabbed his head.

"Right there, Flash," I pleaded, grinding my pussy against his face.

He gripped my thighs, pulling me closer as his tongue traced tiny circles around my clit.

Shivers raked my body. He knew exactly how I liked it. Many years of fooling around had given him that advantage over other men. His fingers slid through my wetness, causing my body to clench in anticipation.

"You missed me, baby," he murmured against my pussy, his hot breath lashing my clit like a whip.

"Flash," I warned, pushing myself against his face. "Shut up and eat."

"Mmm hmmm," he mumbled, closing his lips around my clit, sucking gently.

Needing something more, I touched my nipples, rolling them between my fingers. Waves of pleasure came over me as I stared at him. Moaning and writhing underneath his touch, I closed my eyes and rode the crest, waiting for it to come crashing down and wash away the stress.

The warmth of his mouth, the flicks of his tongue, the pressure of his sucking, and my fingers on my breasts had me screaming within minutes.

"Fuck," I mumbled, my body growing limp as I sagged into the mattress.

"Damn," Flash groaned, licking his lips as he pushed himself up. Resting on his heels, he stroked his shaft and stared. "Baby, I can't wait to tap that pussy. I've missed you and being deep inside you."

I giggled, grabbing my sides as I rolled over. "Oh my God. When did you turn so wishy-washy?" I asked, gasping for air.

"Fuck you, Izzy. I know you fucking love me," he said as he started to lean over me.

"Wait," I said, putting my feet against his chest, pushing him away. "We're friends, Sam. Nothing more." I needed him to understand this. He and I would never be any more than what we were right now—fuck buddies.

We didn't go for drinks like girlfriends to talk about our lives. He never took me to dinner, unless you count the shit-hole bar in town as a restaurant, or McDonald's. We didn't hold hands, walk along the beach, or snuggle. We fucked and he left. Plain. Simple. No feelings involved.

"I know, Izzy." He swallowed hard, his Adam's apple bobbing, as he looked down at me. "I meant as a friend. I've known you my entire life."

"Just as long as we're clear, Flash." I slid my feet down his chest, rubbing against his hard length before I opened my legs to him. The look on his face was closer to a little boy losing a puppy dog than one about to fuck my brains out. "Come here and kiss me already," I said, holding out my arms to him.

A small smile spread across his face as he leaned over me,

placing his arms under my body. "I thought you'd never ask," he said with a chuckle.

I'd known Flash long enough to know that there was something more he wanted to say, but he always held back. I loved him. Don't get me wrong. We'd gone to kindergarten together, but I wasn't in love with him. I never would be, either.

I grabbed his face as he hovered over me. "Hey," I whispered, "I'm happy you're here."

His eyes lit up as he rested his forehead against mine. "Thanks, Izzy. It's just so hard at times."

"What is, babe?" I asked, moving my arms around his shoulders.

"Being part of the Sun Devils MC. I feel so lonely."

"Get yourself an ol' lady," I replied.

He rolled his eyes, pushing himself up on his elbows. "They're bullshit."

"Come on. I'm sure there's someone you're sweet on, Flash."

"She's not—"

"Babe, listen to me. Everyone needs someone. You need to fill that void."

He sprawled out on the mattress, putting his hands behind his head. "It's not that simple, Izzy."

Resting my head in my hand, I placed the other on his chest. "I know. You have a big heart, and any girl would be lucky to have you, Sam."

He didn't like anyone calling him that anymore, but I was always the exception to the rule. I only used it to help drive home the point. He needed to finally comprehend that he and I would never be a "we."

"Not the one I want, though," he mumbled, blowing out a breath.

My heart hurt for him, but I just couldn't give myself to him in that way. "I'm sorry. You know I love you, but not in that way. You'll always be one of my best friends. You need to forget about me and find someone who's going to love you the way you deserve to be loved."

"Yeah, maybe." He closed his eyes as he laid his hand on top of mine and stroked my skin. "No woman will ever measure up to you, though, Isabella."

"I know I'm pretty fanfuckingtastic, but I'm not the one. She'll fall into your lap when you least expect it," I said as I nuzzled my face against his chest.

"What about you?" he asked, kissing the top of my head.

"What about me?" I looked at him.

"When are you going to find someone to love?"

"Aw, baby. I have my family. I don't need anyone else."

"We all do, Iz. When are you going to stop lying to yourself?"

I winked at him, laying my head back down against his skin as I twirled his dark chest hair in my fingers. "I have as much love as I can handle. I don't want to be tied down. I'm happy with my life. The last thing I am is lonely."

"Liar." He laughed, pulling me flush against his side. "Can we just sleep like this tonight?"

"Snuggle?" I asked, wanting to run out of the room.

"I just want to feel close to someone tonight. Please, Iz. I'm so comfortable like this. I don't want to sleep on the couch."

I bit my lip, feeling shitty about always doing that to him. Having him sleep in my bed always felt too intimate for me to handle. "Fine," I said, hoping I wouldn't regret it later. "Don't get used to it."

"Thanks," he whispered, burrowing his nose in my hair. "Night."

"Night," I mumbled as I closed my eyes.

An overwhelming sense of guilt came over me as I lay in his arms. Flash loved me, and had voiced it many times over the years. I'd always set him straight. Tonight felt different, though. It was as if I'd had a knife and jammed it in his heart. I felt like such a cunt for telling him I wouldn't love him—not in that way, at least.

We'd sworn that it wouldn't be any more than a physical friendship. He'd promised me years ago that he wouldn't fall in love with me. Sam had given me that amazing smile while speaking the words I'd wanted to hear but meaning none of them. I felt the end near for us, because I couldn't handle having to kill his heart and hurt him every time we were together.

Hurting someone, no matter the reason, sucks—especially when they're a friend. Someone who has been by your side and had your back since you were a little girl is an important person. He meant the world to me, but I could never settle down and spend my life with Flash.

I needed to let him down easy, and that wasn't my strong suit. I always spoke my mind, and sometimes I came off as brash or unkind.

I curled into his side, letting my old friend drift to sleep while I mulled over my future without Flash weaving himself in and out of my life through the months. I needed to move on. More importantly, he needed to move on and find himself someone to love.

As long as it wasn't me.

CHAPTER THREE

IZZY

"MORNING, BEAUTIFUL," Flash whispered in my ear as I hugged my pillow, facing away from him.

"Morning," I said, groaning as I stretched.

I wasn't a morning person. I'd slept like shit with Flash in my bed. He'd been a hog and snored no matter how much I'd elbowed him to move. The noise just kept coming. I'd thought about pinching his nose, but I'd also thought that'd earn me an elbow to the face by accident. So I'd covered my head with my pillow, faced away from him, and prayed for him to shut the fuck up.

"Sleep well?" he asked, stroking my arm lightly as goose bumps broke out across my skin.

"Ugh," I whined, turning toward him. "No."

"I slept like a fuckin' rock." He smiled, brushing the hair out of my eyes.

"Yeah, I know," I mumbled.

His slow blinks and sappy smile made my stomach turn. He wasn't staring at me like a piece of meat or a hit-it-and-quit-it kind of thing. His face screamed that he loved me, and it freaked me the fuck out.

"So, what do you want to do today?" he asked, his eyes searching my face.

I bit the inside of my lip. "It's Thanksgiving, Flash. I'm going to spend the day with my family."

"Fuck," he muttered as he stared at the ceiling.

"What?" I asked, pulling the sheet over my breasts as I sat up and rested against the headboard.

"I forgot it's Thanksgiving."

"I'm sure your parents are expecting you."

"No, they're out of town. I'll just do what I came here for and head back to the clubhouse."

Fucking great. I don't want him to be alone on a holiday. No one deserves that. "I'm sure Joe wouldn't mind if you came to dinner. He cooks for an army, just like my ma."

"You wouldn't care?" he asked, looking over at me with puppy-dog eyes.

"No. You know everybody, and my mom has always liked you."

"Your mom is the best damn cook. That's one of the reasons I liked you as a kid. Your mom fed everybody."

"You liked me because I let you feel me up in eighth grade." I laughed, hitting him in the face with my pillow.

"Yeah, that too." He grabbed me by the arms, pulling me down on top of him.

"Flash," I warned.

"I know, Izzy. I'm just a cock to you."

I hit his shoulder hard, making my palm sting. "Fucker, you're a friend, but your cock is mighty fine."

"My cock could use some attention."

"So could my pussy."

"Listen, you greedy little cunt. I ate you so fucking good last night and what did I get?"

"You just said what you got. You got to eat my pussy."

"Izzy," he said, grabbing my shoulder. "My balls are gonna burst. You gotta help a guy out here."

I crawled on top of him, straddling him, and felt his dick already hard underneath me. "Flash, what do I get if I let you?"

"Woman," he said as he swatted my ass. "You'll get to come on my 'mighty fine cock,' as you called it."

"I want two," I demanded, grinding myself against him.

He shivered as a small moan escaped his lips. "Anything you want."

I looked at the ceiling, resting my index finger against my lips as I moved my hips. "Well, my house could use a good cleaning," I teased.

"You'll get what I give you," he growled.

"Oh, I like big, bad biker Flash." I laughed, leaning back and pushing the tip of his cock farther into my wetness.

He tossed me through the air, and I landed on the bed and bounced. I snorted as I laughed. He grabbed the condom off the nightstand and moved his body between my legs.

"I'll show you big, bad biker Flash."

"Shit better be good."

"You talk too fucking much," he said as he rolled the condom down his shaft. "I always do you good, Izzy. No one does it better."

On a consistent basis, he was the best, but I'd had better one-night stands. There's something about the explosion of passion that happens when two strangers get together and there's an undeniable attraction. Clothes get torn, bodies get bruised, and everyone walks away with exactly what they wanted to begin with—a quick fuck, no strings attached.

"Gimme those lips," he said, leaning over me as he stuck the tip of his cock inside me.

"No," I whispered, turning my head.

He stopped all movement. "No?"

"Your breath." I laughed, but it was more than that. It felt too personal, and the last thing I wanted was anything that involved feelings.

"Gotcha," he replied as he jammed his dick inside me, causing me to cry out in pleasure.

"Jesus," I mumbled, pushing my head into my pillow and arching my back to give him better access.

"So fuckin' good," he whispered, rocking back and forth.

I sighed, letting myself get lost in the pleasure and blocking everything out. As his thrusts grew more punishing, I dug my fingers into his skin, trying to ground myself.

Closing my eyes, I listened to our moans as he moved. The sound of our bodies connecting filled the room, mingled with our breathing. He drove me closer to the edge. Each thrust hit my clit, bringing the orgasm just within reach.

Within minutes, I was flying off a cliff. A kaleidoscope of colors filled my vision as the orgasm that tore through me stole the air from my lungs. Flash had that ability. That's one reason why I always welcomed him into my bed.

"Oh God, yes!" I screamed, meeting his thrusts as the orgasm waned. I wanted more, needed more. I wasn't done, and neither was he.

He stared down at me, his eyes blazing as he gritted his teeth, chasing his own release. Picking up the pace, he grabbed my ass and tilted my hips, causing him to slide in farther.

"Right there!" I screeched, kicking my feet against the bed.

"Fuck," he hissed, his momentum quickening to an impressive speed.

Moments later, his movement stuttered as he groaned

though his release. Sweat dripped from his chin, landing on my breast and sliding down to rest in between my tits.

The very last thrust he gave me sent me over the edge. The second orgasm was just as intense as the first and left me a puddle of jelly.

We lay there panting, sweaty, and exhausted. Trying to gulp air as if we were fish searching for water as we flopped in a new atmosphere. I wanted to fall back asleep. My eyes felt heavy as the tiredness I felt went bone deep.

Just as my breathing slowed and my mind started to turn off, my phone beeped.

"Fuck," I muttered, reaching out and feeling around my nightstand. Cracking one eye, I brought the phone to my face, too tired to open both.

Joe: Be on time today.

I rolled my eyes, tossing the phone to the floor. Yawning, I moving away from Flash and snuggled with my pillow. I had hours until I needed to be there for dinner. It was a holiday, for shit's sake, and I needed rest after having listened to Flash snore all night.

Comfortable and sated sleep took me quickly. Everything faded away.

"Izzy," a voice said inside my dream, but I ignored it. "Izzy," the voice repeated.

"What?" I mumbled, annoyed to have my darkness interrupted.

"Izzy," Flash said, shaking my shoulders. "What time do we have to be at your brother's?"

"Two," I muttered, placing the pillow over my head.

"It's one thirty, babe."

I jumped from the bed, my heart racing at the thought of being late. "Fuck. Why did you let me sleep so long?" I grabbed my jeans off the dresser, slipping them on and quickly fastening them. Then I turned to see Flash staring at me. "Get your ass up. We gotta go."

"Is someone scared of her brother?" He smiled, stretching out across my bed.

"No. I just don't want to hear bullshit about being late."

"Pussy." He laughed, climbing off the bed.

"If you ever want my pussy again, you'll move your ass." I threw his dirty clothes at him before he could react. They hit him square in the chest and fell to his feet.

"What the fuck, dude?" he asked, holding out his hands.

"Put something on. You can't go like that," I said, waving my hands up and down.

"My clothes are outside."

I crossed my arms over my chest, highly irritated at this point. "Flash, move it. Stop fucking around. Get your shit and get ready. I'm leaving in ten with or without you."

"Fine," he said, pulling on his jeans before stomping out the door as I walked into my closet to grab a cami.

It was bad enough that I was bringing Flash with me. Joe hated him. Fuck, all my brothers hated him. Hopefully, with it being a holiday, they could put aside their bullshit and welcome him inside. I could hope, but I knew the reality. I'd be playing interference the entire day to stop fists from flying.

Exactly ten minutes later, I grabbed my keys off the counter and threw on my heels. Then I stood by the front door, about to walk out, when Flash rounded the corner looking as good as biker Flash could. His outfit wasn't fancy, but it would do. Time to get the clusterfuck over with.

CHAPTER FOUR

IZZY

THANK goodness Anthony showed up when we did. I wouldn't have to hear Joe's mouth about being the last one to dinner.

"Hey, Anth."

Anthony hugged me, moving in closer to my ear and whispering, "Why the fuck did you bring him?"

I looked at Flash, giving him a smile before responding to Anthony. "He didn't have anywhere else to go." I batted my eyelashes at him as he backed away and gave Flash a once-over.

"Joe is going to shit a motherfucking brick." Anthony winked and grinned.

"Just thought I'd keep the day interesting."

"Hey, man," Flash said as he walked up to Anthony with his hand outstretched.

"Long time no see, Sam." Anthony grasped his hand, shaking it for longer than normal.

"Yeah." Flash flinched from the handshake. Then he flexed his hands as Anthony released him. "It's Flash now."

I rolled my eyes and shook my head. *This shit should go*

over real well with my family. Anthony looked at me, and I shrugged before pinching my nose.

"Stay behind me," I said, looking at Flash and pointing at the ground.

"Why?"

"'Cause Joe won't punch me when he sees you, but by all means," I said, motioning in front of me with my hand. "Go ahead in front if you want a fist in the face as a greeting."

Flash grimaced and sighed. "I don't know why your brother doesn't fuckin' like me."

"Maybe 'cause you've been fucking his little sister for years."

Flash mumbled something under his breath, moving to stand behind me as we approached the door. As Anthony knocked, I fidgeted with my hands, praying that the day didn't turn into a clusterfuck.

"Fucker hated me before that," Flash snarled behind me.

Anthony's fists didn't relent as he pounded on the door.

"Why don't you just open it?"

"This isn't Ma's and I don't just walk in without being told it's okay," he said, landing another blow.

"Pussy," I whispered, moving around Anthony and walking inside.

Flash laughed, following behind me as Anthony grumbled.

"Smells damn good in here." I inhaled deeply.

"Hey, sis," Joe said, walking over to hug me.

"I brought someone. I hope you don't mind." I smiled, looking up into his eyes. I knew I was laying it on thick, but I was just trying to cushion the blow.

"Who?" Joe asked, looking over my shoulder. "Really?" he growled in my ear, grabbing my shoulder.

"Come on, Joey. He didn't have anywhere else to be. He

was in town and I told him he could spend the day with us. I know you made enough food for an entire army." I batted my eyelashes at Joe.

"He's here now." Joe shook his head, staring down at me. "Next time ask, Izzy."

"Okay," I whispered against his chest, giving him a squeeze before ducking under his arms.

Joe held out his hand to Flash as Anthony walked by and grimaced. "Nice to see you again, Sam," Joe bit out through gritted teeth.

"I go by Flash now."

I cringed at his response. I always knew Flash wasn't the most intelligent man, but to reply to my brother in that way was just plain idiotic—or he had a death wish.

"Whatever," Joe said, rolling his eyes. "Welcome to my home." He pulled Flash closer. "If you hurt my sister, I'll fucking bury you. Got me?"

"Easy now, City. I wouldn't dream of it. We're just friends." He stood toe to toe with Joe, gripping his shoulder.

I swear to fuck that all I could see was a train wreck. I thought I was standing in the middle of a Looney Tunes cartoon. There had to be a big kaboom coming at any second. Joe and Flash wouldn't be parting on a happy note, but hopefully they could keep their hands to themselves for Thanksgiving.

"I don't care who the fuck you think you are or what MC you're in. You're still Sam to me and I can still whip your ass. Just so we're clear." Joe glared at him.

Suzy's arms slid around Joe as she looked at Flash. "Everything okay, baby?" she asked.

"Just perfect, sugar. This is Sam, Izzy's friend."

She released him, holding out her hand to Flash. "Hi, Sam. I'm Suzy. Nice to meet you," she said, smiling.

"It's my pleasure, Suzy." He pulled her hand to his lips and gently kissed it. "You have a beautiful home."

"Thank you, Sam."

Joe growled. Honest to motherfucking god, the man growled. I knew that my brother was a caveman, but this was beyond the realm of normal behavior. Flash looked at Joe, his lips turning up in a half-smirk before he turned back to Suzy.

"Joe's a very lucky man. I hope you don't mind me crashing the party." Sam looked to Joe with a shit-eating grin before he looked at Suzy.

Yep—death wish.

"Not at all. Come on in and make yourself at home," Suzy said with a smile before stepping aside and wrapping her arms around my big brother.

"Let's go say hi to my parents, dumbass," I said to Flash, grabbing his shirt and pulling him toward the living room.

"Why the fuck am I a dumbass?" he asked, looking at me with a furrowed brow.

I stopped, turning to face him. "Starting shit with my brother," I whispered, glaring at him.

"Dude, I gotta stand up to the guy. I can't be a doormat. Show no weakness."

"You're a fucking moron." I laughed. "Ma," I said, entering the room.

"Happy Thanksgiving, baby girl." She wrapped her arms around me.

I have the best fucking mother in the world. She had to be the best to raise us as children and come out without a scratch. We didn't make shit easy for her.

"Happy Thanksgiving, Ma." I kissed her cheek before releasing her. "I brought Sam with me." I turned to him and smirked. "He would've been all alone today."

"Aww, Sam, it's so good to see you. How have you been?" she asked as she moved toward him with open arms.

This was pure Mama Gallo. She welcomes everyone and doesn't hold a grudge. I, on the other hand, hold on to shit for too long and always wonder what angle the person is working when they are being nice.

"Mrs. G, looking amazing as always." He hugged her, lifting her off the ground.

She giggled as her face turned pink. "Oh, Sam. Put this old woman down."

"You're not old, Mrs. G. You never will be. You haven't aged a bit since I saw you last."

Flash may be a dumbass and a douche some of the time, but he knew how to talk to the ladies. He'd fine-tuned that skill since we were teenagers. I was immune to his charm.

My pop rose to his feet, moving toward Flash with his arm extended as he offered his hand. "Sam, good to see you, kid. How the hell have you been?" Pop asked, smacking Flash on the shoulder with his free hand.

I turned to look at my brothers. Snarls and glares were the Gallo boys' preferred mug of choice today. I knew deep down that this would be the longest fucking holiday of my life.

There wasn't a cock in the world worth this much bullshit at a family holiday. I just wanted to laugh and bust a few balls. I didn't want to play referee.

"Yo, Joe, is dinner almost ready?" I yelled, plopping down on the couch in an open spot. If everyone had their mouths full, they couldn't be spouting nonsense.

Suzy came flying out of the kitchen, adjusting her sundress as she walked. Her face was flushed and her lips looked swollen. "Food's ready. Go sit down while Joe and I bring everything to the table, please." She turned around and ran into the kitchen.

Flash held out his hand, helping me from the couch.

I smiled at him. "Thanks," I whispered, climbing off the couch.

"Any time, babe. Only thing better than tasting you is Thanksgiving dinner." He licked his lips as a small grin played on the corner of his mouth.

"Jesus. Not smooth, man. You need to work on your lines if that's the best you have," I said to him as we followed behind everyone else to the dining room table.

"What the fuck is wrong with my lines?"

"Totally not sexy. Does that shit work on the club girls?"

"I don't need lines with those ladies."

"Lucky for you then or you wouldn't be getting any pussy. *Ever.*"

"Why the fuck were you gone so long?" Flash asked as we walked into the kitchen. His face was red and he was on edge.

Suzy, Mia, my ma, and I had been upstairs in the war room. It's what we referred to the room as, anyway. It was filled with information about Suzy's wedding. Everything was planned down to the last details. She's anal that way. She's a total overachiever who has never done anything by the seat of her pants. She has plans for her plans. There's no room for error.

Suzy and Joe were getting married in a week. I had been elected to be in charge of the bachelorette party and nothing else. Thank Christ. I didn't want to be responsible for any fuck-ups. I am not a planner. I've winged shit my entire life.

"We were talking and got a little carried away."

Flash ran his fingers through his hair, making it a bigger

mess than it'd already been. "I felt like you threw me to a pack of wolves."

I looked around the room, taking in the sight of my brothers and Pop sitting around the living room. I knew they could be ruthless, but they were harmless.

I ruffled his hair. "Stop being a drama queen."

"Izzy, why do they hate me so much?"

"They don't," I said, sitting next to him at the kitchen table.

"Bullshit," he murmured. "Joey wants to cut my fuckin' throat."

"Nah." I shook my head as I bit my lip. "He just wants you to know where you stand."

"What's his issue?"

"Where would I even begin?" I laughed. "Joe is protective of everyone in this family, especially me. You're in an MC, and for that reason alone, he'd hate you being around me. He knows you fuck me, and that makes him want to rip your cock off and shove it down your throat."

Flash's face paled and his Adam's apple bobbed as he swallowed roughly. "You know I'd protect you, Izzy. You may not be mine, but I'd never let anything happen to you."

"I know, Flash, but Joe doesn't. Let's have dessert and we'll be out of here in a couple of hours. Aren't you happy you came to Thanksgiving Gallo style?"

"Hell yeah." He burped, rubbing his stomach. "The food alone was worth all the trouble."

Suzy walked into the kitchen, giving me a devilish smile as she looked between Flash and me. "Hey, guys. Ready for dessert?"

I nodded my head, smirking at her. "Yeah. I have to get Flash home soon."

"Aww, really? I wanted to play cards or something." Suzy pouted and stomped to the counter to grab the pumpkin pie.

"We can stay," Flash interrupted before I could reply.

I glared at him, not really in the mood to play cards with the family. "Fine. We'll stay."

His smile grew wide as Suzy yipped and jumped up and down. "Heck yeah! I'm so excited!"

As she walked out of the room, I kept my eyes glued to Flash. This was going to be a very long evening.

"What time do you have to head back?" I asked him, hoping it was sooner than later.

"I'll leave whenever we get back to your place. I just have to be back tonight. I don't have a curfew, Izzy." He laughed, standing and walking to the counter to grab the other pie.

I put my head on the table, lightly smashing it against the surface. I hated bringing anyone with me to family dinners, even Flash. I always felt a sense of being restricted or tied down. They were two things I never wanted to feel.

I avoided relationships like the plague. I never begrudged anyone happiness, but togetherness wasn't for me.

CHAPTER FIVE

IZZY

TEARS STUNG the back of my eyes as I stood in the bridal suite at the church and stared at Suzy. She looked amazing. I'd worried this day wouldn't come, especially after the bachelorette party.

I'd kind of fucked up. She'd said no to male strippers, but shit… I never listen. Joe had flipped when he'd caught the scent of the guy as it lingered on her skin that night. Their entire relationship had almost exploded into a million tiny pieces, but their love was too strong. Plus, Joe had decided to take the stick out of his ass and apologize to her for acting like a complete caveman asshole.

I'd marked that shit down on my calendar because it wasn't likely to ever happen again. Gallo men aren't quick to take the blame for shit. They grunt, smile, and move on.

"She looks stunning, doesn't she?" Mia asked, nudging me in the shoulder.

I slowly nodded, unable to take my eyes off her. "She does." I turned to Mia with a small smile. "When am I going to see you in a wedding dress?"

"Oh," she said, her cheeks turning pink. "I'm just waiting

for Mike to ask me."

"Haven't you two talked about marriage?"

"He's mentioned it a time or two, but I'm not pushing it on him." She shook her head and sighed.

"I need another sister-in-law. You're like my sister already, but I need it official and on paper." I smiled, happy that there were finally some females inside the family circle after years of dealing with the boys.

She laughed, tossing her head back, and held her stomach. "You're more demanding than my mom," she said, wiping the corner of her eyes.

"Hell yeah. I've gone too many years surrounded by testosterone. I need vadge in this family."

Mia and I stood side by side and stared at Suzy as she fussed with her dress and checked her makeup before moving closer to the mirror.

"You look beautiful, Suzy," I said, walking toward her.

The dress had a form-fitting bodice with a thick ribbon and a flower around the waist. The V-shaped neckline plunged just far enough to show off her chest. The bottom was comprised of loose tulle that kissed the floor and shifted when she walked. Suzy always looked amazing, but today she glowed.

"I'm so nervous. Why am I so nervous?" she asked, turning toward me and taking a deep breath.

I grabbed her hands, wanting to avoid messing up her dress. "You're going to be fine. Everything is ready. Don't stress."

"What if he changes his mind?" Her eyes grew wide as she said the words.

I shook my head, my mouth set in a firm line. "You can't be serious. My brother is so in love with you. Why would you even think that?"

"I don't know. I feel panicked."

I touched her forehead, thinking she had to be sick. "No fever," I said as I removed my hand. "Calm the fuck down, Suzy. Joe loves you. I've never seen him so sure about anything or anyone in his life."

She blew out a breath, touching her stomach and smoothing the fabric. "I know," she said, looking down at the floor.

"Are you sure, though?" I asked.

"I love him," she stated firmly.

"Is it enough?" I asked, cocking my eyebrow.

"Izzy, you're such a Debbie Downer on love," she said, laughing. "I can't wait until you find 'the one.'"

I doubled over in a fit of giggles. "You must clearly be ill. I don't want 'the one,'" I said, making air quotes. "I'm perfectly happy being single. The last thing I want is a ball and chain to tie my ass down."

"Uh huh," she said, looking in the mirror again.

"Izzy, when are you going to stop lying to yourself?" Mia interrupted.

"You two bitches need to slow your roll. I'm not the dating type, let alone the marrying kind."

"It's time." Ma clapped her hands as she sang the words.

"Someone do my veil. I'm too nervous!" Suzy shrieked, shaking her hands.

"I got it," I said, stepping in front of her and reaching behind to take the thin material. Then I placed it over her face, smoothing it to not block her vision. "Good?" I asked before moving away.

"Yes," she replied. "It's now or never."

"Suzy, you two were meant for each other. I may not want it for myself, but I have no doubt there's no one else out there for my brother."

"You're right, Izzy. Let's do this crap."

I chuckled, trying to cover my mouth. "You don't always talk like a Gallo, but you're one at heart."

She giggled nervously, moving toward the door. I grabbed her short train, not wanting it to get stuck on anything. When Suzy's father saw her, his face lit up like a Christmas tree.

"There's my girl," he cooed, holding out his arms.

"Hey, Dad." She wrapped her arms around him, trying to avoid touching his tuxedo with her face.

He backed away and stared at her. "You look beautiful, Suzette," he said, holding her shoulders and taking her in.

"Thanks," she said, linking her arm with his.

The music from inside the church filled the corridor where we stood. Nerves filled my belly as it flipped inside my body. I couldn't imagine how Suzy felt. Some would say that I love to be the center of attention, but having hundreds of pairs of eyes staring at you as you try to walk in a pair of five-inch heels and not fall on your face has to be daunting.

As I started down the aisle and smiled, I knew that no one was really looking at me. Their eyes were trained on the back of the room, waiting for a peek at the bride.

Joe nodded at me as I moved into the pew and then turned to watch Suzy. He glowed. When Suzy came into view, his face lit up, his eyes grew wide, and a giant smile spread across his face.

I never thought he'd fall so head over heels for anyone like he did for Suzy. I would've never put the two of them together and thought, *Fuck yeah, that'll work*, but for some odd reason, it had. Her innocence had captured his attention, but we all knew she was a freak underneath that put-together-teacher exterior.

Joe looked handsome in his tuxedo. His hair was freshly cut and styled, his face cleanly shaven. Sun-kissed skin made his blue eyes stand out. All of my brothers looked killer today. Rarely did they all dress up, but weddings were the exception. Joe was the first out of the five of us to be married, and we knew it would be a while before another wedding would take place.

Mike and Mia had met months ago and were the next in line. That would only happen if my brother could get his head out of his ass and pop the question. Anthony and I were the two holdouts on relationships of any sort. We were the free birds of the group.

I turned, taking in the sight of Suzy as she glided down the aisle. I could see the smile on her face even through her veil as she locked eyes with Joe. They were in a trance, staring at each other as she made her way toward the altar.

When Suzy stopped at the altar, the priest said, "Who gives this bride away today?"

"I do," her father answered, releasing her hand and lifting her veil. Then he placed a chaste kiss on her cheek before stepping back.

Suzy and Joe mouthed some words to each other, which looked like "I love you," as they held hands. After, they made their way to the center of the altar and stood with the priest.

I sat back, watching the beginning of their happily ever after. I wiggled my nose, stopping the tickling sensation from the tears that threatened to fall.

Even someone such as myself, someone against the entire institution of marriage, could grow misty-eyed at a wedding. I couldn't have been happier to have Suzy officially become a member of the Gallo family. It only took twenty-something years for me to finally have a sister.

Today would be a new beginning. The Gallo family would be forever changed.

CHAPTER SIX

IZZY

STANDING in the reception line had to be the most mind-numbing experience of my entire life. Greeting people I didn't know, welcoming them, and thanking them for coming to my brother's wedding—totally fucking exhausting.

Then there were the people who liked to pinch my cheeks like I was still a five-year-old girl. It took everything I had not to slap their hands away and keep a smile glued to my face. By the time the line waned and I was able to hit the bar, my face hurt from my fake smile and my feet were screaming for relief.

I kicked off my shoes, pushing them under the bar and held my hand up to the bartender.

He sauntered over with a giant smile on his face. "What can I get you, darlin'?"

I leaned against the bar, putting my face in my hands, and stared him down. After the hour of awesomeness that was the receiving line, I wanted a drink and nothing more. I didn't feel like flirting or small talk.

"Jack, straight up," I said without cracking a smile.

"Single or double?"

"Double, please."

As he walked away to pour my drink, I turned and took in the room of people. The wedding was massive. Between Suzy and my ma, I think they had all of Tampa Bay crammed in the room.

"God, I need a drink," Mia said as she walked toward me.

"As bored as I am?" I asked as I leaned back, taking the pressure off my feet.

"At least you know all those people," she replied, motioning toward the bartender.

"The fuck I do. I know maybe half, and even then, I'm sketchy on their names."

"There's a small army here," she said. "Martini, please. Make it dirty with two olives."

"Someone looking to get a little buzzed, like me?"

"Just need to take the edge off," Mia replied. "Weddings make me itchy."

"Like you're allergic?"

"No, Izzy." She shook her head and laughed.

"Well, what the fuck? Clue a sister in."

We turned toward the bar, picking up our drinks and clinking them together.

"I feel I'll always be a bridesmaid and never a bride."

"You have Mike." I sipped the Jack, letting it slide down my throat in one quick swallow.

Mia sipped her martini and winced before her lips puckered. "I could be an old hag before he finds just the right way to ask me to marry him."

"Fuck tradition. Ask him already."

"He'd die," she said, bringing the glass to her lips and looking at me over the rim.

I held up my hand, snapping my fingers for a refill. "He'll

get over it. Make a deadline, then. If he doesn't ask by a certain date, then you ask him."

"Maybe," she replied, setting her drink on the bar. "I wouldn't walk away if he doesn't ask. I love him too much."

"He loves you too, Mia. It's really sickening how often I have to hear about you." I laughed, tapping my fingernails against the wooden surface as I waited for my drink. "I love you, of course, but Jesus. The man talks about nothing else except for you and the clinic."

She hit my shoulder, causing me to laugh. "Would you rather him talk about Rob and working out all the time?"

Rob was my brother's trainer before he quit fighting. Rob and I had had a "thing" for a short time. It'd ended badly. Mostly for him, though, since my knee had found its way to his balls and he'd ended up on the floor.

"Well, lesson one is don't refer to women as bitches."

"I'm sure he learned his lesson," she said, and laughed. "I've heard more than once about your wicked, bony-ass knee. I think he still has a thing for you, Izzy."

I turned, holding my glass near my lips. "Ain't no way in hell am I ever dating him. Never. Ever. He's a total asshole."

Mia's laughter turned into a fit of giggles as she held on to the bar to maintain her balance. Tears streamed down her face and her dark eyes twinkled in the lighting. "I know he is. Total douche, but he has a soft side."

"Mia, stop trying to get me to hook up with Rob." I sipped the Jack Daniel's, the feeling of the first shot already making its way through my system. My legs felt a little wobbly and my core warmed. "I don't want a boyfriend and I certainly don't want him."

"Someday, Izzy, you're going to meet that guy. One who makes your belly flip and toes curl. The electricity between you two will be undeniable. You just haven't met the right one."

"He's like a unicorn, Mia. Totally fictional bullshit."

She shook her head, finishing the last sip of her martini. "He's not. You just haven't found him yet. I feel those things when I'm with Michael."

"You're obviously mentally impaired," I chortled.

"I can't wait to see the day someone has you all in a fluster. You're going to be totally fucked."

"Mia, babe, there ain't no man tough enough to handle all this," I said, motioning down my body.

"Uh huh," she clucked, her shoulders shaking from laughter. "I can't wait to see the damn day."

"It's dinnertime, ladies," my ma sang as she walked through the bar area. "It's time to take your seats."

"I could use a little food and a damn chair," I said, wondering how I'd make it to the table with my feet feeling like someone was rubbing hot coals on them.

"Me too," Mia said, following behind me.

We both walked gingerly toward the table that was placed on the dance floor and facing the entire room. I felt almost like a zoo animal as I sat down and looked around the large ballroom.

I ate my food and chatted with Mia throughout the dinner. Joe and Suzy were interrupted so many times with clinking glasses that I didn't have any idea if they were able to consume half their meal. It was cute, and at some point, I thought Joe would tell them to use their fucking forks to eat, but he didn't.

Suzy did that to him. She chilled him out at times when he was ready to burst. I knew he wanted the day to be special, and did everything in his power to make sure it was perfect.

Even held his tongue when I know he had to be biting it so hard that he drew blood.

"I'm hitting the bar again after dinner," I told Mia, hoping she'd join me.

"I'm in," she replied. "Until Michael drags me on the dance floor."

"I wish you luck with that." I laughed, placing the last bit of pasta in my mouth.

I didn't get up immediately. My mother would have given me the stink eye if I'd looked too eager to run to the bar. I sat there staring at the crowd, smiling, and making small talk with the others at the table. Sipping my wine, I counted the minutes until I could stand again on my aching feet and drink myself into oblivion.

Weddings, even my brother's, were bullshit. There was no fucking way in hell I'd be standing on the dance floor later, knocking over girls to get a bouquet of flowers. I wasn't looking for some symbolic nonsense that I'd be the next one walking down the aisle and giving up my freedom. Fuck tradition.

CHAPTER SEVEN

IZZY

AFTER DOWNING countless drinks and chatting up Mia and all the long-lost family members who'd shown their asses at the wedding, I turned to see a very red-faced Suzy enter the ballroom. Joe stood by her side, but he looked calm—besides the small smirk on his face.

"Hey, sister," I said as I walked toward her. "I'm so excited to be able to say that and it be true. I've always wanted a sister." I wrapped my arms around her, squeezing her a little too tight.

"Can't breathe," she whispered.

"Man up," I said, releasing her.

"I'll be back, ladies. I'm going to grab a drink at the bar with my boys," Joe said before he kissed her cheek and left us alone.

"Where's your sister?" I asked, looking around the crowd.

Suzy had a sister, but they weren't close. The Gallos were closer to her, and more of a family than hers would ever be. I felt bad for her, but it made me love her more.

"Don't know and don't give a shit either." She shrugged and looked at the floor.

"You know you've turned into a badass with a potty mouth, Suz."

She smiled, shaking her head. "City. It's all his fault."

"I'd like to think I played a part in it, too." I laughed.

"You're always getting me in trouble, Izzy."

"Me?" I asked, holding my hand to my chest.

"Always."

A man cleared his throat next to us and we both turned in his direction. "Excuse me, ladies. I don't mean to interrupt."

"Well then don't," I slurred, looking the stranger up and down. Handsome, well built, great hair, and totally doable. Maybe I shouldn't have been such a bitch, but then again, Jack was talking after I'd consumed more than necessary.

"Don't be rude, Izzy," Suzy said, turning to face him. "How can I help you?"

"I'm a friend of Thomas's, and he asked me to drop off a gift on his behalf." The man held out an envelope and waited for her to take it.

I took this moment to study him further. His muscles bulged underneath his suit as he held out his hands. His eyes were green, but I couldn't tell the shade. His jaw line was sharp and strong.

"Is he okay?" I asked. I hadn't seen my brother in so long, and information wasn't freely flowing lately. He worked undercover for the DEA and was in deep with an MC in Florida. I wanted him home, safe and sound.

"He is, and he's very sorry he couldn't make it," he said, looking down at me.

"Don't mind her," Suzy said to him, her eyes moving from me to him. "Thomas is her brother."

"Ah, you're *that* Izzy," he said, his lips turning up into a smile. "I've heard a lot about you."

What the fuck did that mean? I snarled, not entirely liking

the shit-eating grin on his face. "And you are?" I asked, holding out my hand for him to take.

"James." He slid his hand along my palm and stilled. "James Caldo."

"Never heard of you, Jimmy," I said, trying to knock him down a peg. I didn't like that he had heard of me, with his "*that* Izzy" comment, and I'd never even heard his name.

He brought my hand to his lips and placed a kiss just below my knuckles. "Perfect."

His lips scorched my skin. An overwhelming sense of want came over me. I felt the urge to jump into his arms and kiss his very full lips. My toes curled painfully in my shoes as I stared at his mouth against my skin. As he removed his lips from my hand and brought his eyes back to mine, I wiped all evidence of want from my face.

Suzy coughed, ruining my fantasy and bringing me back to reality. "Thanks, James. I'll give this to Joseph for you. Why don't you stay and enjoy the wedding?" She smiled at the man.

"What?" I asked, turning toward her. Suzy played dirty. Her angel act was just that—an act.

"We have plenty of food, and I'm sure the Gallos would love to talk with you about their Thomas," Suzy said, grinning like an idiot.

I gave her the look of death. What in the fuck was wrong with her?

"You can keep James company tonight, Izzy. You didn't bring a date."

She did not just say that. If it weren't her wedding, I swear to shit I would've smacked her. I could feel my cheeks turning red as his eyes flickered to mine.

"I'd love to stay. Thank you. Izzy, would you like a drink?" he asked, still holding my hand in his.

"Only because Suzy would want me to be a gracious host," I said, looking at her out of the corner of my eye.

"I don't want to put you out or anything. I'm a *big* boy and can handle myself. I just thought you could use a drink to unwind a bit. You feel a little tense, and that mouth of yours could get you into trouble."

Obviously, he was full of himself. Trust me when I say I can smell a cocky bastard from a mile away. I grew up with enough of them to sniff them out across a room.

"I don't need a babysitter, Jimmy, but I'll take the drink."

"It's James," he said, squeezing my hand.

"You two kids play nice," Suzy said before she waved and walked away.

"Bitch," I mumbled under my breath as I turned back toward the bar.

"Excuse me?" he asked, gripping my arm as he pulled me backward.

I stopped and faced him. "Are you going to release me anytime soon?"

"Highly unlikely." He smirked.

"Jimmy, listen. I don't know what your deal is or who the fuck you think you are, but no one touches me without permission."

With that, he released me, but not before squeezing my arm. "You'll be begging for my touch."

I glared at him, floored by his cockiness. "Obviously you know nothing about me then." I left him in the dust.

I leaned against the bar, feeling him behind me as I motioned to the bartender. At this point in the evening, I no longer had to verbalize my order. He knew it.

"Like what you see?" I asked as I kept my eyes forward.

"Your brother didn't do you justice."

Resting my back against the bar, I asked, "What exactly do you think of me?"

He smiled, stepping closer as he invaded my personal space. He brushed the hair from my cheek, running his fingertip down my face. "You're prettier in person. You are tough as nails, just like your brother said, but I can see the real Izzy underneath."

I snarled, feeling all kinds of bitchy. "There's no hidden me underneath. This is who I am. I make no apologies for my bitchiness or candid comments."

"Oh, little girl, you're so much more than a smart mouth." He leaned in, hovering his mouth just above mine.

I held my breath, silently debating if I wanted him to kiss me. I had to be crazy. There was nothing about this man I liked, besides his face. His words were infuriating, his attitude was obnoxious, and the fact that he thought he had me pegged made me want to slap his face when he spoke.

His eyes searched mine as I stood there not breathing and just keeping myself upright against the bar.

"You're an asshole, Jimmy."

He didn't back away. Instead, he held his ground, pressing against my body. "It's James," he murmured.

I swallowed hard, my stomach flipping inside my body like I'd just gone down the giant hill on a roller-coaster. "Still an asshole," I whispered, my tongue darting out to caress my lips and almost touch his.

"Doll, I never claimed to be nice." His lips were turned up into a grin so large that it almost kissed his eyes.

"Can we drink now?" I asked, wanting to move our bodies apart. The heat coming off him was penetrating my dress and causing my body to break out into a sweat. The pop and sizzle I felt inside was more than just the alcohol. James, the asshole, did naughty things to my body, and I needed distance between us.

"Don't you think you've had enough?" he asked without moving out of my personal space.

I placed my hands against his chest and pushed. He didn't budge or falter as I pushed again.

He tipped his head back and laughed. "Is that all you got?"

"Fucker. First off, I have more, but I don't want to cause a scene at my brother's wedding. Second, I haven't had enough. You aren't my father and you don't get to tell me when to stop drinking. Last time I checked my driver's license, I was old enough to make that choice for myself." I crossed my arms over my chest, trying to put some space between his torso and mine.

"Let's get one thing straight, Isabella." His hot breath tickled the nape of my neck as he put his mouth against my ear and spoke. "I will have you in my bed tonight."

I rolled my eyes and pursed my lips, trying to hide exactly how excited that statement had made me. I didn't want to date the man, but shit, I wanted to fuck him.

"You're quite sure of yourself, *Jimmy*." I emphasized his name, knowing it would drive him crazy.

"There are things I'm very sure of."

"Like what?" I spat.

"From the moment I saw you, I knew I wanted to be inside you. When I touched you, I felt something, and I know you felt it, too. There's something between us. I think I need to fuck you out of my system."

"Is that the best line you have?" I hissed, feeling his lips against my ear. I groaned, closing my eyes to let the feel of his mouth on my skin soak into my bones.

"I don't need lines, Izzy," he growled, with his teeth caging the flesh of my ear.

My toes curled inside my heels; I felt him all over my body. No one had ever affected me in this way.

"I'm down for a challenge."

"Doll, there's no challenge with a willing participant."

I pulled back, feeling his mouth slip from my skin, and looked him in the eye. "I was referring to your ability to keep up with me."

Again, he laughed and held his stomach. "Izzy, Izzy. Baby, if you can walk right in the morning without still feeling me inside you, I'd be shocked. I have no doubt I can keep up with you. You'll never be the same after I've fucked you."

"You better buy me a drink, then. I'll go easier on you." I smiled, turning my back to him and facing the bartender. Then I snapped my fingers, pointing in front of me as he smiled and grabbed the bottle of Jack.

Over my shoulder, James called out, "Make it two." He placed one hand on the bar to my right and stood to the left of me. His forearm pressed against my back, holding me in place and leaving me no escape. "What shall we drink to?" he asked.

"My brother," I replied. Thomas was our link. The connection that James and I shared. "What did he say about me?" I asked.

James smiled, turning his head to face me. "That you're his favorite sister."

"Jackass, I'm his only sister."

"I know." He laughed. "He told me you're hard to please."

I shook my head. "I'm not. I'm just picky and I don't settle."

"Can't fault you there. He's proud of you."

"For what?" I asked, looking at him, stunned.

"He's proud of the strong woman you've grown into, and I'd have to agree with the little bit of you I've experienced."

"Ha," I said. "I learned everything I know from my four brothers."

The bartender placed our shots on the bar and started to walk away.

"Hey, can we get two more?" I asked before he could get too far.

He nodded and grabbed the bottle, making two more drinks.

I lifted my glass, waiting for James to pick his up before I spoke. "To Thomas." I tipped my drink, clinking the glass with his before downing the liquid.

I watched over the rim as James swallowed it and didn't wince. His features were so strong and manly. I mean, what the fuck was that? I'd never thought of any one as manly. *Maybe I shouldn't have another drink.*

"Tell me who you really are," James said as he placed his empty glass on the bar.

"What you see is what you get," I said before I licked the Jack off my lips.

"I know there's the Izzy everyone sees and the real woman underneath."

"James, what you see is what you get."

"Are you always so hard?" he asked, brushing his thumb against my hand as it rested on the bar.

"I don't know. Are you always so damn nosy?"

"I think you haven't found the right man to tame your sass."

I turned to glare at him. "Hold up. I need a man, is that what you're saying?"

"No," he said, shaking his head. "I think your tongue is so sharp because you haven't found the man who makes you whole. Someone who crawls inside you so deep that you finally figure out who you are, what you were always meant to be."

"What the fuck?" I asked, scrunching my eyebrows in confusion.

"It's for another day, doll. Sometimes, we just need someone to bring out our true nature."

"Either I've clearly had too much to drink or you're talking out of your ass. I'm going to go with option two."

He cupped my face in his hand, rubbing the spot just behind my ear with his fingertips. "Sometimes, we don't know who we really are until we find the perfect partner to bring it out."

"Jimmy, I think we were talking about one night. You and me fucking each other's brains out and then walking away. Now, you're talking crazy if you think I need you in my life to complete me. I'm certainly not Renée Zellweger and you're no Tom Cruise. I don't need any man to complete me. I'm quite happy with my life."

"Fine. Tell me who you are." His stare pinned me in place.

Swallowing, I didn't take my eyes off him as I thought about my reply. I'd never had to explain myself to anyone. "Who are you, James?"

He shook his head, a small smile on his face, as he laughed softly. "I'm a protector."

I cut him off. "Do you think I need protecting?"

"I don't know," he replied.

"I have four older brothers who have made it their life's mission to make sure I'm protected. It's the last thing I need in my life."

"Can I finish?" he asked, taking a deep breath and tilting his head.

"Yes," I said, gulping hard and searching for some moisture in my now parched mouth.

"As I was saying, I'm a natural protector. That's why I joined the agency. I'm loyal to the core. I know what I want in life, and I never give up until I get it. There's nothing better than a good chase. Once I have my mind set on something, I'll stop at nothing to get what I want."

"Am I your goal?" I asked, smirking and feeling a little playful.

"What if I said yes?" James asked, moving his face closer to mine.

"I'd say you better have a new game plan."

"Are you a secret lesbian?" he teased, the corner of his mouth twitching.

"No! Fuck!" I hissed. "I mean, more power to anyone who loves vadge, but I'm all about cock, baby."

He closed his eyes, his breath skidding across my face as he blew the air out of his lungs. "If you talk about cock one more time, I'm taking you upstairs and fucking you until you can't scream anymore."

"That sounds creepy."

His chest shook as a laugh fell from his lips. "You have to be the most difficult female I have ever met."

"Maybe I'm more woman than you can handle," I purred, running my hand down his chest. Underneath my fingertips, I could feel his muscles flexing. I splayed my palm against his shirt, letting my hand rest against his rock-hard pec.

"Doll, I'm more man than you've ever had. That I can guarantee."

The air between us crackled. Like it did in the movies.

Sparks were probably visible to any guest milling around the bar area.

"Izzy," Mia said, interrupting my moment with James.

I blinked slowly, looking over his shoulder and smiling at her. "Hey, Mia."

"Who do we have here?" she asked, a grin on her face.

"Mia, this is Jimmy, Thomas's friend."

His eyes flashed before he turned to face her. "Mia, it's nice to meet you. I'm James." He held out his hand, waiting for her touch.

"James, I'm Mike's girl." She slid her hand into his palm, shaking it slowly.

"I'd say you're more than a girl." He pulled her hand to his mouth and placed a soft kiss on the top.

She laughed, her cheeks turning red. Did he have this effect on all women? "You know what I mean," she said, batting her eyelashes.

Thank Christ Mike wasn't here to see Mia blushing and flirting with Jimmy boy.

"Mike's a very lucky man," James replied, releasing her hand.

I sighed, rolling my eyes before glaring at Mia. "Where's Mike, anyway?" I asked, feeling a bit jealous of his flirting.

I was bothered that he was flirting with her, but why? I shouldn't have been. I didn't like him. I wanted to use him. That was all. I wanted to have my way with him for one night and walk away unscathed. Jealousy wasn't an emotion I was used to experiencing, and I sure as hell didn't know how to deal with it.

"He's dancing with his ma," she replied, winking at me and mouthing, "Wow," as James turned to look at me before returning his attention to her.

"Would you like a drink, Mia?"

She smiled, nodding. “Always.”

James motioned to the bartender as I walked to stand next to Mia.

“He’s sexy as fuck,” Mia whispered in my ear.

“He’s an asshole, though.”

“Nah, he couldn’t be. He seems to be a perfect gentleman.”

“Maybe you shouldn’t have another if you think he’s not a total prick.”

“You’re just too damn hard on men, Iz.”

“He’s cocky, Mia. He makes Mike and Joe seem like teddy bears.”

“I like him,” she said, her eyes raking over him.

“Hey, slutty Aphrodite, you’re taken.”

“I can look, *putana*. I’m not dead. I can tell you like him.”

My mouth dropped open. “What?” I whispered. “I do not.”

She smiled, nodding at me. “You do.”

“All right, ladies,” James said as he held out two glasses of Jack.

“To love,” Mia said. “And passion.”

“For fuck’s sake,” I blurted, bringing the cup to my mouth.

“I’ll drink to that,” James said, holding me in place with his stare.

I didn’t respond as I slammed back the drink, letting it slide down my throat. Instead, I started to picture sex with James. There was a simmering tension between us. An animal attraction that was undeniable. I wanted to slap him and fuck him at the same time. I wanted to let loose and show him what Izzy Gallo really had.

“Thanks for the drink, James. I’m going to find Mike.

You two have a fun night," Mia said, winking and smiling as she waved and walked away.

"Traitor," I mumbled, turning to face James.

"You want to fuck me?" James asked, taking the drink from my hand.

"What?" I asked, wondering if he would be so bold.

"You in or you out?" he growled with his hand on my hip, gripping it roughly with his fingers.

"I don't even know you," I replied, as his hold on me felt like a branding iron under my dress.

"What do you want to know?" he asked, still touching my body.

"You could be a bad man." That sounded stupid and childish, but I was trying to not seem too eager to jump in the sack with him.

"Would your brother send me here if I were a total asshole?"

He had me there. "No," I admitted.

"Do you know everything about every man you sleep with?" he asked, running his free hand down my arm.

"No."

"Do you want to fuck me?"

I bit my lip, blinking slowly and processing my thoughts. Did I want to? Fuck yes, I did. Was it a good idea? Hell no, it wasn't a good idea. But then again, mistakes sometimes leave the biggest mark in one's life.

"Maybe," I squeaked out.

He released my hip, moving his hand to the small of my back. "Ready?" he asked, cocking an eyebrow.

"Now?"

"Are you scared, little girl?" he teased.

"Of you?" There wasn't a man on this planet who scared me. The fear I felt was from within. It was pointed directly at me. A man wasn't the issue. James was, and the way my body reacted to him had me on high alert.

"Yeah," he said, the side of his mouth turning up into a grin I wanted to smack off his face.

This was where I should've called a time-out. The words I should've spoken didn't come out of my mouth.

"James, I have four older brothers. You hardly scare me."

"But they want to protect you and love you. While I, on the other hand, want to bury my dick so far inside you that I ruin you for eternity."

"You say such beautiful things." I'd be lying if I didn't admit to myself that he made my pussy clench with his words.

"You in or you out?"

"The real question, Jimmy, is am I going to let you in?" I turned back toward the bar and signaled for another drink.

Let the games begin.

CHAPTER EIGHT

JAMES

WHAT THE FUCK was wrong with me? This wasn't how I normally treated a woman I'd just met. There was something different about Izzy, though. I'd felt like I knew her the moment we met. Thomas had filled my head with stories about his little sister and made her bigger than life. Seeing her in person only drove the point home that she was different than other women.

If he'd heard how I was talking to her, he'd have my nuts in a vise, making sure I'd never be able to get another hard-on in my life. I needed to slow my shit down.

"I'm a patient man, and you'll be in my bed before the night is through."

She laughed, her head falling back as her teeth shone in the light. "I can't leave yet," she said, grabbing her drink and swirling the contents inside. "I have to do all the bridesmaid bullshit."

"I can tell by your comment that you believe in true love."

"Fuck love. Don't get me wrong. I'm thrilled for Joe and

Suzy, but the shit isn't for me. Don't say it," she warned, her eyes turning into small slits as she glared at me.

"What? That you just haven't met the right man?" I stood next to her at the bar and leaned my arm against the wooden surface as I faced her.

"Yes. It's not about that. Love makes shit messy," she explained before bringing the glass to her lips.

"Can I get a beer?" I asked the bartender as he walked by, and his eyes flickered to us.

His eyes raked over Izzy, and I saw the hunger burning inside them. I felt an overwhelming urge to rip them from his skull just so he couldn't eye-fuck her again.

He looked to me and snarled as he reached in the cooler, popped the top of a Yuengling, and placed it in front of me. Grabbing the cool bottle, I let my fingers slide over the wetness. Then I wished I could squelch the internal burning I felt for Izzy.

"You sound like a woman who came from a broken home. Thomas speaks very highly of your parents and the love they feel for each other. What turned you off love?" Bringing the bottle to my lips, I watched her as she swallowed hard and played with the glass in her hand.

"It's not love that I have an issue with. It's the battle that ensues because of it."

After pulling the beer from my mouth, I shook my head, trying to make sense of her statement. "What battle?"

"The one every girl I've ever known has gone through. They have to decide how much of themselves they're willing to lose to be with the man they love."

"That's bullshit."

"There isn't a female I know who didn't change after being in 'love,'" she said, making air quotes and rolling her eyes.

"Maybe they brought out the real woman who was always lurking at the surface and too scared to show."

"You can have your opinion, James, but I know what I see."

"Ladies and gentlemen," a man called through the microphone. "If we could have the bride and groom on the dance floor and all the single ladies and gentlemen join them."

"You going?" I asked with a cocked eyebrow.

"It's stupid," she said before taking a sip of Jack.

"You're such a party pooper. Get your fine ass to the dance floor."

"Or what?"

I smiled, shaking my head slowly. "Let's place a bet."

"Whatcha got in mind, Jimmy?" Izzy cooed, rubbing the lapels on my suit jacket with her fingers.

"If I catch the garter, then we ditch this place and head to my room. No questions asked and no lip from you." I'd knock every motherfucker on the dance floor over to get the garter and have Izzy underneath me within an hour.

"Okay, and if I catch the bouquet, then I don't have to go anywhere with you. You leave and I get to spend the rest of the night in peace." She tilted her head, waiting for me to accept that challenge.

"Fuck yeah. I'm game," I said. Then I gulped the last bit of beer as she downed her drink and placed it on the bar. Setting my hand on the small of her back, I guided her away from the bar.

She stood stiff next to me as we watched her brother use his teeth to remove the garter from underneath the dress of his new bride. The crowd cheered when he appeared from the dress victorious. Twirling the small scrap of material in his hands, he raised his arms in victory.

"You ready to lose?" I asked, looking down at Izzy.

"One thing I'm never good at is losing, Jimmy."

"Single gentlemen first. All others please clear the floor," the DJ said as everyone moved away, leaving about fifteen of us to jockey for the garter.

I looked around, sizing up the competition. I was the biggest besides Michael, Izzy's brother. I took my spot to the side, knowing I could move quickly in front of the crowd and snatch the material before it turned into a free-for-all.

As the DJ started the countdown, Joe turned his back, practicing his throw, and the men moved with his motion. I readied myself as my heart hammered in my chest louder than a drum at a Metallica concert. I kept my eyes locked to his hand as he moved, waiting to see it fly through the air.

As his hand jerked back, the material flew through the air only feet to my right. I moved quickly, stepping in front of everyone else, and snatched it easily. The wedding attendees cheered as I turned to Izzy with a sinful smile, and nothing but seeing her ass in the air, waiting for my dick filled my mind.

"Fucker," she mouthed at me as I walked toward her.

"It's all on you now. Better catch that bouquet," I said, running my index finger down her cheek.

She closed her eyes, swallowing hard before opening them. Inside her baby blues was a fire burning so hot that I could see her pupils dilate as she looked at me. She nodded before making her way toward the crowd of women now standing at the ready.

She whispered to Mia, and their eyes flickered to me. A giant smile spread across Mia's face as Izzy glared at me. Winking, Mia tipped her chin in my direction as her smile grew wider. I said a silent prayer as Suzy readied herself with her bouquet and turned her back on the crowd. Mia bent at the knees like an athlete waiting for the gunshot to sound.

Silently, I prayed that Mia could take Izzy down and make sure she didn't grab the flowers. I wouldn't want to lose a bet to Isabella Gallo, and certainly not one as important as this. I didn't need a bet to bed a woman, but I had a feeling Izzy needed to feel like the choice was out of her hands. She needed an out. Needed something to tell herself to make it all okay to spend the night with me.

I should have felt guilty about the bet, but I didn't. Not one fucking bit.

The countdown began, my heart matching the drum roll blaring through the speakers. "Come on, Mia," I whispered.

My palms grew sweaty as I formed my hands into a tight fist, trying to shake out some of the nervous energy. If Izzy caught the fucking bouquet, I'd have a very long night filled with fantasies and jacking off like a twelve-year-old boy.

As the flowers traveled through the air, Mia held out her arm, pushing Izzy backward. Mia jumped in the air, Izzy looking at Mia in horror. The flowers grazed Mia's fingers, sailing over her head to the woman standing behind her.

The redheaded beauty closed her hands around the flowers, jumped up and down, and squealed.

"Fuck," Izzy hissed, turning to me and glaring in my direction.

I smiled, shrugging as I held up the garter and twirled it in my fingers. "You're mine," I mouthed before licking my lips.

The hunger I felt inside when looking at her was unlike anything I'd ever felt before. I'd lusted after women in the past, but the want for her was so intense that I wasn't even sure one night with her would be enough to satisfy the craving.

She turned to Mia, saying a few things, with her hands flapping around. Clearly Izzy was angry, but all Mia did was shrug and smile. Then Izzy turned her back, quickly moving toward me.

"Mia totally fucked me," she said as she stood in front of me, looking up into my eyes.

My lips curved into a smile as I stuffed the garter in my jacket pocket. "I don't care how I get you, but tonight, I'm the only one fucking you, doll."

"Fine," she said, standing with her legs shoulder width apart and her arms crossed over her chest.

"I'll give you one out. Kiss me, and if you feel nothing, I'll let you out of the bet." It could all blow up in my face, but I couldn't be a total prick. I didn't want her to be an unwilling participant.

"Just one kiss?" she asked as her face softened.

"Yes," I said, holding her face in my hand and running my thumb across her bottom lip.

"I'll take you up on that offer, but I don't welsh on my bets."

"It's your only out. So use it if you need to or else we're going to my room. No more waiting."

"Come on," she said, grabbing my hand and pulling me toward the ballroom exit.

I laughed as I followed behind her, letting her lead me into the corridor.

"Over there," she said as she pointed down the hallway near the elevator bank.

"Anywhere you want, doll."

The crowd thinned as we walked to a small cutout near the bathrooms.

"Why don't we go outside for a moment? Grab some air," I said. I didn't want to kiss her outside the bathroom. There were too many wedding guests and it was not sexy at all.

"Are you pussying out?" she said as she stopped and turned to face me.

"Fuck no. I just don't feel like kissing you outside the bathroom. I've never been a pussy a day in my life."

"Fine, but fuck, these shoes are killing me," she said as she reached down and pulled one off her foot. When she removed the second one, she sighed, closing her eyes like she'd had a weight lifted off her shoulders. She shrank by at least three inches, making me feel even bigger than I was.

"Are *you* pussying out?" I asked, teasing her for taking a moment to enjoy the newfound freedom of being shoeless.

"You're fucking crazy. Just know that, once my lips touch yours, there's no turning back. Come on, Jimmy boy. Show me what you got," she said as she pushed open the exit door in the hallway.

We stepped outside, into the cool night air, into privacy. The back of the hotel was deserted as the parking lot light flickered above us.

"So now what?" she asked, turning to face me.

I looked down at her, taking in her body before staring into her eyes. I didn't respond as I stepped into her space and pulled her toward me. Holding her neck with one hand and her back with the other, I molded my body to hers. Pushing her against the brick façade, I hovered my lips above hers.

Her eyes were wide, the deep blue appearing black in the darkness. Her warm breath tickled my lips as her breathing grew harsh. I waited a moment, letting the anticipation build, knowing that the kiss would alter everything. There would be no turning back.

I crushed my lips to hers, feeling the warmth and softness, tasting the Jack as I ran my tongue along the seam of her closed mouth. A small moan from her filled my mouth, causing my dick to pulse. Pulling her closer to me, tipping her head back farther with the grip on her neck, I devoured her mouth.

Her hands found their way to my hair, trying to grab hold, but the cropped cut made it impossible. She dug her nails into my neck, kissing me back with such fervor that I knew I had her. Sliding my hand down her dress, I pulled the material between my fingers and hiked it up enough to touch the skin above her knee. Then she broke the kiss, backing away as she stared at me and tried to catch her breath.

Before she could respond or tell me to stop, I plunged my tongue into her mouth, stripping her ability to speak. Her hands found their way into my suit jacket, gripping my back and kneading the muscles just above my ass. I ground myself against her, pinning her against the wall as I kissed her like a man possessed.

The ember of lust that had filled my body when I'd first touched her turned into an out-of-control wildfire. She shuddered as my fingers slid up her inner thigh, stopping just outside her panties. I rubbed my finger back and forth, touching the edge where the lace met her soft flesh. Her body grew soft in my arms as she moaned into my mouth.

Not waiting for approval, I pulled the material aside and dipped my fingers into her wetness. I slid my fingers up, circling her clit with my index and middle finger. A strangled moan escaped her lips as my touch grew more demanding. She pushed herself against my fingers, wanting more pressure from my touch.

Gliding my fingers down, I inserted a single finger inside her pussy. She was tight, slick, and ready. Her inner walls squeezed against my digit, sucking it farther inside. Moving my thumb to her clit, I finger-fucked her, bringing her to the brink of orgasm without breaking the kiss. She held on to my shoulder, digging her nails in so hard that I could feel the pinch through my suit jacket.

Just as her breathing grew more erratic and her pussy clamped down on my finger, I pulled out. She sucked in a breath as her eyes flew open.

"What the fuck?" she hissed as she glared at me.

"You want to come, doll?" I asked, sticking my finger in my mouth and groaning.

This was just as much of a fucking tease for me as it was for her. To taste her and feel her against me made my body blaze with need and want, and I wasn't sure one night could extinguish the flame.

"What kind of question is that?" she snapped.

"It's simple. If you want to come, you'll follow me to my room or I walk away and never look back."

She placed her hands against my chest, slightly pushing me away from her. Staring into my eyes, she stated firmly, "No strings attached."

"I didn't picture myself getting down on one knee and proposing." I instantly regretted the words. It wasn't that I wanted to propose, but I didn't want her to feel cheap and disposable. Then again, she'd set the stage for that type of statement. Izzy Gallo didn't want to be tied down and didn't want to have to explain shit to her brother. I liked my life and balls too much to tell him that I wanted her in my life.

"Music to my ears," she said, dropping her hand to my chest, sliding it down my abdomen and grabbing my dick. "Let's see if you're as good as you claim, Jimmy."

"Babe, I'm going to rock your world so fuckin' hard you're going to get down on one knee and propose to *me*."

She threw her head back and laughed. Her beauty was amplified when she smiled. With a small burst of giggles breaking free, she tried to speak. "You obviously think highly of yourself." She squeezed my hardness and bit her lip, stifling the laughter.

"I'm done talking," I said as I pulled her toward the door. "Time to put up or shut up, doll."

"I like a challenge," she replied as she touched the door handle.

Reaching in front of her, I placed my hand over hers. Pulling the door open, I waited for her to step inside. When she walked, she shook her hips, and the movement made it almost impossible to keep my hands to myself. I nestled my palm against the small of her back, helping her toward the bank of elevators.

"Last chance to chicken out," I teased in her ear.

"I may have a pussy, Jimmy, but I'm sure as hell *not* one."

"Usually, a mouth like that I'd say is crude, but hearing you talk dirty just makes me want to jam my cock inside to quiet you," I whispered, trying to avoid the attention of the people passing by us.

As soon as the elevator doors closed, I had her against the wall. I claimed her mouth, her tongue sweet from the Jack lingering on the surface as I devoured her. Caging her face in my hands, I stole her breath and replaced it with my own.

When we reached my floor, I broke the kiss. Her body was still as her eyes fluttered open, and her breathing was ragged. I grabbed her hand, pulling her toward my room, a little too eager to feel her skin.

The chemistry was off the charts. As soon as the door closed behind us, I pushed her against the door, capturing her lips. The need I felt to be inside her bordered on animalistic as our heavy breathing and panting filled the room. I grabbed the purse she had tucked under her arm and tossed it over my head, removing any distraction.

I dropped to my knees, looking up at her, and said, "I need to taste you."

She was a vision. She had on thigh-highs that connected to a garter belt and lace panties.

She didn't reply, but she did spread her legs. I cupped her ass, ripping the thin lace material from her body and bringing her forward before I swept my tongue against her skin. I could smell her arousal. I wanted to worship at her altar.

I lifted her with my hands, placing her legs over my shoulders as I feasted on her. I sucked like a starved man, licking every ridge and bump as she chanted, "Fuck yeah," and "Oh my God." I didn't relent when she came on my face, her legs almost a vise around my head. I dug in deeper, sucking harder as I brushed her asshole with my fingertip. Her body shuddered, the light touch against the sensitive spot sending her quickly over the edge for the second time.

I gave her a moment to catch her breath before I peeled her off me and stood. As soon as I did, her lips captured mine; the tiger inside her had been unleashed. Her tongue danced inside my mouth, intertwining with mine. She wrapped her legs around my waist, digging her pussy into my already hard and throbbing cock.

The wetness from her pussy soaked through my dress shirt, searing my flesh. I walked toward the bed, unzipping her dress and resting my palm against her back. I wanted to rip her dress off, take her fast and hard, but I knew I needed to take my time with her. This would be my only shot to have Izzy Gallo, and I wouldn't waste it. I wanted to spend all night inside her and hear her scream my name.

My first instinct kicked in as I pulled her dress down her shoulders. She released my hair, removing her arms from the small scraps of material that encased her. Holding her body with one arm, I slid my other hand up her side and cupped her breast. Rolling her nipple between my fingers, I pulled her body closer and left no space between us. I toyed with the hoop piercing, gently tugging on her nipple to see her pain threshold.

Her breathing grew erratic as her body shuddered against mine. Biting her lip, I moaned into her mouth as I tried to keep myself upright. I had never kissed someone and felt weak-kneed, but with her, it was like my first kiss. World ending. Life altering. Completely fucked up.

She sucked the air from my lungs, capturing my moans as she rubbed her core against me. Unable to wait any longer, I reached between us and plunged my fingers back inside her. Her body sucked them in, pulsing around the length as I dragged them back out. Curling them up, I rubbed her G-spot with each lash of my digits.

Her fingers moved to my shoulders, digging into my flesh as I brought her close to coming. Claiming her mouth, stealing each other's air, and driving each other absolutely mad, I knew I was fucked.

That's the thing about sex. Touching someone for the first time is so intense that you feel like you'll never be the same. I felt that way with her in my arms and my fingers inside her. I knew I'd be changed forever. Izzy was my equal. Her wit, sass, and sexuality couldn't compare to any other woman I'd ever met. How could I go back to average when I'd had spectacular?

I removed my fingers, hearing her hiss at the loss of friction. I shrugged off my suit jacket; my body cooled, but not my need for her. I laid her down, her chest exposed and the bottom of the dress a mess as I pulled off my tie and started to open my shirt.

A small smile crept across her face as she fondled her tits. Taking a deep breath, I tried to calm my insides as I watched her touch herself. Giving up on the slow-ass fucking buttons, I ripped my shirt open, and the buttons flew everywhere.

Fuck slow. I needed relief. I needed her.

The smile melted from her face as I stared down at her. She pulled at her nipples, her eyes raking over my chest. Moving forward, I unzipped my pants. I grabbed her ankles, yanking her to the edge of the bed. Unable to wait any longer, I pushed down my pants, letting my cock spring free.

Her eyes traveled down my body, landing on my dick. Then her eyes perked up and the corner of her mouth turned into a devilish smile.

"Impressive," she said as she cupped a breast in each hand and squeezed.

"Fuck," I hissed, realizing I didn't have a condom.

What a fucking idiot. I hadn't planned on taking her to bed, or else I would've been prepared. This hadn't been in the cards for this weekend, but I'd take the jackpot and ride the wave.

"I got it," she said as she rolled over and grabbed her purse off the floor, pulling a strip of condoms from inside.

Normally, the sight would disturb me, but not with her. "Planning on getting lucky?" I asked, staring down at her.

She laughed for a moment before her smile faded. "I'm not trashy, Jimmy. They're from the bachelorette party."

CHAPTER NINE

IZZY

I KNOW HOW IT LOOKED. Like I was the type of girl who carried around a box of condoms because I never knew whom I'd be fucking from night to night. It was the furthest thing from the truth. Don't get me wrong. I'm not a prude, and I never put down any woman no matter how many partners they've had. Men can do it without being looked at with disdain, and I wanted to high-five every lady out there getting what she wants.

I had distanced myself from sleeping around. Men were a complication I didn't need or want. Flash was my standby. The one I called when I needed some cock and a quick good-bye. Lately, that in itself had turned into an issue and a fucking headache. I loved him, but as a best friend. We had passion and the sex was fantastic, but the spark wasn't there and neither were the feelings.

Flash was like my favorite teddy bear as a kid, but he ate pussy like a pro. He was comfortable. Maybe a little too easy for me, and I'd grown complacent with just okay instead of fucking amazing. I knew I needed to make a change and kick Flash's ass to the curb, but I had to be gentle about it.

Looking up at James, I didn't see anything comfortable or easy about the man. He stared down at me with such passion and burning that I worried he'd burst into flames before my very eyes.

Sitting up, I tore one condom from the strip and threw the rest on the floor. I'd brought a bunch of them to the bachelorette party as party favors and to throw around at the girls. I'd wanted to make sure every cock was covered and that all the girls were safe. It was something I always preached.

"Must've been one hell of a party."

"Oh it was," I said before tearing open the package with my teeth.

I motioned with my finger for him to step closer, batting my eyelashes at him. I needed to taste him before I covered it. I moved, kneeling on the edge of the bed and waiting for his dick to come to eye level. The glimmer of shiny metal made my insides twist and my pussy convulse. There's something about a man with a piercing in his cock.

I grabbed his ass, bringing him closer to my face as I took in all his glory, feasting on him with my eyes. I opened wide, laying his hardness against my tongue and closing my lips around his length. The velvety firmness mixing with the saltiness made my mouth water. I swallowed around his dick, pulling it farther into my throat, and fought the urge to gag. It hit the back of my throat, cutting off my airway as my eyes watered.

Squeezing his ass, I sucked him deeper before pulling out and repeating the process. I looked up into his eyes, watching his head fall back in ecstasy. Digging my nails into his rock-hard muscles, I flicked the underside of the tip with my tongue. His body trembled beneath my fingertips and my body warmed. I felt powerful with him at my mercy.

The apadravya caressed my tongue and tapped my teeth

as I worked his cock. Just as I felt him grow harder and his body shake uncontrollably, I released him, a popping noise filling the room.

His body jerked, his cock lurching forward as if it were searching for my mouth of its own volition. His teeth chattered as he sucked in air and glared at me.

I shrugged and smiled. "Sucks, doesn't it?" I said, and began to giggle.

He pushed me back before grabbing my feet and yanking me to the edge of the bed. I screamed from happiness—his strength had shocked me. I don't know why. The man was huge. He looked like a giant next to me, but I hadn't thought he could move me around like a fucking rag doll. Holding the condom up for him to take, I bit my lip. His cock was red and bulging as it bobbed in the air.

The shiny metal looked like it was ready to pop free on both sides. I couldn't wait any longer to feel it stroking my insides. He slid the rubber over his cock, paying careful attention to the piercing, while I took in the sight of him.

He had strong, broad shoulders covered in tattoos. I wanted to lean forward and get a better look, but I remained in place. If I hadn't known better or had seen a picture of him first, I would've bet money that he was airbrushed. He was too perfect, with all his rippling muscles, hard body, and flawless skin.

He caught me looking, and winked at me. My cheeks turned pink and heated. I don't know why. I was half dressed and had had his dick in my mouth and he'd tasted me. At this point, what was there to be embarrassed about?

He grabbed the bottom of my dress as I lifted my ass and let him remove it. It flew across the room, landing near the door, where we had begun. I held out my arm, looking to touch his skin, and he gripped my wrist and pulled me off the bed. Then I wrapped my legs around his body, trying not to fall to the floor, and instantly captured his lips.

He grunted, grinding his dick against my pussy as I clung to him. Reaching underneath my leg, he grabbed his dick, rubbing it back and forth twice before jamming it inside me.

I cried out, not having expected to feel so full and stretched. But then he stilled, letting my body adjust before he turned and pushed my back against the wall. The rough wallpaper scratched my skin with each thrust. I reached out, trying to grip the wall, and knocked over the lamp. The sound of glass shattering as it hit the floor didn't stop James.

The pictures on the walls rattled as he pounded into me. My tailbone felt like it was being beaten with a bat each time my body slammed up into the wall. With my back on fire, my ass in pain, and my head slamming against the wall, James pummeled me. Sweat trickled from the edge of his hairline, slowly running down his face.

Sweat and I didn't always get along. With him, I wanted to reach out and taste it. See if it had the same salty taste as his dick against my tongue. Just as I leaned forward, going for the wetness to alleviate the dryness inside my mouth, he placed his lips over mine.

Reaching between us, he flicked my clit with his fingers. It wasn't a gentle touch. There were no tentative feels to see if my body was sensitive. Each stroke felt like a slap against my pussy. My insides clamped down, the edge coming nearer as I sucked his tongue into my mouth.

His strokes became harsh and erratic, matching his breathing. I began to bounce off him, my body flying away from his from the forcefulness of his thighs. Slamming back down on his cock over and over again mingled with the flicks, sending me spiraling over the edge and screaming his name until my throat burned. My eyes rolled back in my head, my head slamming uncontrollably against the wall as my entire body went rigid.

He didn't let up his brutal assault on my pussy as I came down from an orgasm that left me dizzy. As he pummeled me over and over again, I gripped his shoulder, letting myself get lost in the moment.

He stilled, his abs clenching harder as he grunted and leaned his forehead against me. Then he sucked in a breath, his body shuddered, and he gulped for air.

"For fuck's sake," he muttered, swallowing again.

I rested my head against the wall, my entire body feeling like jelly. "Yeah," I said, not able to say anything else.

He held me there for a moment before carrying me to the bed and placing me on top of the mattress. He collapsed next to me, his chest heaving as he wiped his forehead.

"Tire you out already?" I asked as I turned to face him.

"Izzy," he said as he pushed the hair that had fallen behind my shoulder. "I'm just getting started, doll."

I rolled onto my back and stared at the ceiling. The room was spinning slightly from the amount of Jack I'd had at the reception. As I was lost in the passion and booze, he'd consumed my entire world and made everything else vanish.

My eyelids felt heavy as I lay there listening to his breathing slow. My mind was cluttered and I wanted to shut it off and drift off to sleep, but my body had other plans—and so did James. The bed dipped and sprang up as he climbed off the bed. A squeak from the shoddy mattress pulled me back to reality. I opened one eye, watching him walk over to the minibar and grab something inside.

"Want a drink?" he asked, dangling a bottle of Jack.

At this point in the night, there were two options. I could either stop drinking and fall asleep or have another and party to the point that, tomorrow, I wouldn't remember what had happened in this room.

"Yes," I said, sitting up on my elbows.

He twisted off the cap, plopped some ice cubes in a glass, and poured the amber liquid inside before handing it to me. I took shallow sips, not wanting to swallow it too quickly. The wetness on my tongue and burn down my throat helped breathe new life into me. We stared at each other, sipping our drinks stark naked. He leaned against the small bar area, while I sat on the bed with my shoulder back, giving him a full show.

Unable to take the silence, I sloshed back the rest of my drink, shaking the glass, causing the ice cubes to clink together. A small grin spread across his face as he placed his cup on the bar and walked toward me.

"What?" I asked before I stared down into my empty glass.

"Gave me an idea," he said as he grabbed his tie off the floor. Then he removed the knot from the silk material. "Lie back."

"Why?"

"Jesus, just lie the fuck back," he growled, taking the glass from my hand and setting it on the nightstand.

The growl had been a little bit scary, but sexy as fuck. A shiver ran down my spine as I crawled up the bed backward before placing my head on the pillow.

"Give me your hands," he commanded, straddling my body.

I swallowed hard, my mouth feeling dry again as I held up my hands and offered myself to him.

"Hold them together. Clasp them."

"What are you going to do?" I asked out of pure curiosity.

"I'm tying you to the headboard, doll." He smiled, snapping the tie between his hands.

My natural reaction in this situation should have been "fuck no," but since I'd had more Jack than I could remember and James was hot as fuck, I said, "Okay," before clasping my hands together and holding them in front of him without a care.

James twisted the tie around my hands, securing it in a tight knot and drawing them over my head to the headboard. "You okay with this?" he asked, leaning over me with his dick in my face.

"Yes," I said, reaching forward with my lips to lick the tip of his cock.

He shuddered as he fastened the tie to the headboard before grabbing a spare pillow and placing it under my head. "This should help your arms."

"It's not my arms I'm worried about." Really, I wasn't. I knew he wouldn't hurt me. Thomas would kill him, and then the rest of the Gallo men would be in line to revive him and kill him again.

He laughed, nudging my legs apart with his knees. "Wait. Something's missing," he said as he climbed off the bed. He walked to his suitcase, rifled through the contents, and returned with another tie. "For your eyes. Lift your head."

"I want to see," I said, pissed off that he wanted to take away my sight.

"It'll be better."

"I've been blindfolded before, Jimmy. I'm not a virgin."

"Did you like it?" he asked, studying my face.

"Y-yes," I stammered, hating myself the instant I said it.

"Good. Head up."

I sighed, lifting my head from the pillow and watching as he drew closer to me before darkness came.

"Comfortable?" he asked as he tied the knot around the back. "Can you see?"

"It's fine. I may fall asleep. Just warning you now," I lied with a smile.

"Impossible," he whispered against my lips, running his tongue along the seam.

I opened my mouth, trapping his tongue between my teeth. Sliding his hand down my torso, he cupped my pussy.

I smiled, still holding his tongue as his hand left my skin. Suddenly, shooting pain radiated from my core, spreading down my legs. The smack of his hand against my pussy sent shock waves through me.

Instantly, I released his tongue and shrieked, "Fuck!" as I tried to free my hands. I wanted to rub my pussy, hold it, and make the sting go away. "Asshole," I hissed.

"Doll, I'm in control. You can challenge me all you want, but I'll get my way."

I grumbled, twisting my body to change the sensation and pulsating heat between my legs. My breathing was fast from the shock of his assault. Laying his hands against my legs to hold them down, he waited for me to calm.

"Can you handle me, little girl?"

"Fuck you," I seethed. "I can handle anything you give." Being full of liquor didn't help with my ability to make rational statements or judgment calls.

I wanted to see his face. Being robbed of my vision made it impossible to read his emotions. The tone of his voice didn't betray his intentions. I hadn't expected him to smack my pussy, and without seeing his hand move, I couldn't prepare for it.

"Does it burn?" he whispered, the bed jostling as he moved.

I nodded, not able to speak without my voice trembling.

The sound of something moving against the woodgrain of the nightstand made me turn to the side. I needed to be able to hear what was about to happen, especially if I couldn't see, but how I'd turned just blocked one of my ears.

I faced forward, waiting for the next sharp sting, when I heard the sound of ice against the glass. I cried out as the cold penetrated through the burn. He held the ice against me, letting tiny droplets of water drip between my legs.

The heat of the slap melted the ice, and the sting of the cold gave way to a feeling of relief. I ground my body against it, craving the coolness of the ice against me. Making tiny circles, he moved the hardness around my clit, making sure to keep it far enough away from the one place I wanted it most.

Goose bumps dotted my flesh as he slid the ice cube up the center of my body, stopping at my belly button, dipping it inside, and resting it there. Then I heard the sound of more ice before a second one touched my skin and both started the ascent toward my breasts.

My nipples were rock hard, throbbing with need, and the thought of the ice touching them had me on edge. I wanted warmth, the feel of his mouth sucking on my tit. My body shook as he circled my breasts, tightening the ring until it landed on the center. The ice instantly cooled my piercings, sending the bite deeper into my flesh.

"Your mouth," I snapped, craving the heat.

"You don't call the shots."

Water dripped down each breast, pooling in the center of my chest. My skin felt like it was on fire except for the spots he touched with the ice and the small stream running down my torso.

Suddenly, his warm tongue blazed a trail up my stomach, sucking the water that had collected on my skin. I lurched forward, trying to offer him my nipple, but he pushed me back down with his palm.

"Be still," he warned, holding me against the mattress.

I gulped, trying to find an ounce of wetness in my mouth, but came up empty. After licking a path to my left breast, he sucked it between his warm lips and drew it into his mouth. My other nipple was still being blasted by the cold, the opposite sensations causing my eyes to roll back in my head as I lay there immobile.

Once he released my left breast, he placed the ice back on my nipple and moved to my right. The sensation overwhelmed me. No longer could I tell if it was water or my own moisture dripping off my pussy.

Squirming, I needed to find something to stop the throbbing and intense need I felt. With the earth-shattering orgasm I'd had minutes ago, I hadn't thought he could have me so close to the edge that fast.

The ice, cupped in his hand, slid down my body to my core and rested against my clit. I sucked in air, the cold more than I could bear without wanting to claw his face off.

After letting the ice slip toward my center, he pushed it against my opening. As he moved his fingers inside me, the ice slid inside too, burning a path as it slid deeper. I hissed as his cold fingers pushed against the ice, filling me completely.

Water started to trickle out between his fingers as he worked them in and out. He adjusted, moving his body farther down mine and lashing at my clit with his hot tongue. I shook my head, ready to explode from the overload of hot and cold. When he added a third finger, a burn settled between my legs and he lapped at my core.

I pulled against my restraints, feeling the need to move, but it was no use. I was his prisoner as he devoured my body, sucking and finger-fucking me.

I began to chant softly, calling his name at first. As my orgasm neared and he curled his fingers inside me, I began to yell, "Yes!" and "Fuck!" over and over again. I couldn't stop pushing myself down on his hand, feeling his tongue slide across my clit. I felt my toes curl as my body grew rigid. Then I held my breath, riding out the wave of pleasure.

Behind the blindfold, my world filled with colors. Vibrant yellows, reds, and oranges danced inside my eyes as I finally gulped air.

I didn't move as he left the bed. My hands were still above my head, growing tinglier by the second. My chest heaved, the hot breath from my body skidding across the droplets of water. The rip and snap alerted me that he was putting on a condom.

He wasn't done with me yet.

Since I hadn't caught my breath, I couldn't speak before he was between my legs again, rubbing the head of his sheathed dick against my cold opening.

"So fuckin' amazing," he growled as he pushed inside.

I mumbled some bullshit even I didn't understand in my post-orgasm haze. He grabbed my legs, placing my knees over my shoulders as he rammed his dick to the hilt. His fingers pulled on my piercings, sending an aftershock from my tits to my pussy as I gripped him tight, milking his cock.

Linking my feet behind his head, I held his body to mine and pushed against his thrusts. The man was a beast. No other way to describe him. There wasn't a moment I felt in control of the situation, and for once, I liked it. Maybe it was the alcohol that had me going against everything I believed in and had allowed me to give up control so easily. I liked to think it was Jack and not James causing me to give in and become complacent.

What seemed like a lifetime passed before his rhythm

slowed and his body convulsed against me. His weight crushed me as he collapsed, drawing breath as if he couldn't get enough.

"Hands," I mumbled as I shook them, hoping to give them more blood. The prickly feeling wouldn't allow me to be comfortable.

He lifted off me, untying my hands before removing the blindfold. I blinked and squinted, the light blinding me. I closed my eyes, trying to stop the pain caused by the brightness.

"My eyes hurt," I whined.

He curled his arms around me, pulling my body tight against his. "Sleep, Izzy," he said into my ear.

The warmth and comfort of being in his arms sucked me in. Peace and sleep came to me as the darkness took me.

CHAPTER TEN

MY STOMACH TURNED as I moved. It felt like someone was hammering a nail into my skull. *Tap. Tap. Boom. Tap. Tap. Boom.* I winced, trying to pry my eyes open from their sleepy state. The little construction worker inside my skull didn't relent as I looked around.

I swallowed, not recognizing the room before closing my eyes again. Where the fuck was I? Last night was a blur. I remembered the boring-ass reception line, dinner that had seemed to go on forever, and then drinks at the bar. Not just any drink, but my best friend Jack, sliding back and wrapping me up in his warmth.

I tried to smile when looking back on the evening, but everything hurt—even my cheeks. *What the fuck happened?* I slowly shook my head, trying to clear the fog that clouded my thoughts. My head fell to the side and I opened my eyes to get another look around the room.

I blinked twice, clearing the haze from my vision, and saw *him.* James. My stomach fell as I looked down his body and then to mine. We were naked, our clothes thrown around the room haphazardly. I'd fucked him. My pussy ached, the muscles in my arms burned, and my nipples throbbed at the memory of the night before.

I thought I'd dreamt being awoken from my sleep for another go, but nope, I hadn't. James was insatiable. Even while asleep, his dick was semi-hard, staring at me as a reminder of the multiple orgasms he'd brought me.

I stared at James, watching him sleep. He looked peaceful and kind and not like the man I'd met the night before. James had a sharp tongue, a commanding tone, and an air of authority about him. Everything that made me run for the hills and hide. My body liked him, though. Fuck, even my mind tried to tell me that he was a great guy.

I knew better than that. No man, especially one like James, would make me change my mind on love and relationships. He'd promised me a night with no strings attached, and that was exactly how I wanted it.

Saying goodbye was overrated. I didn't feel the need to chitchat and thank him for the amazing fuck. Once I had a good grip on the side of the bed, I slowly pulled myself up, praying that the room would stop spinning. Then I turned toward him, waiting to see how heavy a sleeper he was and if I could slink out unnoticed.

I climbed to my feet, holding my head as I collected my dress and panties from the floor. I had to pee like a motherfucker, but I couldn't risk him waking and finding me in his room.

After placing my panties in my purse, I opened my dress and stepped inside. I zipped it, keeping my eyes locked on him and holding my breath. Then I strapped on my heels, looked around the room one last time to make sure I hadn't left anything behind, and made my way toward the door. Before I turned the handle, I turned and stared at James.

He really was beautiful when he was sleeping. His rock-hard body covered in tattoos, his cock ready for more, and his beauty was enough to suck any girl in, but not me.

A wave of guilt overcame me, but I pushed it aside as I opened the door, trying to avoid waking him. As I entered the hallway, I exhaled and clicked the door closed. I swear, fucking hotels and their loud-ass doors pissed me off more than anything.

A man passed by, looking me up and down, and I felt like a tramp. Dressed in my gown from the night before, my hair a mess, and probably with makeup out of place, but fuck it. I straightened my back, standing tall as I walked to the elevator.

Pushing the elevator button, I glanced back toward his room, silently chanting, "Please don't come out," over and over again.

I couldn't calm my breath as my heart pounded inside my chest at the thought of him finding me in the hallway trying to sneak out.

When the doors opened, I ran to the back of the elevator and held the walls as if they were my lifeline. I'd made it inside without being discovered. I relaxed, almost sliding down the faux-wood walls, allowing the enormity of the situation to hit me.

I'd fucked my brother's friend. I'd fucked him more than once. I'd left without saying goodbye. Would he come after me? Was he a man of his word? There was so much I didn't know about James.

I'd never been the type of girl to sneak out without so much as a goodbye. The night before started flashing before my eyes. Being tied to the bed, the feel of his fingers inside me, the way he'd fucked me, how he tasted—instantly, my body responded. I wanted more, but I closed my eyes and tried to cool off. There was no way in hell I'd allow myself to go there again.

I needed to forget James Caldo.

CHAPTER ELEVEN

JAMES

MY EYES FLEW open as I heard the click of the door closing. Reaching over, I felt the empty space that was still warm from her skin. Groaning, I rolled over and stared at the door. My first instinct was to run after her and drag her back to my room, but I fought it. It wasn't right. Izzy and I weren't meant to have more than a night together… at least not yet.

I'd have my time with her again. There was a connection that couldn't be denied, but she wasn't ready. She still had wildness to her. A rebellious attitude that felt the need to fight against the norm, and that included relationships. Izzy wanted to be the badass chick who didn't need anyone in her life, but that was the furthest thing from the truth.

Her tough shell seemed impenetrable, but I'd witnessed the small crack and peered inside. I could see the fire in her eyes, love in her heart, and the wild animal waging a battle inside. I needed to break down the walls, but timing was key. I couldn't chase after her. I was all about the chase, but not yet.

Her brother, Thomas, and I were tied together through work. We had a mission, and I couldn't do anything that may put his life in danger. Izzy would have to wait until the Sun Devils MC was removed from the equation and Thomas was free from the club.

Throwing my arm across my face, I could smell her on my skin. Inhaling deeply, memories of the night before flooded my mind. I'd never felt weak in the knees before *her.* The electricity in the air as we touched could've lit an entire house and possibly blown out a few light bulbs in the process.

If I said that it didn't sting a little that she didn't stick around to say goodbye, I'd be lying. Izzy was as affected by me as I was her, and she had to slink away before she would have to confront the feeling I invoked in her last night.

I knew I'd have her again. She couldn't escape the inevitable. The connection we felt was undeniable. I'd let her go… for now. I knew in the end she'd be mine.

A chase would ensue and I'd get exactly what I wanted—Izzy Gallo.

MEN OF INKED CHRISTMAS

MIA

Stone's clapping as Pop bounces him up and down on his knee. "Stone, my boy. This is a special year." Stone laughs, drool running down his chin like a ribbon of melting snow, but Pop doesn't care. He loves Stone too much to care his pants are covered. "You don't realize it, but this has been the best year of our lives," Pop tells him, beaming with excitement. Stone claps again, his little head bobbing with each dip as Pop raises him higher and into the air.

They're adorable together. Stone loves his grandpa the most. Sometimes I think even more than he likes Michael or me. As soon as we walk in the door, he reaches for Pop to take him and won't leave his arms until we leave. It usually involves tears, as if we're taking away his favorite blanket.

"Not only were you born, but the Cubbies won the World Series too," Pop tells Stone with a smile that stretches from ear to ear.

I place my hand over my stomach, missing the feel of him moving inside me. It's hard to believe he's already nine months old. Time flew after Lily was born, but with Stone I thought it would move slower. Instead, it moved so fast it's almost like I'm watching it all take place before my eyes at double speed. It feels like yesterday that I found out I was pregnant. It was a shock to me, but even a bigger shock to Mike. After she nagged him mercilessly, he finally gave in and got a vasectomy. He was one of the unlucky one percent who went through the procedure unsuccessfully.

When he found out we were having another baby, he was excited. He claimed this proved that his manhood and virility couldn't be stopped. Naturally, he'd think it was a good thing.

"Baby, you want anything?" Mike asks, taking a seat on the armrest of the chair and wrapping his arm around my shoulder.

I glance up at him, and he's staring at Stone with the biggest smile. There's something about a man and his son. When the doctor announced that we had a boy, I thought Mike was going to beat on his chest and hold him high in the air, beaming with pride. The man prayed every day for a boy.

Don't get me wrong.

He loves his baby girl. God, Lily has him wrapped around her little finger. She always has. From the moment she was born, Mike was a goner. The little princess can do no wrong in his eyes, and she knows it. He doesn't realize it, but soon she'll be a teenager, and he's going to be in for a rude awakening.

"I'm good, love. Just watching your dad and Stone." I smile up at him, watching him as he gazes at them with the biggest grin. There's pride in his eyes every time he looks at his son.

"They love each other, huh?" Mike's thumb strokes the exposed skin on my shoulder that is peeking out from my new sweater. I still don't get why it's missing part of the sleeves, but the sales lady told me it's all the rage. I feel like I paid the same amount for a portion of the clothing.

"Yep, it's weird, almost."

"Yeah."

I place my hand on his knee and rest my head against his rock-hard chest. "Where's Lily?" I ask him, closing my eyes for a moment, listening to the steady beat of his heart

Two kids and years later and I'm still utterly and completely in love with this man. He still has the ability to make my insides quiver with anticipation when he's near.

People said we wouldn't last. A fighter and a doctor. Hell, it was probably a bet I would've taken before I really knew the man.

On the outside, he's a massive wall of muscular testosterone, but on the inside, he's nothing but a soft, loving human being. Except when he's in the ring. Then he's a beast. He transforms into someone I don't know. Someone who would pound another man's face in without even blinking. I'd never admit it, but watching him fight turns me on.

"Somewhere in the backyard with Gigi and Nick." He leans down, placing his mouth next to my ear. "We can sneak upstairs and do it in my old room." His teeth find my lobe, tugging gently. "Everyone is busy, the kids are being looked after."

I melt into him as the noise around us fades.

His lips skid across the skin of my neck before his teeth dig into my favorite spot. "Come on, Doc. I need your special medicine."

My skin breaks out in goose bumps, and I'm more than eager to steal a few moments away with my husband. Time alone has been minimal since Stone arrived. And sneaking away for a quickie sounds perfect.

"You're on, big boy," I whisper.

Mike stands and grabs my hand, pulling me up from the couch and heading toward the foyer. Pop's so engrossed in

Stone that he doesn't even see us leave. Everyone else is sitting outside, watching the kids play and chitchatting while dinner is in the oven. Ma's in the kitchen, cooking and still trying to teach Suzy how not to burn food.

I giggle softly as Mike drags me up the first few steps. When I don't move fast enough for him, he hoists me over his shoulder and jogs up the grand staircase, taking two steps at a time. I bite down on my lip to stop the squeal bubbling from my throat that would be loud enough to draw attention to us.

When we're inside his room, Mike kicks the door closed and we both freeze, holding our breath because we figure our cover's blown.

"Shit, that was close," he whispers, choosing now to be quiet. Mike loosens his grip, making my body slide down his front. It's like cascading down an old-fashioned washboard.

I can feel every ripple and dip of his abdominal muscles until my feet touch the floor. Even then, my body is plastered against his, humming with excitement at his nearness. "Training has done a body good," I tell him with the biggest smile, while my hands dig into his rock-hard sides.

When I met him, I thought he was built like a brick house, but I was wrong. Over time and with more training he seems to be getting bigger and harder. There isn't an ounce of fat on the man. A year ago when he told me he wanted to get back in the ring, I was worried. After such a long absence, I wasn't sure his body could handle the grueling training and snap back.

But, damn. Mike proved me wrong.

"Whatcha thinking, Doc?" He quirks an eyebrow with a smirk. "You look like you want to eat me."

A slow, easy smile spreads across my face as I stare up into his caramel eyes. "Just thinking about how lucky I am to have you."

"Baby," he whispers before leaning forward and placing his lips against mine. He snakes his arms around my back, one hand tangling in my hair and holding me still as he kisses me deeply.

More than anything, I want to savor him, take my time making love to him, but we can't. Backing away, I say, "Michael, we don't have much…"

"Shh," he murmurs, tightening his grip on my back before he trails a line down my neck to my chest with his soft lips. He pulls my hair gently, and my body follows, giving him better access to the opening in my V-neck sweater.

I grip his biceps, digging my fingernails into the skin just underneath his T-shirt sleeve. I'm hot, but not from the overly humid December Florida air. Instead, it's from the way my husband is touching me. I shouldn't feel as needy as I do. He woke me up in the middle of the night last night, spreading my legs wide and slipping inside of me before I could fully wake. The hazy memory of it makes my skin tingle.

Reaching under my skirt, he pulls my panties down and tosses them over his shoulder before I quickly undo his pants, pushing them to his ankles. He turns us, pressing my back against the wall next to the door. His kiss deepens, growing more demanding as he presses his hot erection against me.

Lifting me by the ass, he boosts me into the air, lining our bodies up perfectly before crashing his mouth against mine. I'm breathless and needy, wanting to feel him buried inside of me and needing another orgasm like it's part of my life source. Mike runs the tip of his cock through my wetness before pushing inside, and my legs wrap around his back, taking him deeper and wanting all of him.

He starts with long, languid strokes, causing my slow-burning desire to ignite into a wildfire of lust. The heels of my bare feet dig into his ass and try to pull him forward quicker. The leisurely pace teases me, taunting me with an orgasm that's just out of reach.

"Faster," I moan, digging my shoulder blades into the wall and bearing down on him.

Mike smirks and grips my ass cheek rougher in his palm as he increases his strokes. He's pounding into me; the photo on the wall next to my head bounces with each thrust. My toes begin to curl, and my muscles strain with the building orgasm.

Mike's grunts become deeper and his hips move faster, slamming into me so roughly that my back begins to ache from the assault against the wall. The mix of pleasure and pain, along with his massive cock inside me, sends me over the edge.

Mike covers my mouth with his when I get a little too loud and quickly follows with his own climax. Even after we both catch our breath again, we don't move. It's too quiet, too comfortable to pull apart and go back downstairs. We both have the same thought. We want to stay in this bubble of bliss for as a long as possible.

"Mike!" Joe's voice echoes through the hallways outside the door.

We both make a face at each other, knowing our moment is gone.

"I love you," I whisper to my husband, who is still buried deep inside of me.

"Love you too, Doc." He smiles and slowly lowers my feet to the floor. He starts to pull up his pants when there's a knock at the door.

"Yo, asshole. Get your cock out of her and come downstairs."

Our eyes meet, and we both break out into laughter. We weren't as sneaky or probably as quiet as we thought we were. Joe doesn't care. He and his wife, Suzy, have snuck away more times than I can count to do it all over the house. In reality, every person in this house has, at one time or another. Gotta get it when you can.

"Coming," Mike tells him as he fastens the top button on his jeans.

"Do I look okay?" I ask as I shimmy my panties up my legs and try to right myself.

"That shade of pink is amazing on you."

I give him a "What the hell are you talking about?" look and move my hands over my outfit, showing him there's not a thread of pink on me. "Pink?"

He steps forward and rests his hand against my face, stroking my cheek with his thumb. "You have that well-fucked glow about you." He smiles.

The pink he's referring to turns into the brightest shade of red. "Damn it," I grumble.

He kisses me with tenderness, his hand still on my face, and the embarrassment that flooded me moments ago vanishes. We're not kids anymore. We weren't sneaking off to have premarital sex. The one thing I've learned about the Gallos, even his parents, is that everyone has a healthy sex life.

"We better go," I tell him when I feel the dull ache between my legs starting to return.

He nods and adjusts himself in his pants. "Going to be a long day. I may pull you into another room later."

I press my hand between his solid pecs and smile up at him. "I may just let you."

***

When we walk down the staircase, trying to act like nothing happened, Joe's waiting in the foyer with the girls. His arms are crossed in front of him with Lily and Gigi on either side of him, and from the look on his face, I'd say the girls are in trouble…again. They're staring at the floor as tears trickle down their splotchy red cheeks.

I drop to my knees as soon as I'm in front of Lily. "What happened?" I move my eyes between Joe, Lily, and Gigi. My heart's racing because I can't imagine what has them in tears.

They've grown up so fast. Too fast for my liking. The biggest problem is they're thick as thieves and usually getting into some sort of trouble, but rarely are they in tears.

"Our lovely children thought it would be funny to convince Nick to strip down naked and run through the neighbor's yard."

I'm shocked. "What?" I gape.

Mike places a hand on my shoulder as if to steady himself. "Why in God's name would they do that?"

Joe blows out a breath and clenches his fist. "Well, I guess Nick has a crush on the neighbor girl. Our innocent little girls told him that the way to get her attention would be to run through her yard naked, singing 'Jingle Bells.'"

I have to bite the inside of my cheek not to laugh. Jingle Bells? These two little mischief-makers will be the death of Joe and Mike. They have no idea what's coming because we haven't even hit the teen years. It's going to be hell.

Mike digs his fingers into my shoulder. "What the heck were you two thinking?" His tone is biting.

"Dad," Lily says with a sniffle.

"Don't Dad me, li'l girl. Why did you tell Nick to do that?"

Joe glances down at Gigi, quirking an eyebrow, waiting for her to respond. "You have anything to say, Gigi?"

"Well…" she says, kicking at the tile floor with her eyes downcast.

"Lily, why?" Mike pipes in when Gigi pauses.

"Listen," Gigi says and looks me right in the eyes. "When my mom and dad want to show each other how much they like each other, they always get naked. We wanted to help Nick get Poppy's attention." She glances up at her father with a sad smile. "We didn't know we did anything wrong, Daddy."

"You too, Mommy," Lily says to me. "You and Daddy wrestle sometimes, and you said it was just how you show each other you love one another." And I'm horrified and a little embarrassed.

Joe's face is pale, and he looks more uncomfortable than I do. "We'll talk about this later. You and Lily go wash up for dinner. We'll see if Santa comes tonight. You two just earned a spot on the naughty list," Joe tells them.

"I told you it was wrong," Lily tells Gigi with a snarl. "I'm not going to get my tablet for Christmas because of your stupid idea." Lily rolls her eyes and starts to walk away, dragging her feet with each step.

Gigi peels away from Joe, walking next to Lily, and swings her arm over her cousin's shoulder. "Don't worry," Gigi whispers. "Santa's already in the air, and our gifts are in his sleigh. You'll get your presents."

The girls seem to forget that we can hear them. Even though they try to whisper, they're doing a shitty job of it. They've never been able to be quiet a day in their lives.

"You think?" Lily asks, glancing at Gigi.

Gigi nods. "Next year, we have to be extra good now, though."

"Darn," Lily says.

"I know. It's going to suck."

Joe, Mike, and I look at each other and bite back our laughter until the girls disappear to the back of the house, and then we lose it.

Joe sobers first and rubs the back of his neck. "We're in so much fucking trouble with them."

"Ya think?" I laugh.

Mike shakes his head, rubbing his forehead with his fingertips. "So much fucking trouble."

"Where's Nick?" I ask.

"Getting his ass chewed out by Thomas." Joe smiles. "I'd hate to be him."

Mike pulls me into his side and kisses the top of my head. "Poor kid."

"What are we going to do, Joe?"

"I think we're going to have to talk to them about nudity and sexuality."

"Fuck," Mike groans. "They're ten, for shit's sake."

"Dude, they just made Nick run around with his cock waving in the air. I think it's time for that talk," Joe laments.

"Jesus," Mike says. "This is Mia's department."

I slap his stomach to give him a reality check. "This is an us department, jerk. I'm not talking to Lily about sex by myself."

Suzy strolls into the hallway, glancing into the living room behind her. "Why do Gigi and Lily look like they've been crying?"

Joe wraps his arm around her waist when she's close enough and hauls her into his side. "You don't wanna know, sugar."

"Can't we have one day of peace?" she asks, hugging him tightly.

"I don't think I'll ever have another day of peace with three girls to raise."

We all laugh because we know his words are a sad, sobering truth.

"Wait til they date," Suzy says, looking up at her husband.

The moment Lily starts dating, I know everything is going to spiral out of control in a hot minute, and I dread the day. Mike isn't going to let a boy near his baby girl without a fight.

"I'm locked and loaded when that day comes."

"Me too," Joe tells Mike with a nod.

"You two are crazy," Suzy says with a small giggle. "Boys aren't that bad."

"Walk with me," Joe tells Suzy, placing his hand on the small of her back and ushering her out of the hallway. "Let me tell you what Nick just did."

Mike and I are trailing behind them, waiting for when she finds out exactly what our innocent angels encouraged their little cousin to do.

Joe whispers in her ear, and I know the moment he says the words because she stiffens. She stops walking and turns to face him. "What the frick? Seriously?"

"Afraid so."

"Oh, my God. We're horrible parents," she says, covering her face with her hands.

"No, we aren't," I tell Suzy, knowing exactly how she feels. "We're human. But it's time for the birds and the bees."

"This is bullshit," Mike says, being the pain in the ass he is. "Pop never gave us that talk. I don't even know what to say to a girl."

My eyebrows draw downward as my head jerks back. "He didn't give you that talk?"

Mike and Joe both shake their heads.

"Well, what the…"

"Pop just said to use a rubber and gave us each a box of forty-eight when we turned sixteen."

My mouth falls open. "You can't say that with girls," I tell them. "So, you better figure something out because I'm not doing it alone."

"They're ten," Mike reminds me, as if I forgot that little fact, and crosses his arms in front of his chest.

"Naked," I remind him. "They think that's how you show someone you like them."

Mike winces. "Don't remind me."

"What's going on?" Izzy asks as she rounds the corner and almost barrels straight into Suzy.

"The girls got in trouble," Suzy says but leaves out all the gory details.

"Thank God I have boys." She smiles proudly, finally not complaining about having a baby girl to love.

"Hey, Izzy. Did Mom or Dad give you the birds and the bees talk?" Joe asks.

I'm sure she got a different treatment than her brothers. There has always been a double standard when it comes to parenting children.

"Mom did. I think I was like twelve."

"What did she say?"

"I didn't even know half the shit she was talking about. Basically, she told me to wait until I was married to let anyone touch me down there. She told me that it was the most sacred gift you could give anyone."

Mike almost chokes. "She did?"

"No, ya dumb fuck. She told me to wait until I got married because men are assholes and will say anything to get in my pants. She gave me a box of rubbers and brought me to the gynecologist and put me on the pill too. She figured it didn't matter anyway. With four brothers, I'm sure she assumed I'd never get laid, so why worry."

That isn't an option for Lily and Gigi.

We aren't ready for that yet. Lord, I don't know if I will ever be ready for that.

"Izzy!" James's voice carries through the house like a roar. "I need you."

"Goddamn it. I swear, Trace thinks everything should go in his mouth. I bet he's eating the Christmas ornaments again. He should be over this phase at his age."

"Oh, gawd," I groan and dread the day when Stone starts to eat everything in sight, including Legos and other objects that aren't meant for consumption.

"Fuckin' James takes pictures of it for his Instagram. Asshole thinks Trace is the funniest little thing ever. I'm going to junk punch him soon."

"Bullshit," Mike coughs out. "I'd like to see you try. Bet your ass gets whipped."

Izzy winks, smiling at her brother. "Only if I'm lucky."

Mike's face scrunches at her words. "Yuck."

"Oh, stop the bullshit. You know you love to spank my ass," I tell him with a small giggle, but my cheeks heat at the thought of him buried inside me and his hand coming down on my ass repeatedly.

He places his hand on my ass cheek and gives it a firm squeeze. "Fuck, I love making that ass pink, baby. When I do, your pussy grips…"

"Hey," Joe says, motioning around the room. "There are children around here, man."

"Right," Mike says and bites his lip. "Have kids, they said." He rolls his eyes and groans. "They'd be fun, they said." His lip curls and he growls. "All fucking lies."

Suzy interrupts Mike's pity party. "You guys should really stop swearing so much around the children."

"I'm sorry. You're right. I'll make an announcement before dinner."

"This should be interesting," I mutter because swearing has become almost a second and more expressive language since I've become a member of this family.

"It's best for everyone if we find big-people words to use instead of the dirty ones."

"Yes, Mrs. Gallo," Mike teases her in a whiny, little kid voice because she just pulled out the teacher tone.

"You better behave, Michael, or I'm going to have Mia give you detention."

Mike stares down at me with a cocky smirk. "Only if there's oral involved."

"Boys only think about one thing," I say, shaking my head. But to be honest, when Mike's around, it's always on my mind too.

He beams with pride. "Yep."

Ma walks in with the biggest tray of appetizers I've ever seen. "They're almost here," she says with excitement. "I never thought I'd see the day when Franny got remarried."

Two weeks ago, Fran and Bear tied the knot.

"They've been gone forever," Mom says as she sets the tray down on the coffee table near Pop, who's still holding Stone and watching the video replay of the Cubs winning the World Series for the hundredth time.

"Ma, it's been ten days since they left for their honeymoon. Calm down," Anthony tells her, coming out of the kitchen with another tray of food.

His words earn him a glare from Ma. "Hush your mouth. My best friend has been without any type of cell reception or internet for ten days. Do you know how that killed me?"

"Killed me too," Pop says sarcastically over his shoulder.

Ma gives him a death glare. "Shut up, Sal." She pushes us out of the way when there's a knock at the door, making a beeline for the foyer.

Mike and I settle onto the floor of the living room just as Fran and Maria start squealing with delight in the foyer. Joe and Suzy walk away, heading toward the front door, while the rest of us stay put. Pop's still holding Stone, Izzy and James are off with Trace somewhere, Max and Anthony are curled up on the sofa, and Thomas and Angel are standing in the backyard, watching Nick "the Streaker" like a hawk.

The kids are running around the house, their screams of happiness while playing carrying through the sprawling two-story house. The cacophony only dims when they run out the open sliding doors lining the back of the house, but they quickly return and do it all over again. They're making a circle pattern—up the staircase, around the top floor, back down, out, and back again. I'm exhausted just watching them and more than a little jealous of their endless energy.

Mike's hand is resting against my middle, stroking my stomach slowly. "Maybe I knocked you up again, Doc," he whispers in my ear, and I can feel his smile against my skin. Diapers and sleepless nights weren't my favorite, but they definitely weren't Mike's thing.

"If there's a baby inside me, Michael, I'll never have sex with you again," I whisper back, but we both know it's a lie.

"There's the big guy," Anthony says when Bear and Fran walk into the room with Ma close behind. "What the hell do I call you now? Uncle Bear?" Anthony scratches his head in confusion.

"You're an idiot," Thomas tells Anthony and shakes his head in disgust.

Pop climbs to his feet, placing Stone on his hip, and wraps his sister in a half hug. "Franny, you look relaxed."

Fran steps back, laughing nervously as she slides back under Bear's arm. "I spent ten days in bed with this big lug. I should be in a coma."

Stone yanks on Pop's beard and giggles, distracting him from Fran's statement. "You little stinker." Pop lifts him in the air, exposing his stomach, and gives him a sloppy raspberry against his belly button.

"Why don't the girls go into the kitchen and work on dinner, and the boys can stay out here and watch the kids," Ma says, hooking her arm with Fran's and trying to pry her from Bear's body.

"Sure," I say, climbing to my feet after kissing Michael. I've been in the family long enough to know "work on dinner" is code for drink and gossip.

"We'll hold down the fort out here," Joe tells Suzy when she stands as I pass by her and pull her with me, needing a glass of wine and a little girl talk.

By the time Suzy and I step foot in the kitchen, Fran already has seven wineglasses on the island and Ma has started to pour the wine.

"Sit," Ma says, motioning toward the stools with her chin. "Fran, we want to hear all about it."

"I'm going to need more wine if we're going to talk about old-people sex."

"Stop being a brat, Izzy. You're not too far off from being old," Ma teases.

Izzy gasps with wide eyes. "I'm in my thirties, Ma. I'm far from a senior citizen."

"You're no spring chicken anymore, sweetheart," Fran says, grabbing a glass from the countertop and lifting it near her mouth. "Just yesterday, I was in my thirties. Goes by in the blink of an eye. You'll all be old soon enough."

Each of us grabs a glass, silence falling over the room as we all take a larger than usual sip, contemplating Fran's words.

Every year, time moves faster, and nothing I do makes it slow.

"So, how was the honeymoon?" Suzy asks first as the rest of us continue to drink.

Fran rests her elbows on the counter, leaning forward and holding her wineglass in one hand. "I've never experienced anything like it."

Izzy sighs loudly before guzzling the wine, holding it with both hands.

"Bear is an animal in the sack. I can't believe I can even walk after it all." She snorts against the back of her hand. "The man should've been an acrobat."

"Sounds like you had a great time," I say, feeling slightly awkward hearing about their sex life. She's not my mother or aunt, but I've grown to think of her as a friend and I love her.

"Girl, there's something about a big, muscular guy twirling you around and bending you like you're a Twizzler."

"You mean a pretzel," Max corrects her, finally entering the conversation.

"Whatever. Who knew I was so damn flexible?"

"Anthony does this thing with his…"

Izzy grunts. "Not enough wine in the world for this conversation." She grabs one of the bottles off the counter and heads back toward the living room. "I'm going to sit with the guys and watch the World Series for the millionth time. At least that won't make my stomach turn."

When Izzy storms out of the room, we giggle loudly.

"She's such an uptight princess sometimes," Max says, rolling her eyes. "We have to hear about her chains and whips all the time, but Lord forbid we talk about one of her brother's cocks."

"I don't like hearing about Sal and Maria. It took me

years not to want to throw up every time Maria would talk about their sex life," Fran admits.

"Well, shit. Who else was I going to tell? You're my best friend." Maria fills our wineglasses before refilling her own. "Fran, later you can tell me all the steamy details. We don't want to make the young ones in the room faint."

"Thank you, baby Jesus," Max mutters into her glass.

"It's time." Ma pushes a stack of plates in front of Suzy and me, and we know the routine. It's the same every week and is like a well-choreographed machine. Half of us set the table and get the troops set, while the other half prep the food and carry it out.

Someday, the men will do something more than watch sports and bullshit.

MIKE

I get Lily situated at the children's table before coming to sit next to Mia and Stone at the adults' table. "Did you get her something to drink?" Mia asks just as my ass touches the chair.

I climb to my feet again even though I'm so hungry I feel like I could pass out at any second. "No," I grumble. "She's ten. Her legs aren't broken."

I know I'm a whiny bitch. I love my kids and wife, but there's a limit to my selflessness and it seems to be when I'm hungry. Keeping my body in tip-top shape isn't easy.

"Just do it," Mia orders me with a piercing stare while she cuts Stone's food into the smallest pieces possible. By the way she's stabbing at the meat, I'd say I pissed her off.

After pouring Lily a glass of milk, I collapse into the chair next to my lovely wife and begin to fill my plate without talking. Everyone is chattering around me, but I'm too hungry to do more than grunt.

"Should you be eating all those carbs?" Izzy asks, pointing at my plate with her fork.

"It's Christmas. This is my cheat day." I narrow my gaze at my nosy sister. "Mind your own business."

"When's the next fight?" James asks as he hands me the giant pan of lasagna.

"In a month," I tell him, scooping out the biggest helping I can get away with without getting yelled at by Ma.

"We'll all be there, son," Pop says, which makes me smile.

My big and sometimes annoying family has been nothing short of amazing. They've always supported my choice to fight, and even after I quit and decided to go back, they followed my every move. Even Mia. I thought she was going to have a coronary when I told her I missed it, but the woman told me to follow my dream, even if it included pounding someone's face in. I remember when we first met, she hated the idea of me being a fighter. She said it went against her oath or some bullshit as a doctor to watch me beat the piss out of another man. But I saw the fire in her eyes the first time she saw me fight. It turned her on, and she couldn't deny it. Even to this day, she protests violence, but I always get pussy after a match.

Max wipes Asher's face. I've never seen a baby eat as much as that little man does. When he gets older, he just may give me a run for my money.

"Let me do that, baby. Just eat," Anthony tells her, taking the napkin from her hand.

His unusual selflessness and tenderness earn him funny looks from the entire table. Anthony isn't known for his soft side, but he's changed over the years. Between Max and his kids, he's turned into a smartass teddy bear instead of the reckless manwhore he used to be.

If I'm being completely honest, all of us have changed.

I'm still an asshole, but Mia makes me want to be a better person. I'm still a work in progress, but I'm getting there.

"Fine spread you have here, Mar." Bear jams a chunk of meatball into his mouth and moans. His lack of table manners sometimes makes me look like a gentleman. I think it's why I like him so much.

"Thanks, Bear." Ma smiles. "Shit. We didn't say a prayer and our thanks. Sal, sweetheart, can you start?"

There's a collective groan before forks clank against everyone's plates. I bow my head and hope the kids get so out of control that we eventually skip finishing and go back to eating.

"Behave," Mia says and puts her hand on my knee.

"Higher," I whisper with a smirk.

"I'll go first," Fran says, standing up and looking around the table. "I'm thankful for my family and my new husband. I never thought life could be this good."

"Babe, I love the hell out of you," Bear tells her and then stands. "I'm thankful for my wife and friends around this table and those who couldn't be with us tonight. And thanks to Maria for the amazing food that's getting cold."

I knew I liked this guy. My stomach rumbles, and in order to speed shit along, I stand next before Bear can put his ass in the chair. "I'm thankful for my family and my little surprise, Stone." I glance over at my little man as he shoves lasagna in his mouth with both hands.

The kids are eating at the next table, but no one seems to care. Back in the day, Ma would've knocked us into next week for not listening and saying thanks, but not the grandkids—they always get a pass.

I tune out after Mia says her thanks and stare at my plate. It's like the food is taunting me, the aroma wafting up from the dish, making my mouth salivate.

Pop stands, clinking his fork against his wineglass, even catching the attention of the kids. "Let's bow our heads for a prayer."

Everyone grows quiet, even the kiddos, and we bow our heads and wait. Pop clears his throat before he speaks. "Today, as we're gathered here together, I want to thank God for the amazing lives we have and that everyone is happy and healthy. Not only am I blessed with such love, but…"

He pauses and gets choked up. I roll my eyes because I know where he's going before he even says the words. There's only one thing Pop loves as much as his family. The Cubs. I'd never seen him as happy as he was the day they won. His life had been made.

"But my Cubbies winning the World Series was the best day of my life. I can die a happy man."

"For the love of God," Ma mutters. "I wish everyone a happy and healthy New Year. May we continue to be blessed in the coming year. Amen."

Joining everyone else, I say, "Amen." And I quickly do the sign of the cross before grabbing my fork and digging back into my food.

After twenty minutes of gorging ourselves on an obscene amount of food, the women clear the table and kick our asses happily back to the living room, putting us in charge of the kids. We spread out around the room, leaving enough space for our other halves when they return.

I settle into the couch with Stone in my arms. He's in that familiar food coma too. His eyes are heavy and his blinks long and drawn-out. He's fighting it, unlike me. I prop him on my shoulder and rub his back, making tiny circles until he's fast asleep

I doze off somewhere in the middle of the conversation

about the Cubs. The topic has become boring to me, although Pop is still as excited as the night it happened.

"Daddy." Lily yanks on my pant leg.

"Yeah?" I don't open my eyes.

"Can I snuggle with you, or are you still mad at me?"

I glance down at her and smile. She's chewing on her index finger and staring at me while she turns her body from side to side. I pat the cushion next to me, careful not to wake Stone. "Come here, sweetheart. I always want your snuggles. I love you."

A giant smile spreads across her face. She looks so much like her mother that she takes my breath away sometimes. She climbs on the couch, settling in the crook of my arm and resting her tiny hand on my stomach. "Do you have a baby in there?" she asks into the fabric of my shirt.

"No, Lily. No baby. It's only food. Only girls can have babies. Remember Mommy and I told you that when she was pregnant with Stone."

"That's not fair. I don't want to ever have a baby. Men should be able to have them too."

Joe chuckles next to me after hearing Lily's statement, and I pull her closer to my side.

"Just stay away from gross boys, and you won't have to worry about getting pregnant."

She sticks out her tongue and makes a gagging noise. "Boys are gross, Daddy."

"That's my girl." I pray she'll always feel this way.

"I'll never love a boy the way I love you," she says, melting my heart into a pile of goo.

I lock this memory away because I know soon she'll be dating and will forget the words she just spoke. Someday, I'll have to have a man-to-man with her new beau, and it isn't going to be pretty. Soon, probably sooner than I want, I'll be threatening the life of some asswad horny teenager about putting his filthy hands on my daughter, and Lily will hate me for it.

If she's ever going to get married, it'll take a hell of a man to survive my hazing. I don't know of many fools who will willingly subject themselves to me for a piece of ass. The way I figure it, if he sticks around after dealing with me, then he'd have to be doing it for love.

When the ladies return, gift opening starts. Only the kids get gifts anymore. The main event, as I call it, takes hours. There are so many gifts in the room we'd need twenty Christmas trees to set them under. It's obscenely beautiful. The kids are glowing as they take turns opening their presents.

"We have a great life," Mia says, curling into the spot where my little girl had been an hour earlier.

"I wish we could freeze time, Doc. I don't want them to ever grow up."

"I know." She kisses my cheek, nuzzling into my neck with her face. "I love you, Michael."

"Love you too, Mia." I pull her closer, careful not to smash Stone. Somehow, he's sleeping through all the noise and shrieks as each present is opened.

"We gotta wake him up." She strokes his cheek. "Stone, baby, wake up, sweetheart," she whispers. "He'll keep us up all night, otherwise."

"We're going to be up all night setting up Lily's presents anyway. Might be nice to have him with us."

"I thought we could make love by the fire." She smiles up at me and bites her lip.

She doesn't have to say another word. I pull Stone from my shoulder and cradle him in my arms. "Stone," I whisper repeatedly until his tiny eyes flutter open. He smiles up at me in a sleepy haze before Mia takes him from my arms.

I glance around the room, taking in the moment. My parents are on the floor with the kids, happier than I've seen them in years. Ma's beaming with pride, and Pop's already trying to make sense of the chaos of wrapping paper, boxes, and presents.

Joe and Suzy are snuggled on the floor beside the tree with Rosie, Gigi, and Luna. I don't envy the man. There's so much estrogen in that house, I'm surprised he hasn't gone mad.

Max and Anthony are whispering to each other with Asher and Tamara in front of them, ripping open their presents and throwing the wrapping paper backward onto them, but they don't seem to care.

Thomas and Angel are next to us on the couch. She's sitting in his lap with her legs hanging over the side closest to us. Nick's by Pop, showing him the new baseball glove as they talk about how someday he'll play for the Cubs.

Izzy's leaning against James as she sits between his legs with the kids near her feet. Trace, Mello, and Rocco are like three hellions, throwing things and tossing presents to their cousins like wild animals.

When I look to Fran and Bear, they're oblivious to the chaos in the room. They're into each other. It's nice to see them both finally happy. I never would've imagined that they would be a perfect match, but they are. He balances her nutty with his crazy, and somehow, they work perfectly.

Even my cousin Morgan showed up with his beautiful wife Race. They were late, which is normal for them. Their excuse this time is Race's ovulation schedule. Instead of being here with us, they've been at home fucking like animals, trying to get pregnant. It's a reason I can get behind.

I take it all in and try to memorize this moment. The room is filled with so much love and happiness, it's almost too much to comprehend.

I wish I could hit pause and keep us here, in this moment, forever.

How I've become this lucky is beyond me. I know the moment is fleeting. Time moves on. We're getting older. The kids are growing up and will soon take our place.

… the Gallo Family Saga continues. Please visit *menofinked.com/inked-se* to grab the next special edition paperback.

Want a signed copy for your bookshelf?
Visit *chelleblissromance.com* to learn more.

ABOUT THE AUTHOR

I'm a full-time writer, time-waster extraordinaire, social media addict, coffee fiend, and ex-history teacher. *To learn more about my books, please visit menofinked.com.*

Want to stay up-to-date on the newest Men of Inked release and more? Join my newsletter.

Join over 10,000 readers on Facebook in Chelle Bliss Books private reader group and talk books and all things reading. Come be part of the family!

See the Gallo Family Tree

Where to Follow Me:

facebook.com/authorchellebliss1
instagram.com/authorchellebliss
bookbub.com/authors/chelle-bliss
goodreads.com/chellebliss
amazon.com/author/chellebliss
x.com/ChelleBliss1
pinterest.com/chellebliss10

Men of Inked

MYSTERY BOX

DELIVERED EVERY 4 MONTHS

SPECIAL EDITION PAPERBACKS & EXCLUSIVE MERCHANDISE!

CHELLEBLISSROMANCE.COM

Want a behind-the-scenes look at the chaos of my author life? Maybe you want early sneak peeks and other kickass treats.

CLICK HERE to join the fun or visit *menofinked.com/news*

…and as a special thank you, you'll receive a free copy of Resisting, a Men of Inked novella.

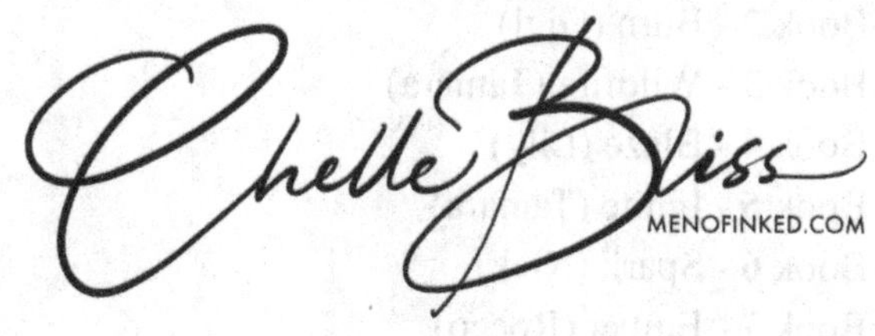

MEN OF INKED SERIES

"One of the sexiest series of all-time" -Bookbub Reviewers
Download book 1 for FREE!

- Book 1 - Throttle Me (Joe aka City)
- Book 2 - Hook Me (Mike)
- Book 3 - Resist Me (Izzy)
- Book 4 - Uncover Me (Thomas)
- Book 5 - Without Me (Anthony)
- Book 6 - Honor Me (City)
- Book 7 - Worship Me (Izzy)

MEN OF INKED: SOUTHSIDE SERIES

Join the Chicago Gallo Family with their strong alphas, sassy women, and tons of fun.

- Book 1 - Maneuver (Lucio)
- Book 2 - Flow (Daphne)
- Book 3 - Hook (Angelo)
- Book 4 - Hustle (Vinnie)
- Book 5 - Love (Angelo)

MEN OF INKED: HEATWAVE SERIES

Same Family. New Generation.

- Book 1 - Flame (Gigi)

- Book 2 - Burn (Gigi)
- Book 3 - Wildfire (Tamara)
- Book 4 - Blaze (Lily)
- Book 5 - Ignite (Tamara)
- Book 6 - Spark (Nick)
- Book 7 - Ember (Rocco)
- Book 8 - Singe - (Carmello)
- Book 9 - Ashes - (Rosie)
- Book 10 - Scorch - (Luna)

THE OPEN ROAD SERIES

Wickedly hot alphas with tons of heart pounding suspense!

- Book 1 - Broken Sparrow (Morris)
- Book 2 - Broken Dove (Leo)
- Book 3 - Broken Wings (Crow)

ALFA INVESTIGATIONS SERIES

Wickedly hot alphas with tons of heart pounding suspense!

- Book 1 - Sinful Intent (Morgan)
- Book 2 - Unlawful Desire (Frisco)
- Book 3 - Wicked Impulse (Bear)
- Book 4 - Guilty Sin (Ret)

SINGLE READS

- Mend
- Enshrine
- Misadventures of a City Girl
- Misadventures with a Speed Demon
- Rebound (Flash aka Sam)
- Top Bottom Switch (Ret)

- Santa Baby
- Fearless - (Austin Moore)

View Chelle's entire collection of books at menofinked.com/ books

To learn more about Chelle's books visit *menofinked.com* or *chellebliss.com*

www.ingramcontent.com/pod-product-compliance
Lightning Source LLC
Chambersburg PA
CBHW010356310726
48979CB00006B/1061

* 9 7 8 1 6 3 7 4 3 1 6 2 7 *